With Great Sorrow

THE PADDY SERIES
BOOK THREE

LISA BOYLE

With Great Sorrow

Copyright © 2022 by Lisa Boyle. All rights reserved.

This novel is a work of fiction. Any references to historical events, real people, or real places are used fictitiously. Unless otherwise mentioned in the Author's Note, names, characters, and events are products of the author's imagination, and any resemblance to actual events, places, or persons, living or dead, is entirely coincidental. No part of this book may be reproduced in any form or by any electronic or mechanical means, including information storage and retrieval systems, without written permission from the author, except for the use of brief quotations in a book review.

ISBN: 978-1-7366077-4-9 (Ebook)

ISBN: 978-1-7366077-5-6 (Paperback)

Copy Editor/Proofreader: Constance Renfrow

Cover Designer: Rafael Andres

This book is for my great, great, great, great uncle.
An immigrant, a Union soldier,
and a prisoner of war.

Rosaleen

Chapter Two

Emmett had enlisted months ago, but the regiment didn't have enough men to fill it until December. They wanted Irishmen. In addition to the regiment that had left in June, there were to be two more Irish regiments from Massachusetts. But even after Thomas Francis Meagher himself came to recruit, there weren't enough men. So, the Irishmen who enlisted in Framingham for the 29th Regiment were instead included in the 28th to create a single, complete Irish regiment. They were to be part of Meagher's Irish Brigade, and nothing could stop my husband from joining. Not even my worry. Not even his own ambitions to become a city councilor.

I understood his enthusiasm more than I cared to admit. We had attended Meagher's speech in September. Steven sat on Emmett's shoulders at the rear of a packed event hall. I watched beads of sweat creep down both of their necks as we listened to Meagher convince the Irish to fight. To fight for and beside the men who had treated us—and treated him—so poorly for so long. Still, we had risen.

Slowly but surely. And we would continue to rise. Only here, in America, was that possible. If democracy failed here, where would it survive? If there was any hope for self-rule in Ireland, we must first prove that it could exist here. We could not let the Southern aristocracy break from the Union simply because they weren't getting what they wanted. They mustn't be allowed to tear at the fabric of democracy.

Besides, England favored the South, which meant there was a possibility that we could fight them, too. If not in this war, then afterward. We would train now. We would start with the traitors in the South and then move on to the occupiers of our homeland.

The Irish were roused. Their patriotic fervor was deafening. Many of the things Meagher said that day, I had said before. Paddy had said them before. But coming from a real, in-the-flesh Irish hero, those words meant so much more. I felt my heart swell with pride. Tears came to my eyes. Emmett danced around the hall while he waited to sign his name to become a soldier, and Steven, still on his shoulders, clapped and laughed. I would have signed up that day, too, if they had let me. We all felt proud. Proud to be Irish. Proud to prove our worth.

And so, I ignored the sinking feeling in my stomach. Was I to let the man who had brought me back to life sacrifice his own? I couldn't even think of it. Like the other women left behind, I put one foot in front of the other and ignored reason and likelihood.

I had made plans to be in Boston for Christmas. To take Steven and Mr. Joyce and celebrate there. Mairead would feed Cocoa. Mr. Joyce would complete all Christmas orders before we left.

Emmett and I had bought a house on the outskirts of the Acre not long after starting our work with the city. Our wages were much higher than they had been at the mill and machine shop. At first, I was appalled by how high they were. A few years later, we convinced Mr. Joyce to leave his work at the canals and do what he truly loved. We bought him tools and cleared out the small shed that sat opposite the privy behind the house, and Mr. Joyce began taking orders to fix broken chairs, tables, dressers, desks. Soon he was honing his carving skills, engraving beautiful designs into chests and cradles. Now, he was the most sought-after carpenter in all the Acre. Though he was no longer doing the backbreaking work of a laborer, he kept his strong, broad physique, and the contentment he found from his new profession made him appear more at ease than he'd been in his younger years.

It was only a week till Christmas when Phillips asked to meet. His note was brief, as always. At first, Phillips and I had only met in empty parks, the backs of churches, at the train station. But eventually, he grew to trust me and I him, and now we met at his home study.

When Phillips had presented himself as the "fixer" for the mills all those years ago, I could never have imagined just what that meant. But once I was folded into his operation, I got a glimpse at how important his work was to the "Boston Associates"—the mill owners. He shielded them from scrutiny, solved problems before they even arose, obliterated obstacles from their business paths. He shielded me and my secret, as well, quelling any whispers of my true identity. Though this meant there were some topics that were now completely off-limits to Paddy, I was surprised by just how much criticism of the mills he *did* allow. "Paddy's voice needs to stay authentic," he always said.

I walked briskly down Middlesex Street toward Phillips's neighborhood, wrapping my arms tight around myself to brace against the biting wind. A wind tunnel always formed at the crossing of the three streets ahead of me. My nose tingled, and my cheeks stung. I knew Emmett was still in Boston, still at Camp Cameron, and I wondered if he was warm enough.

Phillips's enormous house sat at the very end of the street, overlooking the Merrimack River. It was overly ornate in every way imaginable—just like Phillips. I knocked on the door using the iron knocker shaped like a buffalo. I smiled to hear light-footed steps. The door opened.

"Maggie!" I cried, stepping into the foyer. We embraced before she took my coat.

"Rosaleen," she said. "Come in from the cold," although I already had. Maggie was nearly old enough to be my ma and sometimes fussed over me as if she was. Her dark-brown hair was streaked with gray and always pinned back to perfection. She was a bit plump in a way that someone who was paid well could be and muscular enough to move large furniture all on her own. She squeezed my arm.

"How are you doing?" she asked. I shrugged.

"As good as is to be expected, I suppose," I said. "And how are you? I don't believe I saw you at the train station."

She sighed.

"I was there," she said. "We were all a bit distracted, weren't we?"

I nodded.

"Emmett will look out for John," I said.

Maggie gave me a grateful smile. "I know he will."

John was Maggie's son and barely eighteen years old. He had been eager to join up. The boy was full of energy and optimism, and Maggie was powerless to deter him.

"We shan't keep him waiting, though," Maggie said, gesturing toward Phillips's study.

"He's eager to see me, then?" I asked.

"Oh yes," she replied.

I walked to the study and tapped lightly on the closed door.

"Please," Phillips called from inside. "Come in."

Chapter Three

I sat in the emerald-colored chair across from Phillips's desk. At first, he did not look up. His dark hair shone with pomade, and a pair of glasses perched on his nose. His mustache was perfectly groomed. He was hunched over a newspaper: *The Boston Pilot*. Even upside down I would have recognized the paper anywhere. I loathed its editor, and yet, it was him I had to thank for recruiting more Irishmen to fill my husband's regiment.

"Donahoe," I said. Phillips nodded, still reading.

"What vile things is he printing now?" I asked.

One side of Phillips's mouth curled. "Oh, you know," he replied. "The usual. You're aware of how upset he was when Butler declared escaped slaves contraband of war."

General Benjamin Butler had recently told Confederate officials directly, under a flag of truce, that he considered slaves who made their way to Union lines to be "contraband of war." Therefore, he would not turn the enslaved back over to the Confederates when they sought refuge with Union troops. If they were indeed property, as the

Confederates insisted, then they were our property now. To do with as we pleased. So, we freed them. It had caused quite a stir.

Phillips sat back in his chair, pulled up his newspaper, and read: "'The white men of the free states do not wish to labor side by side with the Negro.'"

He scanned down the page a bit and then read again: "'Not one volunteer in a hundred has gone forth to liberate the slaves.'"

"I . . ." I started, but Phillips held up a finger.

"One more," he said. "You'll like this one best. 'Nineteen of twenty Negroes will not accept emancipation, because they love their masters as dogs do, and plantation life is the life nature intended for them.'"

He set the paper down, eyes sparkling in anticipation.

"That man's head is stuck so far up his own arse, I am shocked he can do so much as dress himself in the morning, let alone run a newspaper. He is a detriment to all of society." I sighed. "But you know my opinion of him already."

"And how would you like a chance to respond?" Phillips asked. "Perhaps it is time we shift our efforts toward the Irish community in Boston."

I raised my eyebrows. "And how would we do that?" I asked.

"The Boston Associates' new newspaper, *The Commonwealth*," he said. "I've convinced them to publish Paddy. We need a voice from the Irish community."

"That's the newspaper furthering the goal of emancipation, isn't it?" I asked. He nodded.

"Correct. We need to convince—and prepare—the

people of Massachusetts to accept the inevitability of emancipation."

"And why do the Boston Associates care so much for the slaves' freedom?" I asked. "Weren't they still partnered with slaveholders only a year ago?"

Phillips smiled again. He always seemed to know what I would ask and still reveled in me asking.

"Indeed, they were," he said. "But you must not forget Bleeding Kansas. Where did all of John Brown's weaponry come from? The man, God rest his soul, did not have the means to procure it himself."

My mouth hung open. "Are you saying the Boston Associates funded the abolitionists in Kansas?"

Phillips said nothing, but his smile grew.

"But why?" I asked.

"Truthfully, because free labor is more profitable than slave labor, and it is better for the spirit of a free society as well. Slaves can't purchase goods."

I shook my head. "If free labor is more profitable than slave labor, why are there still slaves?"

He had clearly anticipated this one, too, because he immediately tore into his explanation.

"Because slave labor is still wildly profitable," he answered. "It's the only way Southerners have ever done it, and they must cling to the ways that have brought them such enormous power and wealth. They are afraid of losing that. But surely it is better to pay a man wages for his work and allow him his freedom to do with those wages as he pleases. Those wages will come back again and again when he buys clothes for his family, new furniture for their home, a railway ticket. Those wages will come back to society. Back to all of us. This is the spirit of a free people. We can settle for nothing less. We must not allow these Southern men to stifle the growth of this country."

He certainly knew more about the economics of it all than I did, and it clearly wasn't a moral matter for him.

"Why now?" I asked. "Why didn't they put a stop to it before?"

"Because, had we tried, we would have been in danger of being cut off entirely from our cotton supply. Which would have shut down this whole city and harmed all the workers along with it," he replied. "But the Boston Associates have always been against the *spread* of slavery. Now, we can crush it for good."

I grinned. "If only I had known this whole time that you were an abolitionist."

Phillips laughed heartily.

"I have no opinions other than the ones I'm told to have," he said.

I looked around his study. At the books. At the large paintings of Montana.

"And your idealization of the West?" I asked. "Were you told to have that?"

He smirked and, ignoring me, slid a blank paper across his desk. "I have thought of some arguments in favor of emancipation that might grab the attention of the Irish."

I picked up his pen and dipped it in his ink. I listened to what he had to say as though I did not listen to the Irish every day in our pubs and parlors. Still, Phillips always had valuable insight.

"Taxes," he began. "A nation-wide wage labor system would reduce taxes. The working Irish subsidize slavery when they pay taxes on anything. Alcohol, pigs, tobacco. Clearly slaves don't pay taxes, but their owners aren't paying taxes for them, either. At least not what they should be. Remind them of that."

I wrote it down.

"Donahoe loves to talk about the Constitution," Phillips went on. "The Constitution allows slavery. He falls back on that every time he runs out of ideas."

I nodded. I had yet to find an argument around that one.

"Tell the Irish of constitutional amendments and how they have benefited from them. Most of the Irish were not here—were not even born—when the last amendment was passed."

"Do you think there could be an amendment outlawing slavery?" I asked.

He nodded but said, "It's doubtful. But *they* don't need to know that. What they need to know is that these things can be changed. It's the beauty of a democracy. If the people are in favor of change, then change can occur."

"But the Irish appreciate the assurance that the Constitution brings," I said. "That some king or queen can't make their life hell simply because they want to. They like that the Constitution provides the correct way of doing things."

"Of course," Phillips said. "The Constitution exists to protect the people from an oppressive government. And that is the reason for amendments. Those can only come from the people. In this case, it would protect the people from the South holding the economy hostage."

I nodded slowly.

"And . . . anything else you can think of," he said. "Become Paddy."

I chuckled. "Paddy is a clever man. He'll think of something."

"I'll need that by the fifteenth of January," he went on.

I stood up. "I'll see you then," I said. "Happy Christmas."

Phillips had already moved onto something else, writing intently.

"Happy Christmas," he murmured, absently.

Chapter Four

We awoke early on Christmas Eve to catch the train. The world was still dark and sleeping as our shoes clopped against the cobblestones, and occasionally a bird tweeted a greeting. None of us spoke.

Mr. Joyce's mind was probably still poring over the rocking chair he had completed yesterday. Thinking of the way the chair curved, the special design of the armrests, and knowing that it would fit little Lizzie Ryan perfectly and bring her joy on Christmas. He might have been thinking of church, too. Feeling some sadness that he would miss Christmas Mass at St. Patrick's.

Steven was excited. He couldn't wait to see his Boston family. Miss Susan, who always bestowed gifts upon him and made silly faces when she thought no one else was looking. Marie, Gil, baby Jane, and Levi. Levi was considerably younger than Steven, but Steven still loved to play with him, being kind and gentle, teaching and leading. Lydia, Zeke, Angel, and Eliza. Who all always taught him something he hadn't known before. But most of all, his

Uncle Ronan. Not truly his uncle, but still, his very best friend and closest confidant.

As for me, I was busy trying to think of anything but Emmett. If I did, I might cry, and it had only been two weeks without him. It was far too soon to be crying.

Steven lagged behind to walk next to Mr. Joyce, and I heard their quiet voices behind me just as we reached the railway station.

The train came exactly on time, and we chose seats near the front. Steven took the window. He hadn't stopped talking to Mr. Joyce. He rarely talked so much.

As we pulled into Boston, the day began to brighten. Although the sun wasn't visible yet, it was stirring. Before we disembarked, Steven put on his kepi cap that looked just like the one his da had worn the day he left.

The walk to Ronan's was noisy. There was chatter on the streets, and men strode by with morning newspapers tucked under their arms, in a hurry to get to wherever they were going. For most Yankees, Christmas Eve was still just another day.

I watched Steven knock on Ronan's door and remembered another little boy who'd stood at that same door, but much less eagerly. It startled me to think they were the same age—this little boy and that one. But then, the door opened, and the young man who appeared reminded me of just how much that first little boy had grown. Ronan's face was sharp now, his hair parted on the side, grazing the tips of his ears. He grinned at Steven, grabbed his coat, and hurried out the door.

On the sidewalk, he squatted to get level with Steven.

"Happy Christmas, lad," he said.

"Happy Christmas, Uncle Ronan." Steven hugged him. "Da left for the war."

"Your da's a brave man," Ronan said. It was a kind thing to say, considering how I knew Ronan felt about the war.

"Will you go, too?" Steven asked.

The corner of Ronan's mouth curled into a smile.

"There won't be any fighting left to do once your da's through with 'em." He looked at me and stood. I grinned and hugged him tight.

"Happy Christmas, Ronan," I said. "How are you doing? You look wonderful."

He hugged me back. "Happy Christmas, Rosaleen." When he pulled away, I studied his face. He looked truly happy. Truly content. "I'm feeling grand," he said. "You must be missing Emmett."

I felt my lip tremble but bit it quick and tried to smile. "Of course I am," I said. "But I'm gettin' along."

He pulled me back in for a quick squeeze. Then he shook Mr. Joyce's hand vigorously.

"Happy Christmas, Mr. Joyce," he said, as Mr. Joyce slapped him on the back.

"It's good to see you, Ronan."

As we walked to the inn together, I leaned close to Ronan and whispered, "Can we attend church with you tomorrow?"

"I thought you and Emmett went to that other Baptist church." He practically spat the last words.

"We only go there to meet with our abolitionist friends. And certainly not with Mr. Joyce," I said. "You know he won't go."

"I suppose," he said. "But stay away from Aunt Maureen. You know how she feels about you."

I nudged him. "We still haven't killed one another after all this time. I think we'll make it through Christmas Mass."

~

"Happy Christmas!" Miss Susan said, swinging open the doors of the inn.

When I hugged her, her gray hair tickled my cheek.

"Thank you," I said. "And thank you for having us."

"Eileen and Eddie are coming, too," Miss Susan said, pulling away. Eileen had replaced me at the inn when I moved to Lowell. She still did the same job I had done: waiting tables, shopping at the market, changing and washing the sheets. She had met Eddie at the docks, married him a few years ago, and now they had four children.

"You'll have a full inn!" I laughed. "How will there be room for any guests?"

"There won't," she said. "I've decided to close for the holiday."

I gasped. Miss Susan had never closed the inn. Not even for a single night.

"Truly?"

"We all need some family time," she said, touching my cheek. "Florence is coming, too."

I smiled. Florence was Miss Susan's closest and oldest friend. "It will be wonderful to see her. This is joyous, indeed."

Just then, I felt a pang of sorrow. If only Emmett could

be with us. He would be so happy to see everybody. Miss Susan must have seen my face fall.

"He's missing you, too," she said. "You can count on that."

I nodded but said nothing. Levi ran circles around our skirts, and I crouched down and caught him in my arms. He giggled. I squeezed him tight and jabbed my finger into the ticklish bone in his side. He squealed even louder with laughter. I planted a kiss on his cheek.

"Where is your ma?" I asked. He pointed to the kitchen. Of course. Marie would be preparing breakfast. I had almost forgotten we all needed to eat.

I stood up and introduced Miss Susan to Mr. Joyce. They had yet to meet, both being so busy in different cities. I knew Miss Susan was unlikely to ever leave the inn, even for a day, but in recent years, I had urged Mr. Joyce to come to Boston with me on many occasions. I was grateful he had finally agreed.

"Miss Susan," I said. "This is Mr. Joyce. Steven's grandfather."

They shook hands.

"It's lovely to meet you after all this time," Mr. Joyce said.

"I agree," Miss Susan said. "I hope you'll find the inn a pleasant stay."

"Oh, I'm sure I will," he said, craning his neck to look all around. "You run this place all by yourself?"

I studied them, standing across from one another, and realized that they were close in age. Yet, neither of them had slowed down at all. Miss Susan grinned and winked.

"Oh no," she said. "I have Marie. And Eileen. And if I

ever get too old to do it anymore, I'll give all its charm and headaches to Marie."

I was glad to hear her say it. I had always hoped the inn would go to Marie. My gaze wandered to Ronan, standing awkwardly just inside the door.

"You remember Ronan, don't you, Miss Susan?" I asked, loudly and in his direction. He shuffled over and shook her hand.

"Good morning, ma'am," he said.

"Of course I remember you, Ronan," she said. "You've grown since I last saw you."

He gave her a simple smile and nod.

"Happy Christmas, ma'am."

Ronan was always quiet and formal around my friends at the inn—except for Eileen and Eddie. He hadn't spent much time around Yankees or Black people, and his apprehension was always apparent. To Marie and her family, he was polite—but perhaps only for my sake. The things he must have heard about Black people from his friends and family would have surely made me as angry as Patrick Donahoe's editorials. He would never speak of those things to me, though, so I didn't know how he truly felt.

Still, I saw him watch Steven and Levi chasing each other, and a look of fondness passed over his face. Like he wanted to join the game.

Voices came from the dining room, and when I looked over, I saw Gil, Zeke, and Lydia—who was holding Marie's youngest, baby Jane—seated at a table together. Marie's husband, Gil, had gotten thinner when he quit drinking, and now, his time in the militia had slowly hardened his soft edges. His belly no longer stuck out over his pants when he sat down. His shoulders lifted instead of slouched. Lydia's husband, Zeke, looked no older than the first time I had met him more than ten years ago. I wondered if the man would ever age. And Lydia looked as lovely as ever. Her round face and clear skin only wrinkled around her eyes, where her smile often reached.

Next to their table was another, where Lydia's children, Angel and Eliza, sat hunched together over a magazine, heads just touching. Eliza was the same age as Steven but much more outspoken.

The adults were laughing about something when I walked over. Angel glanced up and met my eye. She grinned and popped up from her seat. We embraced tightly. When we pulled away, I admired her dress. The hoop was enormous. The entire dress was green with gold stitching. There were buttons from her neck to her waist, and the sleeves were wide, narrowing only at the wrist with a dark-blue button, the color of the night sky. Lydia was a striking woman, but Angel was growing into something else entirely. A breathtaking type of beauty. Even during these years that were supposed to be awkward and strange, Angel never seemed to grow too quickly and was never bothered by pimples. Her teeth never became crooked or gaped like those of other children her age.

"This dress," I marveled.

She smiled wider. "Momma made it especially for me."

"If only you had somewhere grand to wear it," I said. "You look like royalty."

She shrugged. I leaned in closer.

"Happy twelfth birthday," I whispered, slipping her a book. She looked down at it. "It's by that scientist you like."

Her eyes lit up, and a smile spread across her face.

"Thank you, Rosaleen! Didn't I tell you that he was there speaking at the debate?"

"What debate?" I asked. She glanced around us, making sure that everyone else was distracted.

"The one about Charles Darwin," she said, real low. "At the Academy of Arts and Sciences."

I raised my eyebrows.

"You didn't go, did you?" I asked.

"Only you would take me to that."

I gasped and pretended to be offended.

"I would never encourage such a thing," I said. She giggled.

"I read about it in the newspaper," she said. "Perhaps one day I can attend. Anyhow, this man—" she pointed to the book, "—he believes that Darwin's theory can exist in harmony with Christianity. And the same for the other laws of science."

"Is that so?" I asked.

"Perhaps Daddy would let me read *On the Origin of Species* then," she sighed.

"Has he read it?" I asked. She furrowed her eyebrows.

"I can't say for certain," she said. "I think he would keep it to himself if he had. It's all too much for Momma."

Suddenly, the smell of breakfast wafted through the dining room, prickling our noses and awakening our deep morning hunger. The kitchen door swung open, and we all turned our attention to Eileen, who was carrying plates stacked with ham and sausage, biscuits and eggs. A collective moan rang out, followed by laughter. Eileen smiled at the reaction.

"I'm going to go help," I said to Angel. She nodded and followed the smell of food back to her table.

I found Marie scooping breakfast onto plates, and I kissed her cheek before grabbing three, settling one into the crook of my arm. I made two more trips before everyone was served. When I went back again for Marie, she was wiping down the counters. She dropped her rag and hugged me.

"How are you doing?" she asked.

I hugged her tighter in response. She rubbed my back.

"I can only imagine. God help me if they ever allow that militia of Gil's to fight." She pulled away and looked in my eyes. "But what Emmett's doing is important. Don't you forget that. He's fighting for democracy. And God willing, one day, the freedom of millions of people."

I finally let tears fill my eyes and fall down my face. Marie wiped them away.

"You can be proud of him," she said.

I smiled through the tears. I was proud.

Chapter Five

The men returned to the inn that night after work. Ronan, too, who, though only seventeen, worked harder and had more responsibilities than half the men my age I knew. In less than half a year's time, he would be of fighting age.

The Collinses were having a grand dinner of their own, but Ruth promised to see us on St. Patrick's Day for the parade. Eddie had left the children with his mother—a much-needed break, he said.

After supper, the inn was full of conversation over tea. Conversation that started quiet but grew louder and louder, vying to be heard over the children's giggles and arguments and shrieks. After tea, Mr. Joyce, Ronan, Miss Susan, Florence, and I all drank a few ales.

"Back in Ireland," Mr. Joyce began, and I smiled. A story was coming. He cleared his throat and scooted forward in his chair.

"We had a neighbor with chickens," he went on. "Lots of people had chickens, of course. Clucked about down the road. Got eaten by dogs, occasionally. But this neighbor. Her chickens weren't like the rest. They had names. They were trained to follow her, to stay, to eat and shite and lay eggs in three different places, and even to protect her! We all know pigs are smart, right? But chickens have got rocks for brains." He stopped and wagged his finger.

"Not Mrs. Buckley's chickens. They looked at you like they knew just what you were thinkin'. Just what you were about to do. One day I see her lining her chickens up in a row, all of 'em waitin' patiently, and I say to her, 'You ought to take those chickens on the road. Give people a show.' And you know what she does then?"

Everyone shook their heads, grinning with anticipation.

"She says, 'Wait till you see this!' And then she brings out a fiddle, and wouldn't you know it, two of those chickens start to pluck it with their beaks! She's got a chicken band!"

Everyone laughed heartily. Mr. Joyce shook his head and sat back in his chair. "Those chickens sure did love her," he said.

"That reminds me of this photograph we took the other day. . . ." Eddie jumped in, telling us about a series he was doing for the paper, taking photographs of city life—including the animals we all lived with. Eileen was right. Eddie would go on and on about photographs if you let him. The business was booming now, everyone eager to have a carte de visite done before leaving for war. A portrait to leave behind with their family. But Eddie's heart was in the newspaper series. He wanted to tell stories with his photographs.

Then it was Zeke's turn. He told us about a new invention called a telephone that none of us understood at all.

"But how do sounds travel through a wire?" Miss Susan asked.

Zeke grinned and launched into a complicated explanation about how sound waves are converted into electricity and back again before Lydia held up her hand.

"Excuse me. What?" she demanded.

"Sorry I asked," Miss Susan said, wearing a look of utter confusion.

Zeke shrugged, still grinning.

"Anytime you change your mind and want to learn about electricity, you just tell me," he said, winking.

"I'd rather chat about this Trent Affair," Lydia said. "It's become quite the contentious topic."

Gil nodded vigorously.

"Whose side do you think England will join?" he asked her.

"They won't join," Marie said. "They've got problems enough with France. They don't want to get tangled up in a war over here."

Gil shook his head. "I don't know. They might just want the South to win badly enough to do it. We know they're already building ships for them. Sending them supplies. That sounds involved to me."

"But to send the British Army to fight?" Lydia asked, eyebrows raised.

"If they do it—if they send over their men—maybe I will fight," Ronan said. "I'd take a few shots at those bastards. I'd enjoy it." We all looked at him. He hadn't said much until now.

"But not those Southerners?" Gil asked. Things got quiet. Even the children somehow sensed the seriousness of his question. Ronan sat back in his chair and crossed his arms.

"It's not my fight," he said.

"And when will it be your fight?" Gil pressed on. "Only when England joins in? What about your new country?"

Ronan shifted. "It was unlawful what the South did, I suppose. But why should I care if they secede?" He shook his head. "I just don't see how it concerns me."

"Gil," I jumped in. "Ronan isn't *of age* to fight yet. He can't and shouldn't be asked to make that decision."

Gil raised his eyebrows and put his hands up as he sat back in his chair.

"Apologies," he said. "Although, it seems as though there are plenty of young men his age who are still signing up, regardless of the official age requirement." Then he muttered, "And plenty of young men his age in *my* militia who are itching to make it their fight."

Marie shot Gil a warning look.

"You aren't exactly helping with recruiting efforts right now," she said.

I turned to Ronan. "Ronan, this war *is* your concern, even if it hasn't been made clear why. Imagine some politician in New York decides they don't like some laws that the federal government passed. They decide to secede. Then Massachusetts is next. You would lose the protections afforded to you under the Constitution."

Ronan frowned. "And what protections have been afforded to me?"

"To earn wages," I said. "To have a home or to own land

if you wish. To vote when you're of age. To speak out against unjust policies. To not have things taken right out from underneath you."

Ronan continued to frown.

"We didn't have those things in Ireland," I said, quieter now. "We have to fight to keep them here. Otherwise, America will no longer be America. It will become like England, ruled by a few with no say from the rest of us."

Everyone quietly sipped their tea. Gil nodded, apparently satisfied enough with my explanation. He knew most white men didn't fight to free the slaves. Ronan only shrugged, but I could see that behind his tough exterior, some doubt was creeping in. Perhaps he was truly considering what I had said.

"Well," said Lydia, standing up and smoothing her skirt. "It's time for these children to get to bed."

"Yes," Marie chimed in. "It is."

Baby Jane was sleeping contentedly in Marie's arms, and Levi was at her feet. Steven and Eliza were playing a game of jacks in the corner, lying on their stomachs and kicking their legs up and down. Angel had been sitting on the floor next to my chair, engrossed in the adults' conversation.

"Come on," Angel said to Eliza as she stood. "Come up to bed."

"Good night," Steven said, collecting the jacks. He placed them in a bag and stood up, rubbing his eyes, looking around sleepily.

Marie and Lydia carried Jane and Levi, and Mr. Joyce busied himself with gathering teacups and plates and bringing them to the kitchen.

"I'll take Steven to bed," Ronan said. "Where are you sleeping?"

"The second room on the left."

As he stood, I grabbed his arm. "Are you all right?" I asked.

"Brought it on myself, didn't I?" he asked with a smirk. He put his arm around Steven and walked him up the stairs.

I still felt a bit guilty. I wanted Ronan to feel as if he belonged here. As if he was welcome. I didn't want him to feel embarrassed, and I knew he tended to withdraw when he felt outmatched. I needed to go easier on him. There was plenty he didn't yet know.

Christmas morning was gray and cold. Ronan, Mr. Joyce, Steven, and I headed to Mass after breakfast, with Ronan leading the way. I walked beside him.

"Tell me more of what you think of the war," I said. "It's only us now."

"Why? So you can tell me I'm wrong?"

I shook my head. "I won't. I'm only curious. What do the men at work say?"

He took a deep breath.

"They're proud of the Irish troops," he said. "For the bravery they've shown. They're worried the war will become one to free the slaves. They don't want any more of them coming up here. And they don't want our boys dying for them They're mad at the South for not honoring the Constitution. But they say it's not our fight."

He looked sideways at me as he said that last part. Maybe he was a little ashamed he hadn't come up with that opinion himself, or maybe he was daring me to argue it.

"I see," I said. "And you agree? That it isn't your fight?"

"Yes," he said. "I agree."

"Well," I sighed. "I would keep trying to convince you that it is, except I have excellent convincing skills and I very much like having you around."

He smiled, and I looped my arm through his.

Ronan's church sat on a corner in the North End. It was a large brick structure with many small windows. The bell tower reached high into the sky—a North Star in its own right, drawing the faithful and obedient from all corners of the waterfront.

The congregants packed inside, crowding the sidewalk and spilling out onto the cobblestone streets. I reached for Steven's hand, and we shuffled into the church and down the center aisle, pushed along by the rest of the people. Ronan ushered us into a pew.

"Aunt Maureen and Uncle Will sit a few rows ahead," he said, speaking low so only I could hear.

"We could have sat with them," I said.

He shook his head and laughed. "No!"

The quiet sounds of light steps, whispers, and muffled coughs were made loud by the sheer number of people and the peaked ceiling. But it soon quieted, and only the occasional wail of a fitful baby could be heard.

This church had a large choir, and the priest was much younger than our Father O'Brien. He wore a pleased smile and every so often rocked up onto his toes.

The first reading came from a different man, a stout deacon who had a calm, contented look in his eyes.

"A reading from the book of Deuteronomy: 'Do Manfully and be of good heart: fear not, nor be ye dismayed at their sight: for the Lord thy God he himself is thy leader, and will not leave thee nor forsake thee. And Moses called Josue, and said to him before all Israel: Take courage, and be valiant for thou shalt bring this people into the land which the Lord swore he would give to their Fathers and thou shalt divide it by lot.'"

The choir sang again, and I looked down at the row of faces beside me. Bored faces, tired faces, concentrating faces. Hands in laps, hands holding those hands next to them, hands rocking babies. One ma silently pointed a warning finger in a boy's face.

When the priest stepped up for his reading, his eyes shone with pride as he looked out at his parish.

"A reading from the Holy Gospel according to Matthew," he said. His voice was deep and loud and strong. "'And entering into the house they found the child with Mary his mother, and falling down they adored him; and opening their treasures, they offered him gifts; gold, frank-incense, and myrrh. And having received an answer in sleep that they should not return to Herod, they went back another way into their country. And after they were departed, behold an angel of the Lord appeared in sleep to Joseph, saying: Arise, and take the child and his mother, and fly into Egypt: and be there until I shall tell thee. For it will come to pass that Herod will seek the child to destroy him. Who arose, and took the child and his mother by night, and retired into Egypt: and he was there until the death of Herod. That it might be fulfilled which the Lord spoke by prophet, saying: Out of Egypt have I called my son.' This is the Gospel of the Lord."

"Praise the Lord Jesus Christ," we said.

He licked his lips and pressed them together before speaking again. "Happy Christmas to you all! I am full of joy to celebrate the birth of Jesus Christ with you."

His brogue sounded like home to me. He was clearly from Cork, though not from the city. He shifted his weight and cleared his throat. His face was so animated when he spoke, but now he let it rest for a moment before furrowing his eyebrows again.

"It might feel impossible, at times, to have a close relationship with God. He is God and we are men. There is an unbridgeable gap between us and Him. And yet, he sent his son, Jesus Christ, to become a man, too. To feel our pain. To carry our burdens. There is much we can relate to, even in the story of his birth. He was born humbly, laid in a manger. Surrounded by all manner of creatures of burden. Donkeys and cows and perhaps an Irishman, sleeping one off in the hay." He grinned at us all, and laughter rippled through the church.

"He was immediately sent away. He was told to flee both his home and birthplace. Most of you can relate to this, as well."

There were no laughs this time. Just a few creaks of the pews.

"He took refuge in a land where it would be safe for him. As did all of you when you came to America."

Now the church was silent.

"And when it was safe to return, God called him home.

You heard Deacon O'Malley read a passage of God calling his people home. Both readings are also about trust. Joseph and Joshua trusting in God to share their burdens, to bestow bravery upon them, and then, to bring them home again."

The faces in my row focused with rapt attention.

"God led each and every one of you to safety by bringing you here. This place is holy. This country is your Egypt. Here, we have been able to lay our burdens at His feet. To feel protected. Now, God is calling on *you* to protect this holy land in return. To protect it from evil forces that are threatening to undo it from within. Will you answer His call? Will you stand tall for Him? For this sacred place? Will you ensure that it will be a safe and holy place for generations to come?"

He breathed in deeply, his chin lifting higher as he concluded: "I believe you will. I believe this, because God has given us something. The same thing he gave to Joshua. He has blessed our people with a natural bravery. Bravery that will be used today to protect America. To protect *our* Egypt. And perhaps tomorrow, He will call us back to our homeland, where we will use that bravery again."

I admired his homily. The passion. The persuasion. If only his next one could be about emancipation. I almost laughed out loud at the thought. Perhaps one day.

He waited a theatrical amount of time before saying, "Let us pray."

Chapter Six

JANUARY 1862

The weeks following Christmas were dreary. Emmett had kept our home loud and lively, and without him, the silence made our hearts heavy.

I had already received a letter from him. Apparently, there wasn't much to do at Camp Cameron other than drill and try to keep warm. I held it in my lap as I stared out the window. Mr. Joyce was in his workshop and Steven was at school.

I ought to write him back, I thought. I was so eager to tell him the news that I would be writing for *The Commonwealth*, and yet, I didn't want to write to him. I wanted to see him. I wanted him to stand in front of me so I could watch his lips break into a smile. I wanted to feel his arms envelop me in a hug. Looking at the letter, I felt flat. As gray as the sky outside. I sighed.

I walked up the stairs to my office in our home. Calvin was in Boston today. As a state representative, he frequently took the train into the city for the day, and as his clerk, I sometimes accompanied him. But today, he'd

LISA BOYLE

gone alone, and I was left to do the work he needed done in Lowell. I had finished it already that morning, and now I was restless. It was time to write the Paddy letter. I hoped I could at least focus on that.

I read over my notes from my meeting with Phillips and thought about my conversation with Ronan. *It's not my fight*, he'd said. Donahoe claimed that emancipating the slaves would make it even less of the Irish's fight. I needed to argue. I needed something—even something small—to make emancipation relevant to the Irish. Perhaps Phillips was right. Perhaps taxes were the angle. I had done some research since our meeting. I began to write.

To the sons and daughters of Erin,

I write to you today to respond to the false and ugly claims made by The Boston Pilot. Like you, I was born on Irish soil. Like you, I fled famine and disease. Like you, today, I call myself an American.

I have read this country's Constitution. You have been told that it allows slavery. This is true. The slave is written into the Constitution as an "other," who is counted as only three-fifths of a person. You, however, are counted as one whole person.

What does this mean? It means that before this war began, when Massachusetts paid the federal tax for services and protections, it paid more for you than South Carolina did for its slaves. How do you think Massachusetts did this? By taxing you more. More for your horse. More for your cows. Your chickens. Your whiskey. Your ale. Your tobacco. All the while, Virginia and Georgia and Alabama and Kentucky paid less.

Much as England stole from Irish land to feed its people, the South stole from your purse to feed its own wealth.

No more. After this war is won, once we make this country whole again, we will pass a constitutional amendment, if need be. But no longer will we pay for feudalism.

Free the slaves! Tax the South!

Signed,

A Paddy

I went downstairs to the kitchen for a cup of tea, bringing the draft with me. Cocoa lazily followed, ambling back and forth. Her hips were tighter than they once had been, and her fur was gray around her muzzle now.

As I waited for the kettle, I paced back and forth in front of the fireplace, reading. A moment later, the front door opened, and Mr. Joyce came in, rubbing his hands together.

"May I read you this?" I asked him. "It's for that Boston paper."

For all of Mr. Joyce's disapproval when he'd first learned I was Paddy, he had long become a voice of critique, one who intimately knew the community and sometimes shared its opinions. He shrugged off his coat.

"Please," he said, joining me at the table.

I read him the letter, and as he listened, he crossed his arms and leaned back in his chair. When I looked up, he was staring intently into the fire.

"A constitutional amendment," he muttered, eyebrows furrowed in thought. "They'll certainly prefer for it to go through a legal process such as the one you're describing," he finally said. "But you still aren't addressing their greatest fears. Will they lose their jobs once the Negroes are emancipated? Will a flood of former slaves, used to working for no pay at all, undercut their precarious positions in this Northern economy?"

I bit my lip.

"The truth is that I don't know," I said.

"You might need to convince them that this won't happen," he said. "Even if you aren't convinced of it yourself. Of course the Irish would like to pay less in taxes. It's fine to tell them about this. You'll certainly educate them on something they weren't aware of before. But it won't be enough."

Phillips read my letter with a smile. He seemed particularly cheery today.

"This will certainly do," he said. "Think about what you'll write in the next one."

"I am," I said.

"Have you got an idea?"

I nodded. "I need to address jobs," I said. "And what will happen after emancipation. Will Massachusetts open the gates and let in a flood of former slaves? That's what the Irish fear most."

"Massachusetts doesn't have gates," he said, "so it's certainly possible. But . . ." He paused to fill his pipe. "After the war, the Irish will be in a better position than they were before it. You have already seen that the Yankees' respect for all of you has grown. The Irish and Negro won't be fighting over the same slice of pie anymore."

His line of reasoning made me uncomfortable.

"You're saying Black people will remain at the bottom. That they'll never rise from their station."

Phillips shrugged and struck a match. He lit his pipe and drew in a drag before slowly releasing the smoke from his lips.

"I didn't say never," he said. "I simply can't imagine it happening soon. Certainly not before the Irish."

I frowned.

"You're upset that the condition of the Irish will improve?" he asked.

"I'm upset that anyone has to settle for less than they deserve, simply because of the skin they were born in or the country they were born to."

He languidly waved away the cloud of smoke hovering in front of his face.

"It's human nature, Rosaleen," he said. "Tribes and all of that."

"But why can't it be about character? Those who work the hardest? Those who are the most honest? Who do the most for their fellow man and woman?"

I knew Phillips enjoyed arguing with me, and I fell into his trap every time. In truth, I didn't mind the challenge, either.

He pointed his pipe at me.

"This is a free market society. We reward those who are clever," he said. "Take you and your family and your friends the Sullivans, for example. You all are the wealthiest families in the Acre, aside from the clergymen. It's because you are clever people."

"And what of the clever slaves?" I asked.

"They have all escaped."

I wanted to slap him.

"You can't believe that no clever man or woman has willingly stayed behind to protect their kin as best they could?"

He took another drag of his pipe.

"Perhaps I shall learn soon enough if you are right," he said.

He smiled broadly.

"What do you mean?" I asked.

"I'll be traveling to the Carolina islands soon," he said. "The islands in South Carolina have been captured. The plantation owners there have fled, leaving behind some of the best cotton land in the whole country, as well as their slaves. We need that cotton. And so, we'll be conducting a sort of experiment. To see just how clever those former slaves are. We'll be sending a shipload of teachers to educate them. We're going to help them to plant the cotton and harvest it."

"And the former slaves will own the land?" I asked, shocked that the Northern businessmen would be so generous.

Phillips's mouth fell into a straight line.

"No," he said. "As of right now, the government owns it."

"But will they sell it to the former slaves eventually?" I asked.

"Perhaps," he said. "Or perhaps it will be sold at auction."

"It ought to be given to them," I muttered.

Phillips snorted.

"But they know nothing of the business side of things. They can't even read and write. How are they to keep ledgers? Conduct business transactions? You would be setting them up for failure. Which is why we are sending teachers to the island."

"How charitable," I said.

He grinned.

"Beneficial," he said. "For them. For us. For the mills."

This, then, was the reason for his happy mood.

"You're excited," I said.

"I am. You know I enjoy new endeavors."

Chapter Seven

MARCH 1862

Steven and I stood at the edge of the Boston Common with Miss Martha and Ruth. I hadn't yet submitted another Paddy letter and Phillips hadn't asked for it, so busy was he with Port Royal Island.

Today was Boston's St. Patrick's Day parade, and the Irish had outdone themselves this year. Smaller parades had been held in the past, but this year's was approved by the city and attended by Boston's most important officials. It would begin right here, in the heart of the city. Phillips was right. The Irish *were* moving up.

I gripped Steven's hand tighter as the crowd grew.

"Ma?" Steven tugged my arm, and I bent down to hear him say, "I'm hungry."

The boy was always hungry. I had slipped an apple into his coat pocket, but it was long gone. Across the street, I spotted a bakery. I turned to Ruth.

"May I leave Steven with you while I get him a treat at the bakery?" I asked. "He's hungry again."

Miss Martha heard me shouting over the noise of the crowd and laughed.

"Of course he is! He's a growing boy!" She reached out, clasped his shoulder, and winked at me. I smiled.

"Would either of you like something?" I asked.

"Oh dear, no," Ruth said. "We feasted at dinner, didn't we, Mother?"

"We did," Miss Martha agreed.

I looked left and right before crossing the street, watching the horses hitched to large, decorated platforms shaking their heads in boredom. I wondered if my old friend Mary still had a hand in those decorations. I dashed across the street. The crowd on the other side was just as packed, and I elbowed and wiggled my way down the sidewalk. I was looking down at my purse, making sure I had brought enough coin, when I accidentally bumped a man's shoulder.

"I'm sorry, sir," I said, and as he turned, I gasped. He broke into a slow smile. I felt myself doing the same.

"Well, that's not a face I've seen in a long while," he said.

"Henry?" I asked.

"Rosaleen," he said. He was certainly older, but the intense dark eyes and strong jaw were the same. I couldn't help but stare. Breathtakingly handsome, as always. Even with a new shadow of pain etched into his face.

I reached out to touch him, to ask how he was, but my hand grabbed nothing. Only an empty jacket sleeve. His arm was not there. I quickly dropped my hand.

"Goodness," I said, still not yet recovered from the shock of seeing him after so many years. "Your arm."

He looked down at his shoulder.

"I still had that the last time you saw me, didn't I?" he asked, frowning.

"Were you in battle?" I asked.

He nodded. "Bull Run. My soldiering career was short-lived."

"I'm so sorry," I said. "I suppose it's difficult to make shoes now, too."

He surprised me by laughing.

"I suppose it would be," he said. "Except that the new sewing machine put me out of a job years ago. Most people don't want to pay for handmade shoes anymore. They're all produced in a factory. I work for my father and uncle now, at the bank."

I nodded, trying to process it all.

"And . . . how have you been?" he asked, with a look of true concern.

"Well," I said. "I'm still living in Lowell. Although I come to Boston frequently on business. I'm a clerk for Representative Calvin Parker."

"That's a wonderful position," he said. Then he looked down at his feet. "Have you got a family?"

"Yes," I said. "Do you?"

He shook his head. "Not anymore. My wife passed," he said. "Not quite two years ago now."

"Oh, Henry," I said.

He swallowed hard and nodded.

"And your husband?" he asked. "Is he fighting?"

"Yes," I said. "Although, I'm not sure where at the moment. He only left a few months ago. Last I heard, he had stopped in New York."

He nodded and put his hand into his pocket.

"I imagine you've come to see the parade?" he asked.

"Yes," I said. "I was going to get a treat at the bakery for my boy."

Henry smiled.

"You've got a son?"

I smiled too.

"Steven," I said. "He's six years old."

A sadness passed over his face, and he cleared his throat.

"Well, it was wonderful to see you," he said. "Please run into me anytime you're in Boston."

I laughed. "Perhaps I will."

"My uncle's bank is right down here." He pointed down the street.

"Now I know where to find you," I said.

"Yes, you do," he said. We stood there for one more moment, looking at one another, before I said goodbye and walked into the bakery.

Chapter Eight

APRIL 1862

Mairead and I stood outside the office of the Lowell Anti-Slavery Society waiting for the news we were certain was coming at any moment. A small crowd had gathered with us, and even though it was April, it was still awfully cold. We wrapped our arms tight around ourselves. We had left the children with their grandparents and enjoyed some whiskey in my kitchen before coming out. Mairead's curly black hair was already falling from her hat and whipping around in the wind. She linked her arm through mine.

"One step closer to getting rid of the awful thing altogether," she said.

"Do you think the war will do it?" I asked.

"It'll have to, won't it?"

I sighed. "Emmett says that everything is different now that General Butler declared slaves contraband of war and they've started flocking to Union lines. That's what he's fighting for. To free the slaves."

"And it's a noble cause indeed," she said.

Dennis hadn't enlisted, and while Mairead was an ardent abolitionist, she hadn't done much to convince him. When the Irish regiments were first being formed, I had been angry that Dennis showed no interest. He and Emmett exchanged heated words on more than one occasion. But we both gave up eventually, and I supposed that argument was now between Dennis and God.

A moment later, a man burst through the door, holding a piece of paper high above his head.

"It's done!" he shouted. "President Lincoln signed it into law! Slavery in DC—in this here nation's capital—has been abolished!"

The crowd hollered and cheered. I seized Mairead and hugged her tight. This was the second piece of good news in just the past week. The first had been an order, also signed by the president, refusing to return runaway slaves, taking Butler's informal declaration one step further.

Under the streetlamp, I could see Mairead's wind-chilled red cheeks and big smile.

"Good work, Rosaleen," she said, and I laughed.

"As if I had anything to do with it!"

She leaned closer. "You had plenty to do with it. Now let's celebrate!"

We ran to the tavern, laughing and singing. The tavern was full and loud at this hour, since many men in the Acre felt the same as Dennis and Ronan. This wasn't their war. Perhaps more would join during the next call for troops. Perhaps not.

We sat in a nook near the door and sipped some more whiskey.

"Do you miss him something fierce?" Mairead finally asked.

"It's the deepest ache, right in the middle of my chest. I can only think of the next time I'll see him. I can't entertain any other thoughts of what may happen. I only imagine being in his arms again—and soon."

Mairead nodded and looked into her glass. I wondered if she felt any shame or only pity.

"Do you remember a long while ago I told you about a young man in Boston who courted me before I came here?" I asked her.

"Didn't he make shoes?" she asked.

"Yes," I said. "That's him. Well, I saw him last month at the parade."

Mairead leaned closer, her eyes wide.

"You did?"

"He lost his arm in the war," I said. "And before that his wife and the job he loved." I shook my head. "He told me to visit him where he works now at his uncle's bank."

Mairead's eyebrows went up even further.

"He sounds lonely," she said. I took a sip of whiskey.

"I feel awful for him," I said.

"How else did you feel?" Mairead asked. "Seeing him."

I felt my cheeks flush. "You know how much I love Emmett," I said. "It's nothing like that."

Mairead shook her head. "I wouldn't see him again. You're lonely. He's lonely. Nothing good can come of it."

"You're right, of course," I said. "But I do feel for him."

"Well, let him find comfort elsewhere," she said. "Even if he must pay for it. Although, if he's as handsome as you've told me, he shouldn't have to."

"Mairead!" I exclaimed. "I was speaking of being a friend! I would never—"

"I know, I know," she cut in. "But I'm sure he has friends already. He doesn't need another."

I sipped my whiskey again and closed my eyes, washing thoughts of Henry right out of my mind.

The next morning, I awoke to a throbbing headache and a letter from Emmett slipped under my door. I dragged myself out of bed, picked up the letter, and headed to the kitchen for some coffee.

I could hear Mr. Joyce pounding away at some poor piece of wood as I heated the pot of water. I rubbed my temple. It had been quite some time since I last drank whiskey, and with Mairead, it was always more than one glass. I waited until the coffee was ready and I'd had at least a few sips before reading Emmett's letter.

March 23, 1862

My love,

I write to you from South Carolina, where we are awaiting orders. Most men in this regiment were sorely disappointed to learn that we would not be fighting under General Meagher as part of the Irish Brigade. At least not for now. We were sent here instead, intended to be part of General Butler's brigade, although as you may have heard, he is on his way to New Orleans, and we are part of an expeditionary corps serving under General Sherman. It is confusing to us, as well, but luckily, I am a mere private and only do as I'm told.

It is awfully warm here already, and many men have fallen sick. I am feeling fine, only sweaty. The locals certainly weren't feeling fine when the soldiers before me arrived. I heard they were clutching their pearls and falling all over themselves to get away from us. Some of them left in their underwear! The slaves they left behind were giddy watching them sail away.

I imagine we'll see fighting soon. Quinn has been teaching us all to shoot a musket properly, which is good, because Pat wasn't putting his musket caps on and nothing was coming from his barrel at all. My new mate, Will, is probably the best shot of all of us. They say hello to you, and Pat blows a kiss. I smacked him for it just now.

Please tell Steven I love and miss him and wish he could see the beautiful beaches here. The way the seabirds hop along the coast, picking things from the sand with their beaks. And tell him that I think of him every morning. I drew him a picture on the back of this letter.

I dream every night of holding you, Rose. Running my fingers through your hair. Kissing all my favorite parts of you.

Don't miss me too much yet. We'll win this war soon.

All my love,

Emmett

I read it three times before tears began to form in my eyes. The coffee had eased the pain in my head, but now my heart ached, and I let myself sob in my chair in front of the fireplace. I tried not to think of how much I missed him. But when I read his letters, I couldn't help it.

Chapter Nine

MAY 1862

I sat in Nancy's dining room as her daughter, Caroline, played with Steven outside. The two of them were the perfect pair. Caroline, feisty and rebellious like her ma, and Steven, honest and serious and always trying to steer her away from her naughty schemes. Nancy's winding garden made for long games of hide-and-seek or tag or even sheriff and robber.

Nancy's green thumb was about the only domestic thing about her, and as soon as Calvin had suggested they hire help, Nancy jumped at the chance. They were both relieved to eat good food again.

We were just finishing tea and sandwiches when I pulled out the paper to read Nancy the latest Paddy letter. I dramatically cleared my throat, and Nancy clinked her teacup with her spoon, calling the empty dining room to attention.

"Here ye, here ye," she said. "Gather 'round and listen to the honorable Rosaleen Doherty write as though she were a man."

I smirked at her before beginning to read:

To the sons and daughters of Erin,

When we talk of the end of slavery, we talk not only of freeing people burdened under the strain of the whip, but also the end of a tyrannical economic system. You are afraid that the Negro will come north and take your job and work for less, but that is only because you are imagining an unchanged world. A world in which the north is the only region to provide economic opportunity.

This will not be the case. With the end of slavery will come a beginning of growth. The South will no longer be stagnant. Factories will open; railways will be built; businesses will thrive. All the things that have been absent from the South—pushed out to make room for the bloated beasts of cotton and sugar and tobacco—will be allowed to prosper.

The South has clung to ways of old. Outdated ways that rely on oppression. That rely on a select few men becoming rich off the toil of many. We will do away with this. We will defeat the wealthy few and welcome the masses into that land of plenty. All men: white and Black, farmer and industrialist, will see the promise before them. The promise of life, of liberty, and of the pursuit of happiness.

Join with me in calling for a new South! A prosperous South! A South without slavery!

Signed,
A Paddy

. . .

Nancy clapped and stood for a moment. "And all in favor, say aye!"

I laughed and said, "Aye!"

"What can I say?" she asked. "I love it, as always." We heard Caroline shriek in delight outside. It made me smile.

Nancy slid a different newspaper across the table. "Have you read this article yet? I think you'll find it intriguing."

I glanced at the headline. It was about General Butler's exploits in New Orleans. I began to read it while Nancy sipped her tea.

"This is fascinating," I said. "Have you read it?"

Nancy shook her head. "I only skimmed it this morning. What does it say?"

"It seems General Butler is having quite the time of it in New Orleans," I said.

"He took the city last month, though, didn't he?" she asked.

"Yes," I said. "Although, it seems the citizens there are having a hard time accepting that."

"Huh."

"It says here that: 'Upon arrival, the Negroes celebrated and blessed the troops while Confederate supporters burned cotton and sugar to keep it out of Union hands.'" I paused to read a bit more. "There is a sizable amount of poor folks, white and Black, inside the city with nothing. Butler is trying to open trade again. Telling everyone outside of the city that they can bring food and cotton through Union lines. That they will be welcomed. Though they must take the Oath of Allegiance in order to do business."

"Why doesn't Butler just feed them himself?"

"It says here he doesn't have enough food to feed them all along with our own soldiers. It seems as though he is also putting the poor whites and Blacks to work cleaning up the city."

"And how is he paying these men?"

"He's using gold, specie, any type of valuable coin. He is confiscating it from those who have funded the Confederacy. He's levying some sort of tax on the rich as a punishment for supporting the enemy."

"Ah, that's right," Nancy said. "Benjamin Butler, champion of the poor."

"I don't know what that man is," I said. "Every time I think I've figured him out, he surprises me. Had you asked me before the war if he was a friend to the slave, I would have said most certainly not. And now here he is, giving slaves a safe haven. Redistributing money from the rich slaveholders to the hands of the city's Black population." I shook my head.

"Perhaps what he's seen this past year has changed him," Nancy said. "Though, I don't understand where the cotton being brought into Union lines is going. It's only valuable if the cotton plantation owners can sell it to us, their enemies. Or if they can sell it to England."

"And selling it to England is the last thing we want. England will give them ammunition in return. We want the cotton to come to us first. And we can decide whether to send it to England or to our own mills."

"So, the cotton is coming to us, then," she said.

"It is," I said, looking up from the article. "It says citizens who are issued permits are authorized to buy cotton with gold or specie in occupied territories. It's happened already in Memphis, and now, in New Orleans."

Nancy's eyebrows went up as she sipped again.

One Tuesday morning, Phillips unexpectedly asked me to meet him at the train station, knowing we both had business in Boston that day. He was adjusting his tie and staring at nothing when I approached. His hat sat atop his valise, which stood on the ground beside him. He was not smiling this time and did not seem at ease.

"Good morning," I said, as I took my place next to him. Our train wasn't set to arrive for another ten minutes.

He said, "I wish it were a better one."

The June sun beat down warmly on my bonnet. The other ladies at the station had shed their coats and shawls and stood straight and contented, like sunflowers in the sun's rays.

"And what's the problem with today's morning?" I asked.

"I've learned some news that I thought I'd share with you. For the sake of whatever friends you still have working in the mills."

Only a few, I thought to myself. Mairead and Dennis, most importantly. We had tried to find them positions with the city over the years but without success.

"Lowell is nearly out of cotton," he said. "Our other mill towns have more on hand. And while we're slowly getting shipments, the rate of acquisition has been too slow. Some of the mills here will be shut down over the next few months."

"Which ones?" I asked.

"I can't say for certain," he said. "But if you've got people at any mill except Butler's, I would tell them to leave Lowell."

General Butler's mill. A woolen mill. The sun, which had seemed so pleasant only a moment ago, began to feel stifling.

"And go where?" I asked, unable to conceal my concern.

"There are a few companies in Lawrence and South Boston where I can guarantee them positions. Lawrence is mill work as well. South Boston is weapons work. Iron foundries."

"Will the iron foundries hire women?" I asked.

"No, but the ammunition factories will."

I was quiet, my mind busy. More people shuffled along, gathering around us.

"Thank you for telling me," I finally said.

"Speak with your friends," Phillips said. He picked up his hat and put it on. "I will need names and ages."

Emmett

Chapter Ten

We had been waiting for eight hours now. More, I suppose, if one counted our whole time in the Union Army. It had been nine months since the 28th was mustered into service.

Not all of that had been spent idly waiting, of course, though it often felt that way. Some of it had been spent truly fighting. Killing Confederates. Pulling the trigger of my musket and watching men crumple to the ground. More men than I could count bleeding to their deaths before me.

Some of that time had been spent doing grueling labor under the cover of darkness on a suffocating island. An island that ended some of the waiting for some of the men. They groaned all day and night from diseases that reminded me of those we'd contracted during the famine. The same fevers. Same delusions. It frightened me in a way that the fighting never had.

Still, some of that waiting had been dull. Painfully lonely. And still other times were some of the best of my life. Even now, as we waited to die by shell or ball, listening to Quinn tell us stories of drunken gamblers and whores he had arrested, we laughed until tears squeezed from our eyes.

"Stop," Pat gasped between wheezes. "Stop or I'll piss mehself."

I shook my head. My cheeks hurt from smiling. Thinking of Quinn finding men in alleyways with their trousers around their ankles took me far away from the mosquitoes biting at my neck and wrists. South Carolina was hot, but the Maryland humidity—even as we inched toward the autumn season—was unexpected. I swatted at one on my hand.

The insects liked to stay close to the water, I had learned, and we were waiting in the woods right by the Antietam Creek. Waiting for orders to cross it now that hundreds of men had died so that we could do so. They had died on the bridge, mostly, shot down as soon as the Confederate sharpshooters had them in their sights. But there weren't enough sharpshooters to get us all, even shooting as they were from high ground, and eventually, our soldiers had succeeded in crossing the creek. We were pushing them back now, the rebel troops that were meant to hold the south side of the creek.

My group of mates had gone quiet again, as we always did after a good story. We were all there, in Quinn's story, instead of here. It would be easy to picture the same scene in whatever town or city these men came from. Most from Massachusetts. Some from Canada. All had alleyways. All had drunks and gamblers and whores and watchmen. We imagined we were there instead of here.

But when the orders came, we would turn once again from men into soldiers. We would do our duty, but our hearts were not in it as they would have been had we been fighting under Brigadier General Thomas Francis Meagher. Even now, as the Irish Brigade was being shot down while trying to overtake rebels tucked into the relative safety of a sunken road, we wished we were among them. Meagher's men were seeing the fear in the enemy's eyes as he realized that what he had believed was folly. He was not, in fact, safe in the sunken road. Union troops were driving the rebels out, and the Irish were there to meet them. Meagher liked his men to have their bayonets fixed and ready. The boys of the Irish Brigade plunged their bayonets into the hearts of those trapped Confederates. Our hands itched to do the same. Instead, we waited.

Quinn's mate from the police force had become a signal officer, which was how we often found out more about the battle than other privates did. Quinn would sneak away when he had the chance and bring back news straight from the messenger's mouth. I looked over at Quinn now; he was still smiling faintly, although with a faraway gaze. I hoped he was thinking of the drunks and not of Nessa and his baby girl, who would be turning one any day now. There was a time for thinking about families, and that time was yesterday. Thinking about them now could make you too cowardly to fight. Though, sometimes the memory of their faces couldn't be ignored.

We all had our last letters to our families securely tucked inside our jacket pockets. Before each battle, some men would open theirs, read it again, add a line or two. There were scribbles along the sides now and at the top.

Small sentiments that couldn't be missed. We pinned our names to the insides of our collars in hopes that, if we died in battle, our letters would make it home. But all of that had been done yesterday. Now it was time to fight. If the orders would ever come.

I patted my jacket to reassure myself that my letter was still there. It was right beside the most recent issue of *The Commonwealth* newspaper. My throat tightened when I thought of the Paddy letter. Of my pride in my wife. I shook my head and tried to follow my own advice. *Now is not the time.*

Then, orders were shouted up ahead. We began to fall in line. The wait had been embarrassing for General Burnside, I imagined. Nothing that morning had gone as planned. This time, it was as simple as a bottleneck jamming up the near side of the bridge. He hadn't known that farther down the creek the water was shallow enough to walk across. I tried not to think of the sad state of our leaders. Even those in our own regiment. They spent their days with the bottle and were ignorant of the ways of war. Not that I wasn't. But at least I wasn't a drunk.

I heard the voice of our company commander. Captain Lawler had been injured in South Carolina and was still recovering. It was a shame, because he was one of the few who was widely respected among the men. Lieutenant Dwyer was left in charge.

"Attention!" he shouted. We lined up shoulder to shoulder, our muskets at our sides. He eyed us with a slight hesitation.

"The bridge is cleared, and it's the 28th's turn to cross. We'll be moving north once we cross the bridge. The enemy's artillery is positioned on the high ground behind the farm, and the skirmishers are posted all around. Keep your eyes up."

He paused to scan the company and then shouted, "Right face! Shoulder shift! Twenty-eighth Massachusetts!"

"Huh!" we yelled in return.

"Forward march!"

"Did yeh know the 51st Pennsylvania wouldn't take the bridge unless they got their whiskey ration back?" Pat leaned slightly into me as we marched.

"No," I chuckled.

"Aye!" he said. "That braggart Ferraro tried to rile them up. Says, 'Burnside has requested the 51st take the bridge. Will you do it?' And one of the men says, 'Will you give us back our whiskey?' Ferraro says, 'Yes!' And then those sons of bitches took that bridge."

I knew Pat was trying to laugh away our fears. I doubted it was true, but it made me smile.

"We should ask for a furlough, then," I said, elbowing him gently.

"Ha! They'll buy us all whores first," he said.

"Now don't go thinkin' about whores right now, Private Clifford. We know you have a soft spot for 'em. Can't have you gettin' all emotional."

"Piss off," he said, but he was smiling. I heard Quinn laughing behind us.

Then we reached the bridge. No one wanted to speak while stepping over bodies. My heart began to beat louder in my ears. My eyes tried to take in every detail of the terrain. Hills, rocks, tall grasses. My ears tried to take in every sound. Shouting, the quick pop of musket fire, the whistle of artillery. The shots sounded lighter than shells. Once we were over the hill before us, I would know exactly what they were.

My heart thumped even louder. My breath quickened. I wiped my sweaty hands along the sides of my pants as we followed Lieutenant Dwyer up the hill. We gripped the rocks and grass, trying to keep our heads down. My boots crushed dandelions.

And then, thoughts of Rose and Steven flooded my mind. The smell of her skin, the soft coos of baby Steven when she'd rocked him in her arms. I felt dizzy but pushed ahead. We crested the hill and started to march closer to the rebel sharpshooters. We were heading toward the dip in the field before the road. The whistle over my head was louder now. The rebel artillery on the opposite hill was firing cases, shots filled with shrapnel that scattered and pelted our advancing line. I could see short bursts of smoke ballooning over top of the farmhouse from enemy muskets—shooting at us. The dip wasn't as deep as I had hoped, but I knelt on one knee behind it anyway and began to load my musket.

"Ready!" I heard Sergeant Cassidy shout. "Aim! Fire!"

I aimed at the farmhouse, fired, reloaded. I bit the cartridge open. Poured powder down the barrel. Dropped in the minié ball. Rammed the ramrod into the barrel. Half cock. Musket cap on. Full cock. Aim. Fire. Again. I thought I might have hit a window. I still couldn't shoot more than twice a minute, although we'd had plenty of practice on the island. Quinn could fire three times in a minute, but he'd been no stranger to muskets before the war began. The next time I aimed, I watched a rebel soldier go down.

"Yah!" I shouted, then fired my own weapon.

A case exploded about fifty yards to our left, scattering dangerously close. We all ducked as chunks of dirt and grass and other things we would rather not identify flew into the air and rained down on our shoulders. Then, we saw a whole regiment moving together to our left. They charged toward the rebel guns. Their heads were ducked, too, anticipating the incoming shots. As they got closer, we all stopped to watch.

"Keep firing!" Sergeant Cassidy ordered. So, we did. But then a loud cheer rose above the noise, and we saw the rebels begin to retreat.

"Huzzah!" our men shouted. We stood and marched forward as the skirmishers retreated, too. There was nothing better than to see their gray backs. I wanted to fire at them as they ran, so we could step over *their* bodies instead of those of our own men.

"Feckin' traitors!" I yelled.

We marched past the farmhouse and closed ranks again. We were close now. The rebels dove behind whatever they could find. There wasn't much. One found a tree. Another a well. The others simply ran.

I heard distant shouting as I reloaded. *We have them*, I thought. *We'll take the city now and trap them. This could be it.*

I fired with purpose and precision, blocking out the yells and groans and pops and booms. It was quiet in my head. I set my sights on the rebel behind the well. He was nicely hidden. I nudged the barrel of my musket instead to a rebel running into the trees. But then, a crash of orders shattered my concentration.

"Private Doherty!" Sergeant Cassidy was yelling at me. "I said retreat!"

"Retreat?" I yelled back. I must have heard wrong.

"Fall back!" he yelled louder. "Our left flank is collapsing. Fall back to the creek!"

I looked to my left as if I could see the collapse myself. I saw nothing. Only the members of my company running back to the creek. This didn't make any sense.

"Now!" Sergeant Cassidy shouted again. I looked at the rebel behind the well. He lifted his head.

Damn this army, I thought.

Chapter Eleven

I picked at my pork and bean stew. It was rarely cooked properly, and tonight was no exception. We had marched south after the Battle at Antietam and were camped along the Potomac River. Lee's army had gotten away, and we had let them. McClellan declared it a victory for the Union. We had kept Lee from advancing further into the North, after all. But it didn't feel like a victory. Not when we had retreated just as we were gaining ground. Not when we heard the stories of the bodies upon bodies in the bloody cornfield. Thousands of men who died so that we could patiently wait for Lee to move back to Virginia unmolested.

"We kept 'em from moving into the North," Pat kept saying. And he was right. But still, we ought to have pursued those men. I took a bite of my stew.

"Just like Ma makes it," Will Malone said, chuckling.

"Your ma makes you pork and bean stew?" I smiled a bit. "You poor bastard. No wonder you joined the army."

"It's a delicacy in Chelsea," he joked.

"Remind me to never go to Chelsea," Pat said.

Alfred Banks emerged from the shadows and sidled up next to me. He was clutching a paper in his hands.

"Have you heard?" he asked me, real low so no one else could hear. I turned. Half his face was lit by the fire. He had long, light-brown hair that hung past his ears and green eyes that always looked tired. His easy smile was plastered across his face as he looked at me in anticipation.

I shook my head and took another bite of stew. I couldn't think of anything I had heard that would make Banks smile in that way.

"The president," he whispered, despite the excitement rising in his voice, "has declared emancipation."

I grinned and slapped him on the back.

"That's great news," I whispered back. I put my bowl down. "Let's take a walk."

We slipped away from the fire.

"Is it in there?" I asked, pointing to the paper. "Can I read it?"

"Not here in the dark." Banks chuckled. "But I'll tell you what it says. It says if the Confederates are still in rebellion by January 1, 1863, all their slaves will be declared free. It says we'll protect them, too. The military will protect any runaway and ensure their freedom."

"Well, that's some fine news, Banks!"

"The men won't like it, though," Banks said, still grinning. "Think they'll still fight?"

"The men who are here will," I said. "They've a duty now. To one another. To those we've already lost. We've only just started runnin' down rebs. And they like it."

Banks nodded.

"Recruiting won't get any easier, though," I said.

"Perhaps it will back home," Banks said. Banks was from Canada and had joined the fight hoping to end slavery. We looked at each other and laughed again. We could share this only with each other, but celebrate we would.

"Should we find some whiskey, then?" I asked.

Banks sighed.

"You think Martell still has some?"

"His wife sent enough for the whole regiment!"

"How did that pass inspection again?" Banks asked.

"She hid it in a turkey," I said.

"What'll we tell him we want it for?" Banks asked.

"On account of you becoming an uncle, of course," I said, putting my hand on his shoulder, steering him toward Martell's tent.

He looked at me, equal parts appalled and impressed at my ability to lie so easily.

"How could I forget?"

I awoke the next morning to the sound of the assembly bugle and only a little regret pounding inside my head. I thought of all the people whose lives were about to change with the promise of freedom. If only we could reach them. I felt a new sense of urgency and thought of Rose as I stared at the top of the inside of my tent. I pictured her face as she heard the news. The way her smile would reach nearly to her ears. The way her skin would crinkle at the corners of her eyes. I would write to her today. I had written to her the day after Antietam to assure her of my well-being. I wished I could rush it to her. Clip it to the wings of a bird. The news of the cornfield and the sunken lane had spread among the troops like a billowing cloud. The newspapers would carry those numbers faster than the post would carry my letter. Many wives had been widowed that day.

When she received that letter, she would feel my frustration. I'd been honest with her, as I always was. If I returned to her, I wouldn't return a stranger.

But now I felt hopeful again. I felt our purpose had been renewed. I needed to share that with her, too. I finally stood, grabbed my pants, and put them on. Quinn's spot inside the tent was empty, as was Malone's. Pat still snored, and I shook his shoulder before walking out to the trees to relieve myself. Just as I was finishing, I heard shouting. I went toward it. Some men stood circled together in the trees. Not men. Officers. I hid myself behind a large trunk to listen.

"He's bringing in some outsider to command it," I heard a voice say.

"Bet he's not even Irish!" another man said.

"Ah, the governor isn't that daft," the first said. "He's Irish, all right. But he isn't one of us! Is he implying that none of us are fit to fill the position?"

I heard a murmur of agreement.

"Any of us would make a fine commander of this regiment!"

I bit the inside of my cheek to keep from laughing. The langers couldn't lead a waltz. I walked away, careful not to step too heavily or snap any branches. Though, by now, they were loudly commending one another on their brave deeds, and it didn't matter much anyway. If our regiment was getting a new commander, I could only hope he was more competent than they.

I found Quinn standing on the other side of our tent, boiling his clothes.

"Up and at 'em today, you are," I said.

"Couldn't sleep," he said. "It's Grace's first birthday."

"How's Nessa doin' with her?" I asked.

"Better," he said. "Says Grace is walking now. I would imagine that her moving around so much would make things harder, but Nessa says Grace is much happier. She likes to take her out of the city for a bit. Let her stumble around. Pull grass from the roots with her little chubby fists."

He pulled a flannel shirt out with a stick. I smiled, remembering Steven at that age.

"I can't picture it," Quinn said, shaking his head. "She was this small, red, screaming little ball when I left. And now she's walking around? Nessa says . . ." He stopped talking for a moment. I waited while he turned his back to me to hang the shirt on a line. He turned back around and cleared his throat.

"She says 'Da' when she sees my picture. Points at it and says 'Da.'"

I could barely see the wetness in his eyes by the moonlight. I stepped forward and put my hand on his shoulder.

"She'll see her da again," I said.

Quinn looked at the ground and nodded. Reveille interrupted us. Quinn pulled some socks from the pot, waved them a bit in the cool air. Both of us hurried to pull our boots on. We never knew what to expect at roll call. Some days they didn't care if we showed up half-naked. Or not at all. Others, we would get an earful about any small infraction. Sometimes a bad hangover was all that stood in the way of us getting strapped to a wooden horse all day.

We lined up shoulder to shoulder in front of the sergeants. The commissioned officers stood somewhat back and to the side. I saw Lieutenant Kenneth Hayes—the most miserable bastard to hold a command this side of the Potomac—scratch his bollocks. My tent mates stood to my right. Banks and his tent mates—Osmond Hall, Hugh McDermott, and Rudolph Klein—normally stood to my left. But Klein was nowhere to be seen, and McDermott's stupid grin told me he knew why.

I looked around as roll call began, hoping Klein would scurry into line, but I saw no sign of him. If anyone would be punished for missing roll call, it would be Klein. Most of the men loved to hate him and see him suffer. The officers especially. They saw him as weak and were embarrassed by him. They would take out their anger—from battle or from a slight or from a petty letter from their wife—on Klein.

Sometimes Klein irritated us all. He had a knack for being clumsy at the worst possible times. Military tasks were tedious, and often, just as a soldier thought he had finished with something, Klein would find a way of ruining it and forcing the soldier to start over. He didn't mean it. His intentions were good. Often, he was trying to help. But he turned situation into disasters. Men like Klein were called "Jonahs"—a title one wasn't honored to wear.

"Klein, Rudolph!" the sergeant called. Luckily, it was still dark.

"Here!" I shouted in the highest voice I could muster.

Pat and Malone snickered, but McDermott shot me an ominous glare. Good. I wished he would start the fight that had been simmering between the two of us for all this time. He was a small-minded man with a temper left unchecked due to his size. Most men backed down when facing his fist. But I was beginning to welcome it. As long as I could land one good blow first.

The sergeant checked his box and continued down the list. After roll call, McDermott didn't look at me or the others. He started off toward the officers, dramatically stomping and swinging his fists. Malone ran up behind him and flicked his ear. McDermott spun around, furious, spittle escaping his mouth and dripping onto his large red beard.

"Damn you, Malone," McDermott growled, lunging at him. Malone danced to the side. He was skinny. Very skinny. And agile. He laughed while he did it.

"Come get me, yeh oaf. Yeh big, fat snitch." He darted away, still laughing.

McDermott pointed a thick finger in my face.

"Yeh covered for that Jonah?" he asked me.

"What did you do to him?" I asked.

"Wouldn't you like to know?" he said. "Yeh aren't to cover for that rat."

I shrugged.

"Didn't," I said. "I heard him myself. He said, 'Here!' in that squeaky little voice of his."

"That's how it's gonna be, huh, Doherty?" McDermott puffed up his chest, and I tried not to laugh at how ridiculous he looked.

"Why don't you take a seat for a minute, big boy?" I said.

"Or you'll do what?" He was close enough now that I could smell his terrible breath.

"Knock your feckin' teeth out," I hissed. "The few you still have."

It's coming, I thought. *Hit me.* But then Pat stepped between us.

"All right, lads," Pat said, leading me away by the arm. "We're all on the same team, remember?"

The breakfast call bugle played, and McDermott hocked an impressive amount of saliva onto the ground.

Chapter Twelve

"Found him," Quinn said, meeting me midway between the company cook and the tents. I placed my breakfast down in front of our tent before following him. He led me to a fence post where Klein was sitting. He had been gagged with a sock. His arms were tied behind him to the post, the word "Jonah" carved above his head. We untied him and took the sock from his mouth.

"What kind of trouble am I in for missing roll call?" he asked, scrubbing his tongue with his palm, trying to rub away the taste of dirty sock.

"We covered for you," I said. "But stay out of his way, huh? No knocking over his coffee, no spilling soup down his back."

Klein's face got red.

"I didn't try to," he said.

"I know." I reached out a hand to help him up.

Pat walked up to us.

"There you are," he said. He surveyed the scene for a moment. "Where were you back there, City Marshal Sullivan? I had to pull this guy—" he motioned to me, "—away from McDermott! Have you gone mad, Doherty?"

I grinned.

"Maybe I'd like to see Emmett level him," Quinn said. "Maybe I'd like to stomp on his ugly face once or twice, too."

Pat looked shocked.

Quinn slapped him on the back and chuckled. "We aren't in Lowell anymore."

Klein stood up but didn't move from the fence post. He looked as if he were afraid to mess something up again.

"Go ahead," I said. "Get your breakfast. You'll be fine."

He swallowed and nodded, and we watched him drag his feet toward the cookhouse. The sun was just peeking out from behind the trees, and Quinn, Pat, and I walked back to eat our own breakfast. We squinted at our food. It was not good. We ate quickly to get it over with.

The day passed same as ever. Guard mounting, a bit of drilling but not enough, retreat roll call, a half-hearted dress parade, and the evening to ourselves. I was writing to Rose when I heard rising voices competing with one another. The absence of laughter. I looked to see who was arguing.

Pat and Malone sat with six other men around a card table made from hardtack boxes. They were squatting or kneeling or sitting on barrels and logs. Pat and Malone weren't speaking, only listening.

"I'm not fightin' for no nigger!" one of the others said. Lots of heads nodded.

"We put our lives on the line out there, our mates *gave*

their lives, and he turns it into *this* kind of war?" another said.

Malone cleared his throat.

"As far as I'm concerned, we're still fightin' for the same reasons we always were. For the Union. For self-government. So that one day we can beat those English scum and kick 'em out of Ireland."

"Yah!" a short man with a full beard agreed.

"No," the first man said. His back was to me, and when he turned his head to spit, I could see how young he was. "This was his intention all along. Him and his Black Republicans. I knew it."

"Why are you here, then?" I called from where I was sitting. All the men quieted. The young speaker turned to squint at me.

"What'd ya say?" he asked. I stood up. I wasn't trying to fight this boy. Because that's what he was. A boy. But there was no use in arguing sitting down.

"Why did you enlist?" I asked. "If you've always known that was what this war was about?"

He got red-faced for a moment, but I interrupted his next thought before he could say it.

"This move is smart, if you think about it," I said. "It'll help us win this war. It'll weaken them from the inside. Those former slaves will come to us whenever and wherever they can. And they'll fight for us, too."

"This is a white man's war! We don't need 'em. And anyhow, I'm not fightin' beside 'em!" He threw his arms up in frustration. He turned back around to the others. "Are you?" he asked them.

A couple heads shook, but no one spoke.

"It's a military necessity," I said. "You fight alongside Yankees, don't you? Some who might have been Know-Nothings. It's no longer Irish against Yankee or Irish against Negro. It's lovers of America, lovers of *freedom*, against landowners who get rich off the labor and suffering of those they see as inferior." I let that sit in the air for a moment before asking, "Doesn't that sound familiar to you?"

A couple grunts of agreement came from behind the boy. The young speaker reached into his jacket and held out a newspaper article.

"But this here—" He tapped it with force. "It says England won't support the South now that he's done this. We won't get the chance to fight 'em now."

"Sure we will," I said, nodding. "When we're stronger. When we've learned how to fight properly. We'll fight them *for* Ireland, *in* Ireland. And we'll win."

"You're damn right we will!" Malone yelled. A few of the men whooped.

Malone jumped up and approached the boy. "Hannigan, those rebs killed your cousin," he said.

The boy looked down and nodded. Malone put his hand on Hannigan's shoulder.

"We can't let them get away with that, now, can we?"

"Hell no," the boy said, quietly, looking back up into Malone's eyes.

"Come on. It's time for tattoo," Malone said. He pointed his finger into the air, and almost on cue, the bugle announced our final roll call of the day.

Chapter Thirteen

OCTOBER 1862

I was standing rear guard, expecting relief soon, when I heard rustling in the trees. I stood up straighter and squinted, but even the sun was not yet visible.

"Who comes there?" I asked, even though it wasn't quite dark anymore.

More rustling. I strained to see what was making the noise. It was no small animal.

Just then, a Black man appeared from the woods.

"Sir," he said. "Don't shoot us."

"I won't," I said. "But I can't drop my weapon, either. Approach."

He was wearing a white shirt that was yellowed and grayed from years of use. It hung from him. His pants were too short. He held a hat in his hand, and he raised it, along with his other hand as he neared. A taller man came up next to him, holding aside the branches to allow them both to pass. The taller man was young, I saw. Almost still a boy.

"My family's a ways back," he said. "But they comin'. We heard we was free if we could find the Yankees."

"Yes," I said. "That's true."

I saw him glance at the young man but couldn't make out what passed between them.

"How many are with you?" I asked.

"Ten," he said. "Besides my son here, James."

"You're eleven and twelve?" I asked.

"Yes, sir," he said.

I knew I wasn't to leave my guard. I looked at the sky, trying to determine the time.

"We crossed the river just last night," he went on.

"What's your name?" I asked.

"Chauncy, sir."

"Well, Chauncy, I'm going to get you to the contraband camp, but my relief hasn't come yet. I think we might want to wait until your family gets here, too."

"That's a fine idea, sir," Chauncy said. James hadn't moved much or said anything.

"You two can sit if you'd like." I motioned to some logs scattered across the ground.

"Oh no, sir. No thank you. I'm still too skittish to be sittin'." He looked exhausted. His body was slightly slumped, and he kept rubbing the back of his neck.

"You sure?" I asked. "It's my job to protect you. You don't need to be looking out for anything here."

Chauncy and James just stared at me in silence.

"Protect us?" James finally spoke. His voice was deep but a little shaky, too. Like he was just trying it on.

"That's right," I said. "The president's proclamation says I'm to protect you."

James cleared his throat.

"We done a good job doin' that ourselves," he said.

"Yes," I agreed. "You did. You made it here. But if you'd like a rest . . ."

"No, sir," James said before I could finish. So, we stood waiting in a small circle, as the sun started to rise. Chauncy looked to be about fifty years old. His face was covered with a short, graying beard, and his forehead bore a couple of slight creases. His hair was receding. James, though, had a full head of healthy hair and round eyes that stared at me with both a curiosity and a fierceness.

When the family's wagon, led by a couple of skinny and tired-looking donkeys came crashing through the woods, it caused quite a stir in the camp. From my right, I heard Malone shout from his post, "Who's there!"

"'Contraband,'" I shouted back, searching the wary faces of the women and children and two much older men sitting atop the wagon.

The wagon arrived just as breakfast was being served, and a few soldiers wandered over to see what the excitement was all about.

"Well, if it isn't a raggedy bunch of pickaninnies," one of them laughed. I watched James grip the branch he held a bit tighter. Chauncy looked away, pretending not to notice the jeers.

McDermott sidled up to me.

"I'd say our contraband camp is about full up," he said. With nowhere else for the runaways to go, separate contra-band camps had been erected wherever the Union Army camped.

"It's not," I assured the group. "We've plenty of room for you. You'll be safe here."

I could feel my face grow hot. I felt ridiculous saying it. I was sure this place didn't seem safe to them.

Chauncy still nodded, though, and stared at me in hopes of some guidance.

I turned and scanned the group of men behind me for someone I could trust. Klein stood off to the side, craning his neck to see the new arrivals.

"Klein," I said, loudly. His gaze darted to me. He looked as if he'd rather crawl in a hole than respond.

"Please go and find the officer on guard and tell him we've got some contraband."

He nodded and scrambled off. McDermott crossed his arms and snorted but didn't take his eyes off the group of freedmen and -women.

"Shoulda guessed you were a Black Republican," he said. "Doherty, the protector of all sorts of wretched creatures."

He glared at the family before leaving. The other men were making monkey noises behind me, and I turned quickly.

"Piss off! Now!" I shouted. "Before I shoot each of you in the foot!"

They kept on laughing as they sauntered off.

"Sorry," I muttered to the group. Chauncy gave me a strained smile.

"We're used to it," he said. "We're used to it all."

James, though, looked as though his mind had left us after that first insult. He stared at my musket.

"How do I get one of those?" he asked.

"A weapon?"

He nodded.

"I'd like to fight, too," he said. "Fight for my family and our freedom. I'd like to kill some'a those Confederates. You kill any?"

"Yes," I said. "Down in South Carolina. Up here in Maryland, too."

He nodded, looking thoughtful.

"That's good," he said.

"I . . . I don't think they're letting Negroes fire weapons yet," I said. "You might be able to help shuttle rounds for artillery. I could certainly put in a word for you."

"What's artillery?" he asked.

"The big guns."

His face lit up.

"I'd like that," he said.

I nodded. Just then, I heard the sound of boots stomping across the wet morning ground. I turned to see Lieutenant Hayes.

"Some contraband, sir," I said, saluting. "They just crossed the river last night. Should I bring them to Colonel Byrnes?"

"I will take them," he said. He walked around the wagon, surveying the group. "You can lead the pathetic beings, I suppose."

I clenched my teeth.

"I mean the donkeys," he sneered. "Come along." And he began walking.

Chauncy and James followed. I walked between the donkeys, guiding them toward Colonel Byrnes's tent.

Colonel Byrnes had only just arrived the previous week, and none of the enlisted men knew what to think of him yet. Many of the officers had hated him immediately for taking what they believed was rightfully theirs.

When we arrived, Lieutenant Hayes was let in right away, and I stood just outside the tent, straining to hear.

"Take them to up to the corps' tents. To General Burnside," Colonel Byrnes was saying. "They'll want to question them about the enemy's whereabouts and movements. Find out if they've seen anything. If they can impart any information."

Lieutenant Hayes scoffed. "I doubt they can tell their left foot from their right, let alone provide valuable military intelligence."

"Don't be so sure," Colonel Byrnes said. "They may prove even more useful than you."

There was silence for a moment, and I wished badly that I could see the lieutenant's face.

"You're dismissed," Colonel Byrnes finally said.

A week later, Lieutenant Hayes was gone. And that wasn't the only change Colonel Byrnes made.

Chapter Fourteen

NOVEMBER 1862

Officers were demoted. Others resigned. Non-Irish recruits joined the regiment in greater numbers. A drum was finally brought in. Roll call, drill, and dress parade were performed with a strict attention to detail. Punishments became more regular, and discipline improved. Hugh McDermott was only one of many soldiers who were less than pleased at this new way of operating. The favorites of the former officers grumbled their way about camp, showing for sick call more often, and taking the longest possible time to perform the easiest tasks.

But Colonel Byrnes gave me hope. Many resented that he was an outsider of the regiment. But he had proven himself to be an adept leader in an artillery unit before coming to us. And he was Irish. For the first time in my military career, I respected the man I was saluting.

On a cold but sunny November morning, the regiment stood at attention for roll call. Colonel Byrnes was not standing a distance away, as usual, but rather right next to the sergeants performing roll call. After all were accounted for, he spoke.

"I have some news," his voice boomed, "that I hope will lift the spirits of this regiment. Governor Andrew has just informed me that the 28th Massachusetts Infantry will, from this day forth, be the fourth regiment of the Irish Brigade."

A few men laughed quietly in disbelief.

"Allow yourself a few moments to celebrate this morning. You are dismissed."

I turned to Pat and saw his grin. We hugged each other tight, smacking each other on the back. I didn't know whether to laugh or cry, so I sort of just grunted. My chest felt as though it would burst. I was speechless. I pulled away, and the rest of the Irishmen were looking at each other with the same look of stunned happiness. Then, Malone started to sing. He had a deep and scratching voice. It was a strange sound to come from the likes of him. But we loved to hear it in a jig.

> *I'm Paddy Magee, sir, from Ballinahee, sir*
> *In an elegant ship I come over the say,*
> *Father Donahoe sent me, my passage he lent me—*
> *Sure, only for that I'd a walked all the way!*

Pat and I joined in. Our voices less harmonious.

> *He talked of America's freedom and glory,*
> *"Begorra," says I, "that's the country for me!"*
> *So, to end a long story, I've come now before ye*
> *To give the opinions of Paddy Magee*

Quinn and a few others joined in next.

> When Ireland was needing and famine was
>   feeding
> And thousands were dying for something to eat
> 'Twas America's daughters that sent over the
>   waters
> The ships that were loaded with corn and wheat

Now, nearly the whole company was singing. Even a few who weren't Irish. We sang enough, as it was, that they knew the words.

> And Irishmen sure will forever remember
> The vessels that carried the flag of the free.
> And the land that befriended, they'll die to
>   defend it
> And that's the opinions of Paddy Magee

Malone hopped up onto a barrel for the next part, wobbled for a moment, and solicited laughter from the men.

> I'm sure none are bolder the musket to shoulder
> Enlisting to learn the soldiering trade—
> With Corcoran fighting, in Meagher delighting
> They swell up the ranks of the Irish Brigade!

Loud cheers rose up at that, drowning out the song for a moment. When it picked back up, I was certain even the artillery boys could hear us.

With Columbia defying the bold British Lion
The sons of Old Ireland forever shall be;
I'll have no intervention if that's their intention—
And that's the opinions of Paddy Magee

We all started for the company cookhouse then, still singing to one another as we went.

That whole day felt like Christmas morning, and we were all giddy with good cheer—like children who had been surprised with candy and toys. We wanted to fight after that. Right then. We couldn't wait to be in front of Meagher, to stand next to the boys of the 69th New York. To look up at that green flag billowing in the wind. To see the Confederates shudder at the sight, and to hear them say, "Here come those crazy Irishmen . . ." with fear in their throats. To fix our bayonets. We were like dogs who could smell the fresh meat just on the other side of the fence.

But it was winter. The season of fighting was over. Byrnes ordered us to begin preparing winter quarters since our tents would no longer suffice. The snow began to come down. We needed log huts. So, we spent our days chopping wood instead of fighting, picturing those gray coats as we plunged our axes into felled trees. We were nearly done setting up the bare bones of the hut when we got the orders.

First Lieutenant Bailey walked briskly over to our row of half-built huts, logs lying here and there in a maze. He stepped over a few before giving up and calling for our attention. We turned and acknowledged, "Aye, sir," with snow falling softly on our shoulders.

"Your wish has been granted, boys," he said. "We're to

meet up with our new brigade in Virginia. Seems General Burnside is trying to fit in one more campaign. Get to packing."

None of our usual grumbling followed. We were too excited. We kicked logs out of the way, slipping on the wet ground as we rushed to our tents, not even angry that our hard work was for naught.

Not one rebel soldier could have felt the way I did that day. Their cause was rotten. Their leaders driven by greed. We had Thomas Francis Meagher. I pitied them.

Once we had decided which of our things were worthy of coming along, we made a bonfire of the rest. Rations had been distributed. Ammunition stored away. And now, we took advantage of the rule suspensions.

When the fire burned bright, we sang a lively song, and when it started to dim, we sang something slower and sweeter. We spoke of the hell of the South Carolina islands and of the crushing defeat of the Second Battle of Bull Run.

"That was back when we were fightin' for somethin'," McDermott grumbled from the outskirts of the group.

"And we're not now?" I asked.

"That president of yours seems to think I signed up to free the slaves." He snorted, "Don't give two shites about those slaves."

"We're fightin' for the Union," Malone insisted.

"No," McDermott said. "He's twisted it with that proclamation. Made it something else. Something ugly. No white man should be fightin' for that. It isn't my business what the Southerners do with those colored people."

"Why do you think they seceded in the first place?" I asked. "For the right to keep their slaves. It's always been about the slaves." The men had grown quiet. This kind of talk always made them uncomfortable. "You should've been paying attention."

McDermott stood up and glared at me across the fire. He was about to walk away, but I had one more thing to say.

"You aren't very good at that, though, are you? Like in South Carolina, when you should've been paying attention but dropped your musket instead and kept runnin' without it."

He stepped closer to the fire. I could see his big, ugly face now, breathing heavily. All the blood had rushed to his head.

"You're a real arsehole, Doherty," he said. "And you better watch your back. Watch your back before you find my bayonet stickin' out of it." He kicked the burning ashes, sending embers flying into the air at me. I tried to shield myself, but I was too late.

"Arrah now!" I yelled as I clawed at my eyes. Something had gotten in there, and it burned like hell. Everyone jumped up. Malone patted at my jacket. A piece must have landed there, too. I could hear the commotion of the others but couldn't see anything.

"Hey, hey! That's enough! Back up, McDermott. We're on the same side here!" they hollered.

"Get off me, damn it," McDermott growled. I tried to

look at him, but everything was blurred, and I only saw a mass of people.

"You and your filthy Black Republicans are scum!" McDermott railed. "Mark my words, Doherty, I will see you dead before this war is over."

"Try it then!" I shouted, lunging toward him and the fire. Figures started to appear in my vision. "Go ahead and kill me now, you coward!"

More grunts and shouts. The men were holding his arms, three on each side. One of McDermott's friends, Griffin, stood in front of him. He put a hand on McDermott's chest and spoke to him in hushed tones. He turned to look at me over his shoulder and then said something else I couldn't hear. Then Griffin nodded at the other men, and they let go of McDermott.

"Not here," McDermott said. "And not now. But you better have those sins absolved by Father Corby. And soon."

Griffin put his hand on McDermott's shoulder and steered him away while we all stared after them. My breathing was still quick, and for a moment, I thought of running after him. But then Malone stepped in front of me and patted my arm.

"You're well," he said. "How many fingers am I holding up?" He lifted his first two fingers up in a V.

"Chucklehead," I grunted. Will hooted.

"Told yeh, you're all right, mate."

I sat back down, still shaking a bit. Still trying to rub the soot out of my eyes. Everyone else slowly sat back down, too, clearing their throats and thinking about how to bring back the cheerier mood.

"I still can't believe McClellan's gone," Pat finally said. Men agreed loudly, glad that someone had said something.

"That man turned us into a real army," Malone said.

"But he didn't go after Lee after Antietam," Quinn said.

"Hell, when did he ever go after Lee?" I mumbled, squeezing my eyes tight and opening them again.

"Come on!" Malone answered, gently shoving my shoulder. "Little Mac loves the Irish. He would've used us if he thought we could beat 'em."

I shook my head. "We *did* beat them. We had them beat. Everywhere the Irish were, those rebel boys were retreating. At the bridge, in the sunken road."

Malone snorted. "They weren't retreatin' at the sunken road. They were bleedin'. Bayoneted through the heart."

I tried to look around the fire, to really see everyone around me. Their details were coming back, my watery eyes drying out, adjusting again. I tried to shake it off. Forget about it. Enjoy myself again.

"McClellan could never have won this war," Quinn said. "But is Burnside the man to do it?"

"We've got to give him a chance," Pat said. "He's bold, we know that."

"Took him four hours to cross a bloody bridge, though," Malone said, and we all laughed.

I realized then how quiet Banks had been.

"Banks," I said. "Tell us a story about Montreal."

Malone rubbed his hands together quickly over the flames.

"Yes, tell us a story, you Canadian bastard."

Banks laughed.

"We've got Irish up in Montreal, too, you know," he said.

Pat slapped Banks on the back.

"Course you do," he said. "We're everywhere. The further the Crown can send us, the more eager they are to do it."

"But it's not far enough," Malone grinned. "Won't ever be."

"Tell us about your Irish, then," I said.

Banks shrugged. "Just like you all, I suppose," he said. "Quick tongues and sour breath."

Pat laughed loudly. "I like that, Banks," he said. "I like that a lot."

Malone raised his cup of coffee like it was a pint.

"To quick tongues and sour breath," he said.

"Sláinte!" I shouted.

"Sláinte!" they all replied.

Eventually, we stumbled into our tents, reluctantly trying for just a bit of sleep. I lay on my back, listening to the fall of a cold, light rain. My eyes still stung, and I found myself trying not to rub them. I thought of what Hugh McDermott had said. A man who wore the same uniform as I did. Who stood beside me before battle. I hated him, but I also took him as a man to make good on his threats.

I turned to one side, then the other. I stared at the tent walls as Pat staggered in. I closed my eyes and tried not to think of the men on both sides of this war who would like to kill me. Instead, I imagined Rose lying next to me, her soft hair brushing my cheek. I dared not think of her smooth skin and the curves of her body. The tent was too crowded for that. I thought of what she had said to me when I told her I wanted to enlist.

"Good," she'd said, running her thumb across my cheek. "They need men like you. Good men. Brave men. Men of their word."

But she had grown sullen and fitful after, and I wondered if she regretted those words. She had never taken them back, though—not aloud. She was too dedicated to the cause. She did cry, loud, heaving sobs the night before I left, clinging to me with all her strength, burying her face in my chest. It was almost enough for me to desert on my first day. I sat on that train, thinking of those sobs, thinking of my son's brave, serious face, and I almost ran off as soon as the train stopped. Instead, my legs shook as I stood, and I could only follow the man ahead of me. It had been the first test. The same feeling came over me before every battle, and every time, I willed my body not to betray me. It hadn't gotten easier.

Eventually, my thoughts of Rose morphed into the dreams of half sleep, interrupted by the familiar tune of assembly. I didn't open my eyes until Pat nudged me.

"Time to get those rebs," he said. "This is the one. This is *the* battle. I feel it deep in my bones."

I groaned. Every battle was *the* battle to Pat. I rolled over.

"I thought Antietam was *the* battle," I mumbled. I could barely see anything, but I could hear that Pat was grinning.

"Nah," he said. "Thought it might be, but I was wrong. This is the one. I know it."

"It's bloody freezing in here," I said. "Did you put out the fire already?"

He clapped his hands together loudly.

"I told you, s'time to go!"

I rolled onto my feet and tried to grab him, but he was gone. *Who has ever heard of a winter campaign?* I thought, as I shrugged my coat on. It seemed General Burnside was trying to prove something. I didn't quite like the feel of that. Still. "The Irish Brigade," I whispered into the early morning, watching my breath steam. "Ha!" I stepped into my boots. Perhaps Pat was right. Perhaps this *was* the battle.

Chapter Fifteen

DECEMBER 1862

We awoke on the morning of the Battle of Fredericksburg covered in frost. It was still dark, and my stiff blanket crunched as I pulled it off and rolled it into my knapsack. We made our coffee and ate our hardtack. As the sun began to rise, the cannons resumed their firing. They had fired at us nonstop the day before, as we crossed the Rappahannock, entered the city, and took cover there. The Confederates were as heavily fortified as they had ever been. Sitting up on Marye's Heights, behind a wall, muskets loaded, guns aimed. We were going to attack anyway. We were going to march toward that hill and try to take it.

We were called into line. I stood shoulder to shoulder with my mates. General Thomas Francis Meagher's hair was perfectly parted on the left side of his head, and it curled inward just at the ends, as did his mustache. His eyes looked solemn, but his mouth was fixed in a determined grimace. He was calm.

"Men of the Irish Brigade," he began. "Sons of Erin.

Warriors of Hibernia. Today, we will march to the hills of Marye's Heights without fear or cowardice. Fire will rain down upon you, but you will not turn and run. They fear your courage. They know just what is coming for them when they see that glorious green flag. Today, we live up to that legend. Today, we do not stop until we reach them. We do not stop until we see their backs in retreat or their bodies pierced with our bayonets. Today, we prove our love for this land. Our love for our fallen brothers. Our love for freedom."

Some men grunted and shouted in agreement. General Meagher's lips curled in approval. Then, he retrieved some sort of plant from a captain standing beside him.

"In my hands, I hold a sprig of green boxwood. There is one for each of you. You will wear these today, tucked under your caps, as I will demonstrate."

He pinned the stem of the boxwood to the inside of his cap with his thumb and pulled it onto his head.

"Be sure that the boxwood is visible. We may be missing most of our flags today, but those traitors will know each and every one of you by these sprigs. They will tremble in fear when you are near enough to know their own fate."

The boxwood sprigs were doled out, and we tucked them into our caps. We turned to one another to be sure they were securely displayed.

"You're glowing, dearest," Pat said, patting my cheek. I snorted.

We were called to attention again, and this time, General Meagher walked down the line to address each regiment separately. When he reached the 28th, he said, "Ah. My Massachusetts men. So long and patiently you have waited to stand at our side. Though we have not yet fought together, your bravery is well-known, and we are honored to fight with you today."

As he passed me, he looked into my eyes, and I was flooded with an ache of purpose. Here was a man who was afraid of very little. A man who had been chased by the Crown and nearly hanged for his words of protest. Who escaped imprisonment on the island of Tasmania and made his way to America. For this fight. To lead us.

"I recognize some of you from my visit to Boston. I am humbled that you answered my call and know that you will not let me down. Indeed, you will make me proud. And you will make our country of adoption proud."

"Huzzah!" we cried.

Next, he addressed the 88th New York. The 88th was, famously, Mrs. Meagher's regiment. She spoiled them, sending them socks and sweets and cookies and special notes. Now, when Meagher addressed them, he began to lose his composure. His lip quivered; his voice wavered. He stuttered and sputtered but quickly pulled himself together to assure them that her smile would be upon them.

How could I not think of Rose in that moment? Of the way she threw her head back sometimes to laugh at my jokes. The desire in her eyes when she rested her head on my chest at night and looked up at me. I felt my stomach turn over and willed my breakfast to stay where it belonged. I did not want to die. I did not want to leave Rose, and I did not want to leave Steven. Tears stung at my eyes, and I blinked them away.

And then we were marching—before I could think of even one more thing—through the city, through the outskirts, past farmhouses with holes in the roofs. Across boards laid over a creek, across a field. I could see the bodies now, lying beside one another, sprawled on the ground up ahead. I could feel the hot stare of death. My feet felt as though they each weighed a thousand pounds. I gripped my musket tighter.

The screaming of the wounded men and of the cannon fire mixed with the screaming in my own head, telling me to run. I clenched my teeth and felt my body shake. But when I looked up at the green flag billowing above me, the screaming in my own head quieted. I was an Irishman. I was part of Meagher's Irish Brigade. I did not run or hide. I fought. *Help me, God*, I silently prayed, and then, a yell erupted from the deepest part of my soul, and I marched on.

Cannon fire surrounded us. There was no escaping it. It landed in front of us and to our right and left. I stepped over one man. And another. The first was dead. The second was not. He held his shin and rolled from side to side in anguish. Soon, there were too many to count. A cannister shot burst about a hundred feet in front of me. Metal shards scattered. I flinched but kept marching. The next one was much closer, and I couldn't help but to duck and throw my hands over my head. Cries pierced through the ringing in my ears. I straightened and felt my face, my chest, my stomach. I wasn't hit. But when I looked beside me, my breath caught in my throat.

No! I thought. *No, no, no. Damn it! Not Pat. Please, not Pat!* He lay on his stomach, blood pooling all around him. I knelt down and rolled him over. His skull had been sliced open, one of his eyes missing. I choked on my cry and then shouted, "No!" Quinn grabbed my arm. "No!"

"Come on!" Quinn yelled. I allowed him to pull me along, not able to take my eyes off Pat's lifeless body.

We were ordered to fire, and so we stooped behind a pile of dead bodies in order to aim. I turned one man's head away, so I wouldn't have to look into his eyes. The Confederates were tucked neatly behind a stone wall midway up the hill, and we had little to fire at. Still, we tried. We watched the minié balls bounce uselessly off the wall, mocking us. I wiped at the wetness on my face.

We stood and marched forward again. There was nothing to cover us, but we were moving toward the rebels anyway. We were in range of their muskets now, and men fell around me. I felt desperate. A man in front of me crumpled. It was Klein. His arm gushed blood. Men of the brigade were breaking off now, trying to find cover behind a fence or at the farmhouse up ahead.

Klein was screaming. He was small enough to throw over my shoulder, and I did, running toward the farmhouse with him that way. I slipped a few times on blood and melting snow but made it there all the same.

When we were inside, I knelt down and set Klein on the floor, propping him up against the wall. Quickly, I wrapped my handkerchief around his wound, tying it tight. He stared at me, eyes wide with shock. Then he looked down at his lap, and we both saw that he was bleeding from his groin, too.

"Are you hit elsewhere?" I shouted at him.

"I . . . I don't know," he gasped.

I tugged at his pant leg, furiously trying to tear off a

strip, but while I was working, Klein slumped over. I kept tugging and ripping until I got a piece. I pulled his leg to the side, and the blood rushed out furiously. I began to wrap it, blood covering my hands, but when I looked back up, Klein's eyes were closed. He wasn't breathing. He was gone.

"Fuck!" I screamed. I buried my face in my hands. I couldn't understand. Pat had been next to me only just this morning. And now he was lying out there, dead. A minié ball whizzed over my head and hit the wall behind Klein's body. "Fuck!" I yelled again.

I reached into Klein's coat pocket to retrieve his last letter and found a photograph there, too. Klein stared into the camera with his hands on the shoulders of a girl nearly his age and a much younger boy. His siblings. I could see their likeness. I stuffed both in my pocket, picked up my musket, and squeezed in next to a man firing from a window. I loaded and fired and reloaded and fired and reloaded again and fired again. I was firing at nothing. At ghosts. And still, I couldn't stop. I thought of the rebel soldier who'd loaded the shot into the gun that killed Pat. My fury overtook me, and I continued to fire on those soldiers I could not see.

Chapter Sixteen

We fired at Confederate caps and eyes and fingers until night fell. We never got close enough to see their gray backs in retreat or their bodies pierced with our bayonets.

Now, in the dark, we could see nothing at all. But we could hear them firing at our men who ran to retrieve the wounded. We finally retreated, taking with us a few wounded who'd sought shelter in the house. We carried them on taut blankets like stretchers, the men crying out in pain, the minié balls bouncing around us.

Malone and I made one more trip to the farmhouse to retrieve more of the wounded. We went right to the man with the most severe injuries, but we soon realized he would not survive the trip to the hospital. And so, Malone held his hand and prayed with him. Then, we lifted a different wounded man onto our blanket and hoped he would not bleed out before he reached the hospital.

The rebels fired upon us as we left, but their aim was weak in the dark.

A second lieutenant from our regiment told us that was enough. We were to stay in the city now. I collapsed on a board amid the rubble that had once been a house and thought of all the dead we'd stepped on in order to get back to the farmhouse. There were more bodies than grass. "Sorry," I said to the dead men a few times. I got up and retched, hands on my knees. I thought of the smells of their wounds. The whimpers of the men who were not quite dead. The way they'd begged, "Please." What did they want from us? A drink of water? For us to end their suffering? They didn't say. I heaved again, but nothing came up.

I awoke the next morning with a jolt. I hadn't retrieved Pat's letters. They were still on him. I needed to get them. I looked around at all the inactivity and was flooded with relief. The sun had nearly risen now, and the men still ambled about, making coffee, uniforms in tatters, hands and faces smeared with blood and dirt. I went to the second lieutenant from last night.

"Sir." I saluted. "I need to retrieve Private Clifford's letters. He was blown to bits."

"General Meagher will be taking stock of the Irish deaths today. A temporary truce has been declared. He's bringing some men with him. They'll get Clifford's letter, if it's there."

"Respectfully, sir," I went on, "his head was blown apart. They won't recognize him as an Irishman without his cap and boxwood."

I could hear my desperation and wished I could make it go away. The second lieutenant's mouth turned down.

"We'll go see the general, then," he said.

General Meagher was limping and haggard. He had clearly not slept. But he was here.

"Sir," the second lieutenant said. We both saluted. "This private wishes to find his friend. Says he won't be able to be identified as one of ours on account of his cap being gone." He cleared his throat. "Blown right off his head."

General Meagher sighed heavily.

"Then come with me, private," he said.

I followed him and his group of men across the field. It was strange to walk upright across this same stretch of land without fear of ball or shot. And for what? Nothing had been gained. The scene was worse in daylight, and I was grateful I had not eaten. As I stared across the field of bodies, I felt defeated. How would I find Pat? I tried to remember how far we had marched when he was hit. I toed shoulders and heads, looking for Pat. Green boxwood sprig after green boxwood sprig after green boxwood sprig poked out of caps, hung into lifeless eyes. It was like walking through hell. I wanted to run—out of this field, out of this city. But I couldn't leave Pat. He wouldn't have left me.

When I finally found him, I recognized only the split in his head. I remembered it so vividly. His long, lanky legs were tangled among others. I looked away from his mangled face and searched his pockets. I found two letters. One addressed to his ma and another to a woman named Lizzy. I tucked his letters next to Klein's.

"You were a good mate, Pat," I said. A tear fell from my

face onto his hand. I wiped my eyes with my forearm. "We'll have a drink for you soon."

And with that, I left him there. The nurses would come next to see if there were any left to save. I saw none. Most of these men would be buried where they lay. All the better. Pat's ma shouldn't have to see that.

On my way back down to the city, I saw a green flag. It was riddled with holes and wrapped around our flag bearer's dead body. I wept.

We crossed back over the Rappahannock that night and were immediately called to picket duty. We stood at the banks of the river with our muskets loaded, daring the rebels to come close enough.

Do it, I thought. *Come after us.* I waited for any movement, any sign of a fight. I was wound so tight, my teeth ground together.

And then, out of the corner of my eye, I saw a shadow in the night. Someone was crawling along the inside of the riverbank—away from me, away from our company, moving east. I trained my musket on him but realized he was on our side of the river. When he turned, I could see his bushy red beard in the light of the moon. His sour, down-turned mouth. It was McDermott. My finger hovered over the trigger. Plenty of men were killed by friendly fire. And at this time of night, there was only one thing he could be doing down there: deserting. He would deserve it. My breath was steady, but the longer I waited, the shakier my hand got. Finally, I lowered my musket. Someone else would find him. He was too big to hide. Too stupid to avoid his fate. Let them drag him back to camp, where he could be properly shamed. Executed. He scurried away, tripping over his enormous boots. I closed my eyes and imagined him drowning in the black waters of the Rappahannock.

We barely slept and ate our breakfast the next morning around the fire. Quinn and Malone and Banks and I were all quiet.

"Did Hall and McDermott make it?" Quinn finally asked. "I haven't seen them."

"Hall was killed," Banks said. I cleared my throat.

"And McDermott is gone," I said. "Made it through the battle just fine but slipped away last night."

"You saw him?" Quinn asked. I stared into the fire. Quinn shook his head, and we scooped our cornmeal from our bowls, scraping the bottoms.

"Remember when we were in South Carolina, and Pat was shitting himself?" Quinn asked.

I laughed out loud without meaning to.

"He was cursing and praying all at the same time," I said.

"He told me if he made it out of that alive, he was buying us all a good time with the girls in Washington when we got back to the North," Quinn said.

I shook my head. "Anyone know who Lizzy is?" I pulled out the letter to show them. Malone reached for it, but I pulled it back.

"Can't we read it, though? Clifford would want us to," Malone said. He was probably right, but I tucked it away.

"Let's preserve Lizzy's modesty," I said. Malone rolled his eyes.

"How about that time Pat showed up for dress parade without a shirt on?" I said.

"That's right!" Malone exclaimed. "He had burned all his shirts! And showed up with just a jacket on."

Quinn chuckled. "Those bloody bugs."

"He burned one shirt and then another," Malone added.

"We told him to wait for his mother to send a fresh one," Banks said.

"But he burned them all." I laughed.

We smiled, remembering Pat's impulsiveness. His stubbornness. His love for his mates. Then, Malone started to sing.

> *It's whiskey in the mornin', whiskey in the night*
> *Another Irish soldier lad has fought his final fight*
> *We'll toast him till we're drunk, boys, and dowse*
> *the candlelight*
> *And tell them Patrick Clifford is comin' home*
> *tonight.*

His eyes were wet, and we looked at each other desperately, wishing we had some whiskey. We watched Banks get up and come back with something under his arm. It was what was left of the bottle we had started months ago. I didn't know he had any left. He raised it up to us.

"Shall we drink to Clifford?"

I lay awake, alone, in the tent Pat and I had shared. It was so quiet. No snoring or grunting. No fluttering of the tent walls whenever Pat rolled over and knocked them with his long legs. I turned onto my side and propped myself up. Reading Rose's letters always helped. I lit my candle and reached into the pocket where I kept them. But they weren't there. I dug deeper, as if they might be hiding in some corner. I shook out my jacket, my shirts, turned my knapsack inside out, but they were gone. All of them. I shouted and kicked at my things. I wanted to tear the tent down. Pat was gone. My letters were gone. I wasn't drunk enough for this. When Malone found me, my knuckles were bloody from punching the ground. He wrestled my arms behind my back and held them there.

"You're all right, mate," he said. "You're all right."

Rosaleen

Chapter Seventeen

JANUARY 1863

I stood next to Reverend Edson, my arm linked through his. We were waiting to hear a speaker, same as when we'd first met. I'd been just a girl then. So afraid and yet the reverend was so kind. We stayed close friends through all the trials that followed, and he helped me in my times of greatest need, even though I was Irish and a Catholic.

The hall we stood in now had replaced the one in which we'd first met—rebuilt larger and grander, it was unrecognizable now. A railway depot had been added to the bottom level—the same depot where, last year, my husband had left for war.

A sadness washed over me, but just then, the reverend put his hand atop mine and smiled at me.

"Did you know I officiated his wedding?" he asked. I smiled back at him.

"I did not know that," I said. "Is he a member of St. Anne's?"

"Hardly," the reverend said, chuckling. "He has never been much of a churchgoer, despite my best efforts. But we have been close friends ever since I helped him avoid expulsion from school as a boy."

"General Benjamin Butler was nearly expelled from school?" I marveled.

"Are you truly surprised?" he replied.

I laughed. "I suppose not."

"Much like you, the general has always had a mind of his own," Reverend Edson said. "But he is also a good man."

"Hmmmm. He has done much to hinder the antislavery cause," I said.

The reverend looked thoughtful for a moment.

"I don't believe he means ill," he finally said. "He believes he is simply being neutral—though you and I both know there is no such thing in the fight to end slavery."

I nodded. "I've read that his time in New Orleans has changed his mind," I said.

"I suppose we're about to find out the truth of it," he said.

We stood at the front of the room, and though I could not see him, I knew Phillips was in attendance, too. He would never miss such an event.

When General Butler entered the room, the quiet, casual conversations became an uproar of cheers and applause. He smiled and raised his hands in a manner that said he was both humbled and pleased. He was thankful, but really, it was all too much.

He was a rotund man. His uniform flared out at the bottom, away from the largest part of his belly. His hair was visible only on the sides of his head, where it stuck straight out to the side.

"Thank you for this gracious and beautiful homecoming!" he announced.

More cheers filled the hall. He gripped the podium on each side and smiled widely at us.

"I do know someone who wishes dearly he could be here, but sadly, he could not attend."

Everyone quieted.

"Jeff Davis!"

A woman beside me laughed, high and melodious as a ringing bell.

"He's anxious to find me and punish me for my deeds in New Orleans."

The crowd shouted their disapproval.

"To think that they would approve of their ladies acting in such a disgraceful manner! Taunting our soldiers on the street! Our morals are starkly different from those of our enemy. We value hard work, dedication, equality, responsibility. They value pomp and wealth. Social niceties."

He nodded as the crowd shouted some more.

"At the beginning of this war, I didn't want to believe that its cause was slavery. I had friends in the South who owned slaves. They told me they treated their slaves kindly. Better even than the North treated their immigrants and factory workers."

His face grew serious.

"I read *Uncle Tom's Cabin*, like most of you here today. I was convinced that it was nothing but exaggerations. Propaganda! Today, I say to you, it is not. If it is untrue at all, it is only because it is too generous to the slaveholders and their ugly institution. What I saw in Louisiana was despicable. It is not so easy to look away when the truth is staring you in the face. These so-called friends of mine had lied."

The audience was so quiet now I could hear the general's steady breathing.

"The Negro can never again be a slave. Slavery has no place in the future of this country!"

The audience cheered wildly at this, and the general waited until they quieted.

"The president has recently enacted the Emancipation Proclamation. We must welcome the Negro into free society. We must employ him, give him land, allow him to vote and to send his children to school."

The reverend and I clapped loudly.

"It is the only way forward. And trust me when I tell you these men are ready to work and to fight! They are eager to become a part of our free society. Allow them to take up arms against their former masters! With their help, in a year's time, this war will be won. The Confederates will be defeated."

Though I heard the general's words, I couldn't believe they were coming from the same Benjamin Butler who had so bitterly decried the abolitionists' efforts, calling them zealots and radicals, and insisting that slavery was allowed under the Constitution. He used to say that we ought to leave the South alone about slavery—that it wasn't our business.

"Wage labor is not only the best thing for our country's economy, it is the best thing for our country's soul!"

Thunderous applause echoed off the walls. The reverend and I raised our eyebrows at one another. The general smiled and waved and walked offstage, shaking hands as he made his way through the crowd. I watched him until he paused at the back of the room. Someone led him to the side. To our side. I craned my neck to see who it was. I could only make out the man's hat, but I would recognize that hat anywhere.

Chapter Eighteen

Once the crowd began to dissipate, the reverend and I approached Mr. Phillips and General Butler. Phillips was still speaking in hushed tones when Butler noticed us.

"Reverend Edson!" he bellowed, his face lighting up. He shook the reverend's hand vigorously.

"This is a friend of mine," Reverend Edson said, indicating me. "Rosaleen Doherty."

General Butler took my hand.

"Pleased to meet you," he said. Then his eyebrows furrowed. "Have we met before? You seem familiar."

Phillips's lips curled.

"We have indeed," I said. "I am Representative Calvin Parker's clerk. We worked together on the bill for equal suffrage for foreign-born citizens."

"That's right!" he declared. "Now I remember. There aren't very many women clerks in Boston's political circles. Certainly none as beautiful as you."

LISA BOYLE

I felt my cheeks redden.

"Thank you, General," I said. "Although, I suppose we were on opposing sides when you argued to exclude Black men from the militia."

General Butler looked surprised but then laughed.

"I suppose we were," he said. "As you must have heard, I've since changed my mind."

His eyes twinkled in anticipation of my response. I nodded.

"You have certainly proved yourself a reformed abolitionist," I said.

"You ought to meet my wife, Sarah," he said, leaning closer. "You two would get along famously!"

"Is that so?" I asked.

"She suffers greatly in my absence. With a mind as sharp as hers, our disputes are vital to her well-being. Of course, she is permitted to visit me frequently in the field."

"Rosaleen's husband is fighting in the 28th," the reverend chimed in. "An enlisted man."

"An enlisted man? A private?" Butler looked nearly offended. "Then you are not permitted to visit him at all in the field."

"No, sir," I said. "Though I'm very proud of him."

"Of course you are," he said, composing himself. "As you ought to be."

He clapped his hands.

"My lovely wife is waiting for me at home, and tomorrow, I'm off again to Boston. They are planning quite the event there. The papers used to hate me but now they're hailing me as 'the hero of New Orleans.'" He laughed and slapped the reverend's back. "Suddenly, I am a military genius." He winked.

The reverend laughed, too. "They have not printed the most flattering things about you in the past."

"I only want to get back to fighting," Butler said, though I was confident he was ravenously eating up all this attention.

"And do you know when that will be?" Reverend Edson asked.

"When Stanton gives me back New Orleans, that's when," Butler grumbled.

"You'll accept no other post?" I asked.

"I worked hard down there," he said. "I'm proud of what I accomplished. I'd like to finish the job. Make sure that Negro regiment gets their chance to fight. They want to fire weapons at those bastards, and they ought to be able to."

Butler put his hand on Reverend Edson's shoulder.

"Apologies for my language, Reverend, Mrs. Doherty. I've got to get home now."

Reverend Edson extended his hand, and the general shook it.

"It was good to see you, Benjamin," the reverend said.

"And it was good to see you, too, Theodore," General Butler replied. "Pleasure seeing you again, as well, Mrs. Doherty." He smiled at me. I nodded, and then he was gone.

I looked around for Phillips, who seemed to have slipped away.

"Shall I walk you home?" the reverend asked me.

"Oh no," I said. "Thank you. I'll be off to see Steven from school."

"Do come visit me soon," he said. I kissed his cheek, and he departed. Phillips was nowhere to be seen. *I'll have to pay him a visit later*, I thought as I descended the stairs. But as soon as I stepped out onto the street, a man appeared next to me.

"I was looking for you," I said.

"I know," Phillips answered. "What did you think of Butler's speech?"

"It was interesting," I said. "Do you think he truly believes those things?"

"Yes," Phillips said. "Butler has always been one to speak his mind freely. Despite being a politician."

"What do you think it means?" I asked.

"He'll probably set his sights on the presidency."

"Do you think so?" I asked. "He seems so eager to get back to the field. Or back to New Orleans, rather."

"Perhaps," Phillips said. "But when the war is won, he will run. I'm sure of it."

"Did you hear what he said about the Negroes fighting?" I asked.

Phillips nodded. "Good luck getting the troops to accept that. Especially the Irish ones." He smiled at me.

"If that's a challenge," I said, "I accept it. That is exactly what I intend to do."

My mind raced as I walked Steven home from school. I kept answering him with "Mmmhmm"-s and "Oh"-s, but I only heard parts of what he said.

Though Lincoln had officially issued the Emancipation Proclamation, we were all hoping for something more permanent, and so the focus of *The Commonwealth* stayed the same. We plowed forward, arguing every possible benefit to white people, and occasionally relying on sympathy for the slave.

When we were in sight of our home, Steven charged ahead of me and burst through the door, and I hoped Mr. Joyce could give him more attention than I could. I planned on going straight to my writing desk.

Steven had left the front door slightly ajar, and I prepared to scold him—but then I saw their grave faces. Mr. Joyce had the newspaper spread out, and Steven peered over his shoulder. Neither spoke.

"What is it?" I asked. Normally, Mr. Joyce spared me the details of smaller skirmishes. But we knew a big battle had been brewing. Terror gripped me.

Mr. Joyce sighed. Steven looked at me apprehensively.

"Could you go to the shed, lad, and finish that rocking chair we were working on yesterday?" Mr. Joyce asked him.

My legs wobbled. Rarely did Mr. Joyce deem anything too difficult for Steven to overhear. I was the protective one.

Steven's face fell, but he obeyed.

I took a seat at the table.

"What is it?" I asked again.

He put his hand on my arm.

"Emmett is not listed among the dead," he began. I breathed a sigh of relief, though I knew the lists printed in the papers were never final. More dead always came after. After the injuries festered. After the bodies were more closely identified. Still, I allowed myself to believe this meant Emmett was safe.

"But the battle at Fredericksburg was a disaster," he went on. "Thousands of our men were cut down while trying to storm a well-fortified Confederate hill. It makes little sense, but wave after wave of men were sent to their deaths."

He took a deep breath.

"Someone we know *has* been confirmed killed," he went on. My heart dropped. "Patrick Clifford."

I gasped, and my hand went straight to my mouth. Sweet, funny Pat. Emmett's closest and longest friend. *His poor mother*, I thought.

Tears of relief and sadness streamed down my face.

"I need to visit his ma," I cried. "And write to Emmett. His heart must be breaking." *Because he's still alive*, I assured myself.

"Well . . ." Mr. Joyce pulled a letter from his pocket. "You can answer his. I'm sure he wrote it before the battle."

I nodded but tore open the letter anyway, desperate to hear his voice, if only in my head. My eyes darted down the page. He went on and on about the contraband, which I would have been grateful for just moments ago, but now I only wanted to know when this letter had been written. I finally reached the bottom.

We will be going into battle in only a day or so, but this time, under that green flag! Meagher's Irish Brigade will win this war.

"Meagher's Irish Brigade," I said aloud. "Finally." I wanted to be happy for him, but I was too worried. Mr. Joyce's frown deepened.

"The Irish Brigade got the worst of it. You can imagine what *The Pilot* is saying about it: 'The Irish are cannon fodder. The Irish spirit for the war is dead.'"

My stomach felt heavy with stones. I glared at the bright sun streaming through the window.

Chapter Nineteen

FEBRUARY 1863

My trip to Boston had been planned for some time, and despite the heavy snowfall, Calvin and I stepped onto the train in the early morning of the seventeenth. He had a busy few days ahead, and for much of that, he needed me at his side. But today was reserved for his social meetings, which I was not required to attend, and I was looking forward to spending the day with Marie and Eileen at the inn.

"How is Emmett?" Calvin asked, as we watched the farms and towns flashing past. "Have you heard from him recently?"

"Yes," I said. "He wrote me soon after the Fredericksburg campaign. I was so glad to receive that letter. After reading about all those horrific deaths . . ."

Calvin's eyebrows furrowed in concern.

"Is he in decent spirits?" Calvin asked. "All things considered."

"I suppose," I said.

I thought of Mrs. Clifford in her black dress, her pained

wail, her fingernails digging into my arm when I hugged her at the memorial. Most families could not afford to locate their loved one's body and have it brought home, so St. Patrick's—and many other churches—had begun to hold memorials anyway. How else was one to grieve?

The train slowed as we reached Boston. I said goodbye to Calvin with a plan to meet him in the lobby of his hotel early the next morning.

I walked to the inn with my umbrella held over my head, my boots sinking into the quickly accumulating snow. I shook myself off under the awning and knocked my boots against the brick. Still, large puddles dripped from me onto the dark-blue rug as I paused in the entry-way, reveling in the inn's warmth.

Eileen and Miss Susan bustled about, serving breakfast pies and steaming hot coffee. I left my umbrella leaning against the wall next to the door and started for the kitchen. Miss Susan intercepted me and planted a kiss on my cheek.

"Good morning, Miss Susan," I said. She beamed as she hurried off again.

In the kitchen, Marie looked harried, which was unusual for her. Practically nothing disturbed her anymore. Baby Jane stumbled into me and wrapped her chubby arms around my leg. I scooped her up and set her on my hip.

"Can I help with anything?" I asked Marie.

"I've almost got this all on plates," she said.

Baby Jane grabbed my collar, squeezing it and then releasing it, watching delightedly as the fabric crinkled.

"That child must be getting her last teeth," Marie said,

shoving the last two plates onto the counter in front of her. The door to the kitchen swung open, and Eileen entered. She kissed my cheek, too, before grabbing the plates and leaving again.

"She had me awake all night," Marie went on, collapsing into a chair.

I put my hand on her shoulder.

"Tell me what needs to be done today, and I'll do it. You need rest."

She rubbed her eyes and then opened them real wide.

"I'll be fine," she mumbled.

Lydia came in behind me.

"I've caught up with all my mending now, and I can help, too. Rosaleen is right. Go rest."

This time, Marie didn't argue. She pulled herself off the chair, kissed the top of baby Jane's head, and trudged down the stairs.

Lydia hugged me and baby Jane.

"It's good to see you, Rosaleen," she said.

"It's good to see you, too, Lydia," I said. "How is everything?"

"Oh, everything is wonderful . . . and also a mess." She laughed.

"Would you like to chat about it?" I asked.

Her gaze darted to mine, and I could tell that yes, she was eager to chat.

"Oh, I wouldn't worry you with it," she demurred.

"Please," I said. "And if you only want to chat about the wonderful things and leave out the mess, that's fine, too. But I'd like to hear it all."

"Well, all right," she said.

~

We were stripping the sheets from the first bedroom when Lydia said, "I'll tell you what I'm upset about."

I considered Lydia my friend. My good friend, even. Our relationship had grown alongside my friendship with Angel. Still, Lydia was a private person. It was rare for her to share a strong opinion about much of anything, unless it was to Marie. I wondered if this concern was something she wanted to keep from Marie for some reason. She looked over her shoulder, through the open door, and when she was sure we were alone, she spoke.

"There was a meeting last night at church," she said. "To recruit Negro soldiers to fight in the 54th Massachusetts Infantry."

She spoke quickly, with excitement. She didn't sound upset.

"I saw an advertisement for that in the paper," I said. She nodded.

"You know Gil enlisted a month ago—one of the first to sign up," she said. "That was no surprise. He'd been a part of that Negro militia for years. Well, we were all there last night, and I was hoping Zeke would enlist, too. I know I ought to be eager to keep my husband at home and safe, but I want so badly to win this war. I can't describe how it feels to be this close to freedom for us all. I wish they'd give me a musket. Marie doesn't remember much of that plantation, but I do. Our daddy didn't buy our freedom until I was six years old."

I knew Marie had always felt strange about that. Almost

as if she had failed her older sister by not remembering. But she couldn't have. She'd been much too young.

"I remember it. Sometimes, I even still dream about it," she went on. "And I'd love nothing more than to fight those devils face to face. To give the rest of my people their freedom. I remember one woman in particular. I thought she was old, but she was probably not much older than I am now."

She laughed at the realization.

"When our momma died and Daddy was freed and it was just Marie and me, this woman acted like a momma to us. Taught me things. Told us stories. Her name was Jo."

She tucked the corner of the sheet under the mattress.

"Anyhow, I think about her when I think about the Negro troops fighting. I think about her freedom. So, I was excited for Zeke to join up. I wanted to be proud of my husband."

She shook her head.

"But he won't," she said.

"What do you mean?" I asked. "Why not?"

"He said, 'First, we had to beg to fight when they told us it was a white man's war. Now that they've fully humiliated us, they won't even allow us to be officers. They'll have white men lording over us on the battlefield, too.' He doesn't believe the Black troops will end up doing anything more than the contraband are doing now. Backbreaking labor."

She bit her lip. Her eyebrows were furrowed real deep.

"And he thinks his 'talents lie elsewhere.' That's what he said." She sighed. "I don't know if I should be telling you all this."

"I won't say a word of it to anyone," I said. "I promise. Not even Marie."

"Well . . . it's also that . . ." She stopped fussing with the sheets and looked at me. "You're white." She looked almost apologetic. "I don't want you to judge us. Especially because your husband *is* off fighting."

I put the sheets down.

"Lydia, I love your family," I said. "Zeke is a good man. I know that. I know he has his own reasons for thinking and feeling what he does. It's not my place to judge."

She still looked torn, but the words spilled out anyway.

"Zeke's always been free. His parents were born free. He thinks differently than I do. He has pride—a lot of it—which normally I love. Marie thinks like he does sometimes. But me, I feel like I understand Gil better. Those first six years of my life have never left me."

Lydia frowned at the open door. I fluffed a pillow.

"What's bothering me most is this awful feeling that maybe Zeke is just a coward."

She looked at me with wide eyes, like she couldn't believe she had actually said that.

"Oh, Rosaleen, please don't repeat that," she begged.

I went around the bed to stand in front of her. I took her hands in mine.

"I will never repeat that," I said. "You have my word."

I pulled her in for a hug, and she started to softly sob.

"I get so angry at him," she went on, speaking half into my dress. "How can he look at our children and tell them he won't fight for the freedom of all Black people? And then I get angry at myself for blaming him. The song and dance white folks want us to do just to prove our worth *is* humiliating."

I stroked her hair. I didn't know what to say. She sniffled a few times and then pulled away, dabbing underneath her eyes with her sleeve.

"I'm sorry," she said. "I shouldn't be unloading on you this way."

"Please don't apologize, Lydia," I said. "I'm happy to listen."

She smiled faintly.

"That's kind of you," she said. "Can I tell you one other thing? It's a little silly, but the thought of it makes my heart soar."

"This must be the wonderful part?" I guessed.

She smiled wider. "I've been following the news about Port Royal. Do you know about it?"

I nodded. That was Phillips's wage labor venture in the Carolina islands.

"They've got Black folks going down there to be teachers and ministers for the freed people. I want to do it. I want to go."

I must have looked surprised, because Lydia quickly added, "It's a silly idea, isn't it?"

"No." I shook my head vigorously. "It isn't."

"I've been thinking about it a lot," she went on. "Angel's old enough now to help with her sister. Marie and Miss Martha and Ruth are here. And if Zeke's not going anywhere . . ." Her voice turned a bit bitter. "There will be plenty of people to help with the children."

She had clearly thought this through. She was serious.

"Have you told anyone else?" I asked.

She shook her head.

"I wouldn't even know how to go about doing it. I haven't heard anything through the church."

And then, I spoke before thinking about whether or not I ought to: "I know someone. He could get you down there."

Chapter Twenty

MARCH 1863

Nancy and I sat in the shade of a cherry tree, watching Caroline and Steven race one another.

"Calvin's mother would be beside herself if she could see Caroline," Nancy snorted. "Pulling up her dress like that to run faster. So unladylike."

The children collapsed on the grass, out of breath. Caroline pointed to the sky.

"I adore their friendship," I said.

It was pleasantly warm for March. The snow had slowly melted earlier in the week, and we'd hurried to the park to bask in the sunlight until the next snow came.

I had left Boston with a promise to speak to Phillips as soon as I could, but Phillips was away, in Port Royal. Neither Lydia nor I had said a word about it to Marie, although I wasn't sure why Lydia didn't want her to know.

Nancy took a bite of bread from our picnic basket and spread the newspaper in front of her.

"I see you picked up some trash this morning," I said, recognizing the paper right away.

"You keep saying you want to respond to him, but you won't even read his paper," she said.

"I try," I insisted. "But every time I do, I get so furious. The man is a spectacle, and he is relentless in his pursuit to manipulate his readers."

"Well, you'll need to develop a stronger stomach. You're the only one who can provide the truth to those same readers."

I looked away from the children and into Nancy's accusing gaze.

"All right, then," I said. "Tell me. Read me the filth before you."

She smiled and cleared her throat, before reading aloud: "'The president now plans to recruit Negroes to take up arms and become soldiers in this war. This will be a lasting disgrace to the nation. The Negro's intellect and moral character are lacking and suit him for toil and labor only. To put him alongside our brave heroes fighting this war is not only insulting, it is a sure path to defeat. White troops' morale will plummet. The South will be invigorated in its motivations. And all these noble Irish deaths will be in vain. These Negrophilists who believe in equality among the races have been grossly misled. At one time, we did support Lincoln; but then he had the full promise of constitutionalism about him. But he has changed and so have we. It is now every man's duty to disagree with him.'"

"If he is so much better than the Black troops, let him put down his pen and take up a musket!" I shouted, thrusting my hands angrily into the air. "He is the one lacking in intellect and moral character! He doesn't even understand numbers! The South's motivations matter not if we have the former enslaved fighting for us! What can they do then?"

"None of that is a coherent argument, Rosaleen," Nancy said, folding the newspaper up again.

"I know," I said. "It's why I'm shouting at you rather than writing it down."

"Well, shout away. I happen to be particularly fond of angry Rosaleen."

"Ha!" I said. "Fine! I will! And what is this about the troops' morale? How would he know how the troops feel? He isn't one of them. And maybe—*maybe*—their morale wouldn't be so low if he wasn't writing these awful things! He is positively irresponsible!"

"I can't say I'm surprised that he's withdrawing his support for Lincoln's presidency," she said.

"It was only a matter of time," I agreed. "Lincoln is too radical for him."

Just then, Steven and Caroline came up to us, one with a bloodied knee and the other with disheveled hair.

"What on God's green earth have you two been doing?" Nancy asked.

They giggled.

"Climbing trees," Caroline said, sweetly. "I climbed all the way to the top! There was a nest up there, and I saw small eggs inside!"

"I'm pleased you didn't fall," Nancy said.

"How many eggs were there?" I asked.

"Two," Steven answered.

"Did you go up there, too?" I asked. He nodded.

"Let's get you both home and cleaned up," I said. "The

sun will be setting soon, and I've heard Mrs. Parker is very strict about her student's home study."

Nancy raised her eyebrows at them, and they both giggled again.

"Race you to the corner?" Steven asked, turning to Caroline. But she was already running ahead.

I sipped my tea and gazed out the window beside my desk. Lamps illuminated the empty streets, but there was nothing exciting to see at this time of night here at the edge of the city. I had put Steven to bed hours ago, and even Mr. Joyce had popped his head in to say good night. But Donahoe's words still tumbled inside my head, and I knew any attempt at sleep would prove futile. I bit my lip and tapped my pen and finally began to write.

To the sons and daughters of Erin,

The Negroes have toiled upon land they do not own their whole lives. Working only to have another man reap the rewards. This is not hard for us Irishmen to imagine, because it happened to us. If they wish to fight for that land, if they wish to fight for their freedom, I say we welcome it.

Hundreds come to Union camps every day with hope in their heart and fire behind their eyes. They want to fight. They want to avenge the misdeeds done to them for generations. They want to help us win.

To waste their burning desire for freedom and justice would be folly of the highest order. How many Irish lives will be saved when more soldiers join our ranks? How quickly would this war end?

Allow the Negro to pick up the musket. To stand by our side as we fight for the future of this great country.

Signed,

A Paddy

I set down my pen. My eyes finally felt heavy, my mind clear. Soon, Phillips would return, and I would bring him my letter. I would speak to him about Lydia. I lay down on my bed, spreading my fingers across Emmett's side, and fell asleep.

I awoke in the dark to my bedroom door creaking open. I squinted into the abyss.

"Steven?" I asked, groggily. He stepped into the small glow of the barely lit fireplace, came to the bed, and crawled under the blanket without responding. His back was to me, and I wrapped my arms around him. I kissed his hair, and it tickled my nose.

"I miss him," he said.

"I miss him, too," I said. It had been more than a year since Emmett left. More than a year since Steven had seen his da. Though Steven was older now and Emmett wasn't missing first steps and first words like Quinn was, Emmett was missing his little boy turning into something else. Steven was already much more independent. Much more responsible.

"Will he recognize me when he comes home?" Steven asked.

When, not if, I noted to myself. Steven still had not entertained the more likely thought. Just as I refused to.

"Of course he'll recognize you," I said.

"What if the war lasts another year?" he asked.

"Even if the war lasts another ten years, your da will still know you."

He peered around at me.

"Do you think it will?" he asked. "Last another ten years?"

"No," I said, brushing his hair with my fingers.

"Do you think he's ever afraid?"

"Yes," I said. "I think sometimes he is afraid. He loves us so much. It would be impossible for him not to be afraid of losing us. Or of us losing him."

I heard Steven breathing steadily. His cold toes found their way to my leg, where he pressed against it for warmth.

"And he still fights?" Steven asked.

"He still fights," I said. "That's what courage is. Being afraid and doing it anyway. That's why we must be proud of him. Courage is one of the hardest things to have. And your da has always had it."

"I wish I could hug him," he said.

"I know, darling." I pulled him closer to me and hugged him tight.

"We will send him that wooden boat you are making for him as soon as it's done. He will feel your love as soon as he holds it."

"Will you tell him in your letter that it's supposed to be the boat on which he met you?" Steven asked.

I smiled in the dark. "I will."

Chapter Twenty-One

APRIL 1863

I hoped I wasn't wrong about what I had told Lydia. Perhaps I had overpromised. Phillips was so tight-lipped about most things. I hadn't asked where he was getting the teachers for Port Royal or how many they needed or how many they already had. And he hadn't volunteered that information, either.

He read my latest Paddy letter now, with the same look of amusement he always wore when reading them.

"Paddy is raising his own Negro regiment, is he?" he asked.

"If there is one Irishman in all of Boston who reads this letter and doesn't immediately toss it into the fire when he's finished, I'll consider it a success," I said.

"As always, you do not give yourself enough credit," he said. "This is good writing. There might even be two Irishmen who do not condemn it to the fire."

"There's something I'd like to ask of you," I said, unwilling to put it off any longer. I wiped my palms on my thighs.

"Do ask, then," he said.

"I have a friend," I said. "A Black friend. She's interested in helping out with the Carolina islands. She'd like to be a teacher."

Phillips smiled, which caught me by surprise.

"Excellent," he said.

"Yes?" I asked, tentatively. "Do you think it's possible?"

"More than possible," he said. "Do you think this friend of yours would be interested in doing more than just teaching?"

I narrowed my eyes. I should have known this "favor" would not be free of charge.

"What do you have in mind?"

"The reason I was just in Port Royal is because the government was holding a sale for plantation lands. Quite a bit of it was bought up by New York merchants."

He pursed his lips as he began to pack his pipe with tobacco.

"They'll ship that cotton right to England, you understand," he went on. "This isn't good for our mills."

"And what does this have to do with Lydia?" I asked.

"About two thousand acres of that land was sold to the Negroes in Port Royal. Frankly, that's a pathetic amount. They have saved every coin and every note they earned since they started working for the government, and that's the best they could afford. How can we possibly expect them to compete with men like me?"

He said this with no pleasure or amusement.

"I'd like this friend of yours—if she's up to it—to be a sort of ambassador for me. To arrange to have the cotton from the Negro-owned land come to me and me alone. I will pay them fair prices—more than fair, in fact. They won't get a deal like it from anyone else. But I need them to trust me entirely. I need to be their sole buyer. This Port Royal cotton is some of the best in the world."

"And Lydia," I said. "She'll receive additional compensation for this work?"

"Of course," Phillips replied. "I'm almost offended you would ask." He grinned.

"I'll speak to her," I said. "Though she is quite eager to get down there, so I imagine she'll be willing."

"Do you think she has a mind for it?" he asked. "For the business side of things?"

"Oh yes," I said. "The mind and the personality. She is incredibly likeable. People will want to please her."

"Wonderful," he said. "Speak to her soon, and we'll set up a meeting at my Boston office."

"Of course you would know that she lives in Boston," I said.

He lit his pipe and spoke with it clenched between his teeth.

"I'm not sure how many times I must tell you, Rosaleen. I know everything."

The ale that Miss Susan poured for me warmed my insides right away. I had written to Lydia and told her I hoped we could let Marie in on the secret. So, we were meeting Marie at the inn to discuss Lydia's future.

I was the first to arrive and drank my ale entirely too quickly. Now, I felt a bit calmer, though perhaps still not ready to tell Marie we had been keeping a secret from her.

Lydia hurried in next, slipping in beside me at the table in the back corner.

"What will you tell her?" I asked. I felt like a naughty child, afraid of getting scolded.

Lydia shrugged and unbuttoned her coat.

"The truth," she said. "She's my baby sister. She can't be too mad."

Miss Susan brought Lydia an ale, too.

"Better drink it quickly before Marie sees," Miss Susan said, winking.

Lydia giggled and took a long sip.

"Oh, it's so nice to have a drink every now and then," Lydia said, just as Marie emerged from the kitchen. "But I'm afraid you'll have to finish this one," she whispered. I grabbed it quickly and set it in front of me. Marie tugged her rolled-up sleeves so that they fell around her wrists, and she visibly shivered.

"Has God decided to skip spring this year?" she asked. "It's entirely too cold for April."

Lydia shifted in her seat.

"Now, what is the big news that has caused this very formal meeting?" Marie asked, taking her seat. I smiled nervously, my lips closed.

"There's something I want to do, Marie," Lydia began. "I hope you'll give me your blessing."

Marie's eyebrows furrowed. "What is it?" she asked.

"I would like to . . ." She stopped and sat a little straighter. "I am going down to the Sea Islands in South Carolina to teach the freed people there."

Marie looked as though she couldn't have been more surprised if Lydia had told her she was growing a third leg.

"What about the children?" she sputtered.

"Angel is practically a young woman now, and you know how mature she is," Lydia said. "Eliza is in school for nearly the same amount of time Zeke is at work, and Ruth has agreed to help, as well. The girls will be taken care of. I'm hoping you will help, too, when you can."

Marie looked hurt now.

"Ruth already knows?" she asked. "And I assume Rosaleen." She turned to me. "That is why you're here, isn't it? You're behind this?"

I fought a grin as I looked up at her.

"Why am I the last to know?" Marie asked.

"I was afraid you would talk me out of it," Lydia said, quietly.

"Why would you think that?"

"Because . . ." Lydia looked down at her hands. "Perhaps it's irresponsible of me," she said, quickly. "Perhaps you think I'm abandoning my family. But Zeke . . ." Lydia sighed and looked up again. "Zeke isn't going anywhere. He's made that clear."

A look of understanding passed over Marie's face.

"I want this island to be successful," Lydia went on. "I want the people there to thrive, and I think they can. I want to help make that happen."

Marie nodded slowly.

"Well." Marie took a deep breath. "How will you get there, then?"

"About that," Lydia said, glancing at me. "We've already found a way."

Marie looked at me.

"Some of my acquaintances in Lowell," I said.

"Is this . . ." Marie's voice began to rise. "Is this that rich mill man?" Marie, like all my friends, only knew minor things about Phillips.

I nodded. She glared at me and turned back to Lydia.

"I don't trust that man, Lydia," Marie said. "Men like him don't do things out of the goodness of their hearts. I've warned Rosaleen, but she won't listen. No good can come from associating with that man. He'll want something in return."

"We already know what he wants," Lydia said. "And I'm willing to do it."

Marie looked as though she had been slapped. Her mouth hung open. Then, she pointed her finger right at me.

"How dare you drag my sister into this?" I could tell she was trying hard not to shout.

"I went to her, Marie!" Lydia said. "And it's not as if he's asking me to do something terrible. In fact, I don't think it's a bad thing at all. I think it'll be good."

"Marie, I'm sorry," I practically whispered. "She didn't want me to say anything to you until we knew it was a done deal. I wouldn't have entertained discussion of anything that would put Lydia in danger."

Marie's eyes hardened, and her jaw clenched. She said nothing.

"Please listen, Marie," Lydia said. "I'll be helping the people there. This man—this friend of Rosaleen's. He's offering to buy their cotton at a very generous price. He wants me to help him. To ensure his purchases."

"No," Marie said. "You are not working for that man."

"I want to." Lydia was practically pleading now.

"Why? So he can manipulate you and all those people? How do you know what a good price for cotton is?" Marie spat.

"I know," I said. "I've made him show me the numbers. I know the rate cotton is going for at auction in New York City right now. I don't believe he's trying to trick anyone."

Marie's nostrils flared like an irritated bull.

"I'm not saying he's doing this for our benefit or for theirs," I went on. "I'm saying that we've developed a relationship. He and I. We trust each other. In certain ways, he needs me."

Marie snorted.

"He doesn't *need* you," she said. "It only goes to show how good he is at all of this that he's made you believe he does."

"Marie," Lydia said. "If he asks me to do something that's wrong, I'll tell him no. We're already under their thumb. I might as well do some good."

"Neither of you know how stupidly you're behaving," Marie said.

"Why don't you ever take me seriously?" Lydia's voice rose now, too. "Just because I'm easygoing doesn't mean I'm stupid!"

"Then act like you have some sense and walk away from this ridiculous arrangement!"

Lydia's eyes welled with tears for a moment before she sniffed them away.

"No," she said, steadily. "I'm doing this. With or without your approval."

She stood up and strode out of the inn. I felt an awful feeling in the pit of my stomach. All of this was because of me.

Marie stood next and stared down at me.

"I've never pried into your questionable activities with rich white men," she said, quietly. "Because it was not my business. But you've dragged me into it anyway."

"I'm sorry, Marie," I said. "I'm truly sorry."

She looked me square in the eye.

"Then you'll stop this," she said. "If you're sorry, you'll stop this."

I left the inn and stepped into a carriage that would take me to South Boston. Mairead and Dennis had opted to move to Boston instead of Lawrence. They were wary of more mill closures, and they were right to be. Weapons were a sure thing now, and their factories were in South Boston—an already established Irish community that kept growing and growing with each year of the war.

As the carriage bumped along, I thought of Marie's words. I *could* put a stop to this. Marie knew I could. I could tell Phillips that Lydia was no longer interested, and though he would be disappointed, that would be that. He wouldn't pursue her. Lydia would be angry and hurt and unable to contribute to the war in the one way she very much wanted to.

I looked out the window as we rode toward Congress Street, passing Faneuil Hall. Marie and I had spent much time there, shopping at Quincy Market. I had always taken

Marie's word as truth. She had been the one to guide me when I first arrived in America—was my only friend in the whole of Boston at the time. She was older and educated and wise. She was the one who had taught me to be wary of men like Phillips. But as soon as I had the chance to sit at his table, to influence his decisions with my own power, she told me it was the wrong path.

But Marie was wrong. About all of this. I was convinced of that much. If Phillips didn't buy the cotton grown on the Black-owned land, someone else would surely come along and offer them less for it. At least we could make sure he was good for his word. Lydia and I could hold him to it.

The carriage pulled up to the South Boston postal office, and I paid the driver. Just as I walked through the door, Mairead ran up to me, coat and gloves already on.

"Perfect timing," she said, hugging me. "My shift just ended."

I looped my arm through hers, and we walked back outside, toward her and Dennis's home.

"You look upset, Rosaleen," she said.

"I've gotten myself into a right mess with my friends from the inn," I said.

"Would you like to talk about it?"

I shook my head.

"I want to talk about you," I said, forcing a smile. "Tell me about the postal office. How is it going?"

"It's much better than the mills," she said. "The wages are better. I'm grateful for that friend of yours who got Dennis his job."

I smiled, but it felt strained.

"And Dennis is enjoying his work at the foundry?" I asked.

"He's made some good friends there," Mairead said. "Irish lads."

She shot me a sideways glance. As long as my husband was risking his life, hers would have guaranteed work. I pushed the bitter thought away. One spat was enough for today.

We were at her building now. It was three apartments stacked on top of one another. We climbed the stairs to the second level. She and Dennis and the children had it all to themselves. Upstairs, an Irishwoman watched the children while they Mairead and Dennis went to work. I was happy for Mairead, truly. Her life had greatly improved in South Boston.

"Give me your coat," Mairead said. "I'll put on the kettle"

Chapter Twenty-Two

MAY 1863

Marie had been right. Spring didn't come that year. It already felt like summer when, weeks later, I picked Steven up from school, his anticipation to be free radiating like an instrument's vibrations.

"Two weeks of school left, Ma," he said. "And I'm going to finish Da's boat today!"

"I can't wait to see it," I said. "We've got a letter from him to read, as well."

"Is it a happy one?" he asked.

"I haven't read it yet," I said.

"You'll still let me listen?" he asked. "Even if it's terribly sad?"

"You're almost eight now," I said. I smiled, thinking of how strong and independent he had become.

"I read the papers, you know," he said, getting more serious. "I know it's gruesome."

"Your da tends to be quite honest," I said. "Oftentimes about things the papers aren't printing. I'll read it first and then decide."

"I suppose that's fair," he said, sounding very grown-up.

When we got home, I sat on the sofa by the big window and read Emmett's letter as Steven retrieved the boat from the work shed.

May 19, 1863

My dear wife,

I'm growing tired of it. We ache for a victory. Good, brave Irishmen—who ought to have lived long enough to see their homeland liberated—are dying. Our regiment has suffered greatly. The brigade is only a shell of its former self after Chancellorsville.

General Meagher has resigned as our commander, because he was not given leave to recruit more men. It has been mainly dark days here, with our only respite being the St. Patrick's Day celebration I wrote to you about. We hold those memories tight, but with the general gone, they are bittersweet.

I am afraid, Rose. Every time we go into battle, I am sure I will die. I make my peace with it. I say my goodbyes to you and Steven and listen as the priest absolves us of our sins. And yet, when it is finished and I am still here, I wonder, how many times must I die?

When you answer this letter, please remind me of all the things for which we are fighting. At this moment, it is too hard to conjure them. I can only see the lifeless faces of the boys who were taken too soon. Boys who should have had their whole lives ahead of them. Please remind me, Rose.

Hug Steven for me.

I love you,

Emmett

. . .

Steven burst through the door just as I finished, inspecting the stern of his wooden boat.

"Just a few final touches," he said. When he looked up at me, he stopped walking and talking. He must have seen the horror on my face.

"Is it too sad, Ma?" he asked, quietly.

I nodded and swallowed hard.

"Let's read the one about St. Patrick's Day again," I said.

He sighed and trudged off to get it.

Emmett's letter haunted me, and I found myself thinking often about him silently bidding us goodbye. It kept me awake at night and popped into my head unannounced at the strangest of times. Of course, I had written back promptly, listing all of the reasons why it would be noble to die for the Union Army. Democracy. Our debt to our adopted country. Emancipation. Freedom. Freedom for generations to come, afforded to all. But I'd had to stop four times, and once I was finished, I sobbed violently, though I was careful not to leave any teardrops on the page. Then, I folded it, stamped it, and sent it, along with Steven's wooden boat, which said more than I ever could. *It's worth dying for the Union, because this country is the only home our son has ever known, and look what he can do here. He doesn't have to worry about what he'll eat today or tomorrow or the next day. He can live and learn and create beautiful things. You are dying for your son's future.*

Lydia had sent me back-to-back letters that I hadn't answered yet. In the first, she asked when she could meet with this man Phillips. Everything was ready. Zeke and Angel knew what was expected of them. She had even told most of her clientele that she would be leaving Boston for some time and that they better find a new seamstress.

As cold as things had been between Marie and me, I was set to visit Boston to see Gil off. The 54th was leaving for South Carolina in two days. I needed to be there, and I had decided to go a day early to speak with Marie alone.

I hugged Mr. Joyce hard before I left. Steven was at school, and Mr. Joyce had walked me to the train station.

"Thank you for being such a wonderful grandda to Steven," I said to him. "I feel as if I'm coming apart at the seams these days."

"You're a tough lass," he said. "Don't worry about us. Steven's a fine assistant and a good lad. I'm proud of you both." I squeezed his hands one more time and boarded the train.

When I arrived at the inn, Eileen was cleaning up dinner, and so I helped her, bringing plates and mugs into the kitchen for scrubbing. Marie barely acknowledged me, but I wasn't put off. I joined her at the sink, and we washed in silence. Finally, as we were finishing the last set of dishes, I spoke.

"I know how much you're going to miss him," I said.

She stared into the washtub.

"I'm proud of him," she said. "So proud. But I have this feeling that he isn't coming home. That tomorrow will be the last time our children and I will see him. How do I prepare for something like that?"

She finally looked up at me, her expression pained, her shoulders slumped.

"You don't," I said. "You can't. And after every battle, you'll look desperately through the newspaper for names of the dead, certain you'll see his name listed. But a small piece of you will never let go of hope. That maybe he made it through this one. And maybe he can make it through the next."

She turned away from the sink and leaned against it, crossing her arms in front of her.

"Gil said he won't allow himself to be captured," she said. "Not after what Jefferson Davis said about the colored troops. He'd rather die than allow them to sell him back into slavery. I don't know if I agree with him. I think I'd do anything for the chance to see my children again."

Marie's face contorted for a moment before a few tears fell. I wanted to hug her, but I didn't know if she'd welcome that.

"I don't suppose that's the sort of decision any of us would want to make. But that's why Davis said it, isn't it? To scare Black men away from enlisting. And yet, they filled up Gil's regiment so fast that now they need another."

Marie glanced at me, her eyes still wet.

"There's power in that, isn't there?" she asked. I nodded.

"They're afraid of that power," I said.

"It's like you said in that Paddy letter. Who has more fire in their belly? The Black man does. The Black man has the most."

I nodded again.

"I don't want to argue with you, Rosaleen," Marie said, sighing. "But you made me so angry. My sister is not like you. She isn't white. She can't get away with the same kind of antics. This friend of yours won't hesitate to leave her high and dry, and then what? How will she get herself out of a bad situation—in the South, no less? But now you've put the idea in her head, and I won't be the one to stand in her way."

She stood up and wiped her hands down the front of her apron.

"But if anything happens down there and she finds herself in trouble, promise me you will get her out."

"I understand, Marie," I said. "And I will."

Lydia wore her best gray-and-maroon dress to our meeting with Phillips, her hair parted pristinely down the center and pulled into a tight, low twist. She took off her matching hat and held it in her hands as we stood before the door to Phillips's Boston office. She pulled her shoulders back and lifted her chin as I knocked.

"Come in," he said.

"Mr. Phillips," I said, as soon as we entered, "this is Lydia Johnson. Lydia, Mr. Phillips." She curtsied.

"Hello, sir," she said.

"Hello, Lydia. Please sit." He gestured to the chairs in front of his desk, and we both sat.

"I understand you would like to teach the freed people in Port Royal," Phillips said.

"Yes, sir," Lydia said. "I believe their island could be very successful. I would like to help with that."

Phillips nodded. "They've already shown great progress

and an eagerness to learn. They respond particularly well to their Negro teachers. I believe you'll be able to help. Now, Rosaleen has explained to you the other part of the proposal, hasn't she?"

"Yes, sir," she said.

"And you think you'll be able to help with that, as well?"

"Yes, sir," she said again. "It will be a relief, I'm sure, for the new Negro landowners to have a reliable buyer with excellent prices."

Phillips smiled. "I'm glad to hear it. I'll be taking a trip down in early August. Will you be ready to leave then?"

Now, Lydia smiled. For the first time that day, her nerves finally seemed to calm.

"I will," she said.

"Perfect," Phillips said. "Then I will meet you at the docks at Long Wharf sometime during that first week of August. Rosaleen will let you know the date as it draws near."

Phillips stood and extended his hand to Lydia. She shook it eagerly, grinning.

"I look forward to working together, Lydia," Phillips said.

"Yes, sir. Me too."

On our walk back to Lydia's home, she couldn't stop talking.

"I'm going, Rosaleen!" she said, hopping a bit. "I'm really, truly going. Oh, I simply can't wait! What will I do with all this time? I want to leave tomorrow!"

I laughed. "I'm sure Zeke will find plenty for you to do."

She smirked. "You're probably right. My poor girls will

have to teach him how to do everything." She suddenly deflated. "I'll miss them greatly," she said.

"And they'll miss you," I said. "But they'll be so proud of their ma."

Lydia beamed. "You think so? You don't think I'm being selfish?"

I shook my head. "The girls will be fine. And they'll be able to see that they can make a difference. Because their ma did."

"That's what I want," she said. "Especially for Angel. An ordinary life won't be good enough for that girl."

I took Lydia's hand in mine.

"She has a wonderful example."

Chapter Twenty-Three

JULY 1863

For days, the newspapers printed news of troop movements, small stories of bravery and loss, and I could not read them. But Gettysburg was in Northern territory. The outcome of this battle was important.

When news of the Union victory arrived on the third of July, the city of Lowell erupted in celebration. The streets were full. Bands played in the parks. Though Steven and I had to catch an early train to Boston in the morning, we still stayed up late that night, sipping lemonade and whiskey with Nessa and Grace, Nancy and Calvin and Caroline. Everyone was festive. It was as if we'd all made some unspoken promise not to think of the bloody cost of the battle quite yet.

I slept fitfully and woke Steven a bit earlier than necessary. Boston's Fourth of July celebration would be even grander than last year's with this news.

Everything was crowded, starting with the train. Ronan met us at the packed station and tousled Steven's hair.

"Your da probably led the attack against those dirty rebels!" Ronan shouted above the din, grinning.

"Probably!" Steven shouted back. Then he pretended to lift a musket to his shoulder and fire it at Ronan.

"Ouch!" Ronan yelled, covering his chest with his hands. "You shot me!"

Steven laughed. As we elbowed our way to the Common, Ronan would tap the shoulders of people ahead of us and hurriedly glance away, inciting uncontrollable giggles in Steven.

On the sidewalk, a newspaper boy waved the latest issue high above his head.

"Victory at Gettysburg!" he shouted. "Read President Lincoln's remarks!"

I made my way over to him and slipped a coin into his hand. He grinned and tipped his hat.

"Thank you, ma'am!"

I tried to smile, but my heart thumped so loudly I thought I might faint. I tried to breathe deeply as I flipped through the pages, desperately scanning for the list of the dead. His name was not there.

I looked up at Ronan and Steven and felt like crying. It wasn't final, but it was something. Ronan regarded me anxiously. I shook my head and smiled. He smiled back, and a wave of relief washed over me.

As we waited for the parade to begin, Steven and Ronan found a tree across from the Common.

"I'll boost you up," Ronan said. "It'll be a better view!"

"Be careful!" I shouted at them. Ronan only winked. I was suddenly tired. Overly exhausted and only wanting a letter from Emmett to assure me that all was well. I found a set of stairs and slumped down. I didn't care to see the parade.

I ought to be jubilant, I thought. My husband was most likely alive, though that wasn't certain. The Union had won a great victory. And yet, I felt—as Emmett had said in his letter—hollow. I wanted it all to be over with.

Someone sat next to me, then. I glanced up.

"Henry!" I cried.

"I hope I didn't scare you," he said.

"No," I said. "I was only off in my own head."

He nodded. "These victories are hard, aren't they?" he asked, gazing into the crowd. "Just as the defeats have been."

"Yes," I said, surprised he understood. "They are. Why is that? It's easier to be sorrowful after a defeat. Today, I feel like I ought to be celebrating. But I can't."

"I know," he said. "It's all right to be sorrowful. Because we know the cost. The victories don't come freely. They come with too much blood. Too much sorrow. Too many widows."

I choked back a sob. I shouldn't cry to Henry. He would feel the need to comfort me, and I didn't want that. But when I looked at his concerned face, the pain etched across his forehead, I wanted nothing more than to sob into his chest. Instead, I looked away.

"I want you to know that I'm here, Rosaleen," Henry said, quietly. "I'm here if you need me for anything at all."

I looked back at him, into his dark, almost black, eyes. They were so sincere. I nodded, and he got up and walked away. I struggled to breathe. *He meant . . . he meant if Emmett dies*, I realized. *He is here for me if Emmett dies.* I couldn't hold back the tears anymore. They ran down my cheeks. I sat there for many minutes, wishing to simply disappear. Wishing to be anywhere but in the middle of a crowded street. Finally, after my tears had dried, Ronan and Steven found me.

"Are you all right, Ma?" Steven asked. I smiled at him.

"Yes," I said. He looked relieved.

"Shall we go watch the dancers at Faneuil Hall next?" he asked.

"Yes." I stood and brushed off my dress. "Let's go."

Ronan put his arm around my shoulder and pulled me in close. I closed my eyes and allowed myself to be comforted. If only for a moment.

Chapter Twenty-Four

I sat in Calvin's Boston office, sweat dripping down my back. The windows were wide open, but no breeze wafted in, only a creeping fog, which made the room heavy. It was difficult to think of anything but the heat. Calvin was working, though I frequently caught him staring off into the distance, as well, the sweat on his brow gleaming. The draft lottery had been announced only days ago, and the city was tense, everyone was waiting to see if the poorer neighborhoods—the Irish, especially—would erupt into riots like they had in New York. There was plenty of work to be done that day, but with the heat and the uncertainty, time seemed to stand still. It was as if we were all holding our breath. Straining to listen.

And then I heard it. I watched Calvin glance to the street. He had heard it, too. I rushed over to the window, where a boy was running and shouting. *It's happening,* I thought. *It's happening here. Damn Donahoe!*

"They're attacking the police in the North End, on Prince!"

Prince Street? Was Ronan home? Panic rose in my throat. Was Ronan involved? I ran to the stairs.

"Rosaleen!" Calvin called after me, but I didn't stop.

Thoughts of Ronan in the middle of the fight pushed me forward. But then I thought of Marie and Lydia and the children and stopped. Should I go to them instead? Miss Susan would protect them, wouldn't she? As would Miss Martha and Ruth. What could I do that they couldn't? I ran forward again, toward Ronan.

Keep going, I thought. The streets were crowded now with men who wished to see or be a part of the fight. I tried to elbow my way in—tried to think of side streets I could cut through. As I approached the North End, I could hear the shouting, the breaking of glass. People shoved me. The anger was spreading to the outskirts of the crowd, too. I could barely breathe. But I needed to find Ronan. A few paces ahead of me, a man punched a police officer. The officer swung his baton, cracking the man on the head. Two more men wrestled the baton from the officer and began kicking him as he fell to the ground.

My mouth was dry. So dry. I was at Prince Street now. Which way to Salem? I was confused, trying to see over the heads of the men, and now, plenty of Irishwomen, too. The crowd stank badly. I thought I might retch. I was shoved again. Hard this time. I tried to stay upright but fell to my knees. I would get trampled in this. I tried to stand, but just then, a man fell into me and pushed me all the way to the ground.

And suddenly, hands scooped under my arms, pulling me away. I turned to see Ronan dragging me. He looked furious.

"What are you doing here?" he yelled.

"What are *you* doing here?" I yelled back.

He didn't respond, only set me on my feet, took me under his arm, and pushed us away from the fighting. He gripped my shoulder, protecting my body with his. Finally, we broke free. We were at the bridge to Charlestown. Men ran past in both directions.

"Are you daft?" he shouted. "Do you ever think of anyone but yourself?"

"Yes! I was thinking of you!"

"*You* were going to protect *me*?"

Tears formed in my eyes. "You can't be here."

"Look at me, Rosaleen," he shouted, incredulously. I did. He was no longer a boy. At least a head taller than me now. He was lean but strong. He was angry and pained and scared. I knew him so well I could read it all on his face.

"I . . . I'm sorry," I said. He took a deep breath and combed his fingers through his hair. "But if it got you away from this mess, I'm not *that* sorry."

The corner of his mouth twitched. He almost smiled but didn't. I grabbed his hand.

"Come on," I said, leading him away.

"Where are we going?" he asked.

"To talk," I said. We walked along the docks, which seemed to be clearing out, workers running toward the melee. Bewildered managers stood outside their offices, eyeing the abandoned shipments.

"An afternoon stroll?" he asked, irritation thick in his voice.

"What were you doing there, Ronan?" I asked.

"I live there," he said.

"Not right there, you don't," I said. "Were you there to fight? To riot? To beat up police officers?"

"I know *you've* wanted to hit a police officer before," he snarled. "Don't act as if the thought sickens you."

"And what happens if they go to . . . you know . . . the next hill?" I asked, unable to use the disgusting name the Irish had given to the Black neighborhood on the opposite side of Beacon Hill. "Would you go with them?"

"I don't know, Rosaleen," he said. "You would like me to say no. I would like to say no, too. But I'm just so angry!"

I watched a crate topple as the man moving it ran off.

"You aren't even twenty yet," I said. "You can't be drafted. Not for another year."

"I'm not angry for me," he said. "I'm angry for all of us. These men work hard. They have for years. They show up to a job that doesn't pay them enough, and they continue to do it day after day to provide for their families. They've been good citizens of this country, but they want no part of this war! And yet, they're being forced to fight and to die simply because they're poor! And now they must fight to free the Negro? The Negro who will repay him by taking his job right out from under him? Tell me how any of that makes sense, Rosaleen!"

"And so you'll murder innocents instead? Because that is what happened in New York, and it's what might happen here! Today!"

"I'm not going to murder anyone!" He threw his hands into the air as he shouted, "Do you really think I would do such a thing?" I opened my mouth, but he gave me no time to respond. "Would I like to break some windows? Yes, I would! How else are we supposed to get them to listen to us?"

"You think something good is going to come of all this?" I asked. "This behavior is ruining the good reputation the Irish soldiers have built. We are finally being held in high esteem. The Yankees are seeing the good in us. You're willing to jeopardize that?"

"How else am I supposed to be angry? Do you want to tell me how to be angry? Do you want to scold me as if I'm still a child?"

We had stopped walking and were shouting at each other in front of a wide-open warehouse. The smell of fish interrupted my thoughts.

"What do you want me to do, Rosaleen?" He stepped closer, his chest heaving. Sweat dripped from his forehead. He reached his hand up for a moment, as if to touch me, but then he put it back down. "Tell me. Tell me, and I'll do it. You want me to enlist?"

He was pleading now, blinking away the tears that fought to come out. I searched his eyes for the little boy who had stepped off that boat with me all those years ago. Perhaps on this very dock. He was in there somewhere, but I couldn't see him anymore. Still, the thought of sending him off in a uniform and marching him to his death—another person I loved, sacrificed to this war—sent a dagger through my chest.

"Because if I'm *not* going to enlist, then I ought to be over there." He reached his arm out toward where the riot was still raging. "Showing them that I won't do it."

Just then, a thunderous boom roared from the direction he was pointing. The ground rumbled, and we looked to each other with wide eyes. The sounds changed now. Wails and screams pierced the air. Ronan and I raced back toward Prince Street, where men and women were backing away. Some ran southward, others walked in a daze, looking over their shoulders, tripping over things sprawled in the street.

"The armory," Ronan muttered. He took off running, past Prince Street, and I followed him, my heart beating faster as we approached.

The first thing I saw was blood. Cooper Street was wet and sticky with it. The armory stood before us, the windows shattered, one of the doors blown entirely apart, the other in shreds from ax blows. A smoking cannon stood behind the destroyed door from where the soldier inside had fired it. Men and women and a boy lay in front of it, bleeding and crying out, though others were silent and still, tangled together on the ground. Bricks and axes and chains and sledgehammers lay at their sides, some still in the hands of the attackers. People knelt in the blood next to their dead loved ones, crying and screaming.

Soldiers slowly emerged from the armory, muskets raised. Fear rose in my throat as I stared. One of the soldiers was clearly young. Perhaps Ronan's age. His gaze darted from the people on the ground to the people backing away from him. He was sweating profusely.

Before I could stop him, Ronan raced toward the bleeding people.

"Wait!" I yelled, just as another shot rang out.

Ronan fell to the ground. Smoke plumed from the barrel of the young soldier's gun. I looked back to Ronan. He had been hit.

No. My breath left my body. My surroundings began to spin.

"Ronan!" I screamed, as I ran right for him, realizing too late I might be next. But the soldiers didn't shoot me.

I fell to my knees beside him and cradled his head in my lap.

"Ronan," I pleaded. Blood seeped through his shirt, turning everything a dark red.

"Help!" I cried. "Please!" Tears streamed down my face.

"Rosaleen," Ronan gasped. "I'm bleeding." The blood was everywhere now, pooling around us, seeping under my fingernails, into my dress, dying red the strands of lace.

"Ronan," I said, in between sobs. "I'm going to get you help." I tried to steady my voice, but it was no use. "Help!" I screamed. I clutched his hand with all my might. His eyes rolled back, and he closed them and opened them again weakly.

"Everything is . . . so . . . blurry," he breathed.

"Stay with me," I said. "Someone will come help. They must come help!" I looked up and down the street, frantically. Why wasn't anyone coming? The soldiers, still looking for threats, had not lowered their muskets.

"Rosaleen," Ronan said. "I have to tell you something." His breathing was labored. I shook my head.

"No talking," I said. "Keep your strength." I balled up the end of my dress and pressed it to his gaping wound. It soaked through immediately.

"Listen to me," he groaned. "For once. In your life." He tried to laugh, but only coughed and then grimaced. "I love you," he went on before I could cut him off again. "I have always been in love with you."

I stared at him, stunned. He closed and opened his eyes again. "If I was any good at all," he whispered, "it is because of you."

"No." I shook my head violently. "No, Ronan. You've always been good. Your heart is good. I'm proud of you. Of the man you've become."

His smile faded into a frown. His breath grew short and choppy.

"I wish." He paused and stared into my eyes. I had to press my ear to his lips to hear him now. "I wish. So many things."

I pulled away to look at his face, but his eyes had rolled back again, and this time, they had not closed. They were not focused on me. They stared lifelessly at nothing.

I pulled his head into my chest and wailed. His breath was no longer on my skin. My vision blurred, and I could hear only the painful moan coming from deep inside my chest.

When the nuns arrived and began to treat people, the soldiers finally joined them. But it was too late for us. Too late for Ronan. He was gone.

Chapter Twenty-Five

I sat in Ronan's blood for a long time. His head in my lap. The nuns tried to help him for only a moment before realizing it was no use. One of them prayed with me over his body. And still, even when she had moved on, I sat with him. I pleaded with God. I willed Him to bring life back into Ronan's body.

The riot had fizzled out shortly after the blast at the armory. Additional troops had been called in, and with the help of police officers, prevented the Irish from breaking into the gun shops on Dock Square. Priests walked through neighborhoods, urging people to be peaceful and calm. Finally, the rioters went home, and by the time the undertakers came for the bodies—came for Ronan—the city was quiet again.

But I did not go home. I wandered the city, my conversation with Ronan playing over and over again in my head. Ronan's life playing over and over again in my head. What could I have done differently? How could I have saved him? How could I turn back time and change everything?

Back to before the riot. Before the war. Before everything. To the first day we stepped off that boat. *What could I have done, Ronan?*

I stayed in Boston for another week, sleeping at the inn. When it was time for the wake, I walked into Ronan's aunt and uncle's house, where no one said a word to me as I prepared the downstairs. When his body was brought in and laid out, I sat next to him and held his cold, lifeless hand. The boy who could never have what he wanted. A garden for his ma. The woman he loved. I bit my lip as tears fell down my face.

The men he worked with came to pay their respects, seemingly knowing who I was without any introduction. They told me how highly Ronan had spoken of me. How often he would use my arguments as his own. The people who'd lived with him in the house shuffled about, making themselves busy, looking at their feet or their hands or the ceiling, unable to even look me in the eye.

But when Steven and Mr. Joyce arrived, my heart broke into two. Steven's face was the saddest I had ever seen it. He bravely walked up to me, his shoulders back, though his chest moved in and out as he quietly sniffled. He hugged me hard. Then he stared at Ronan for a long time.

"Was he afraid, Ma?" he asked. "When he died?"

"No, darling," I said.

He nodded.

"I'm glad you were with him," he said. He cautiously reached out and brushed Ronan's hair away with the back of his hand.

"I'll miss you, Uncle Ronan," he said. And then he collapsed into me, unable to be strong any longer. Mr.

Joyce gathered us both into his arms, and we stood that way for a long time, holding onto one another. Keeping each other from falling to pieces.

Cocoa would cry, too. Sad, long whines. For weeks. I didn't know how she knew, but she did. I lay next to her the first night I was back in Lowell, and together, we cried for the boy, for the man, we'd not been able to save.

The letter I had been waiting for from Emmett finally arrived. My hands shook as I read it.

July 5, 1863

To my dear wife,

I write to tell you that I am alive and well after the battle at Gettysburg. I hope you receive this letter promptly, because there have been many deaths here, including my good friend Alfred. I will miss him very much. He was the only other abolitionist in my company, and we spoke often of the worthiness of the cause. Even as he lay dying and I gave him some water to drink, he spoke encouraging words to me. He was proud of his service, of his sacrifice, and I am, too.

The victory has been good for us all. We hope it has been bad for Bobby Lee. Perhaps we can track him down and finish him off for good. The morale of the rebels must be very low. I know too well how it feels.

Please tell Steven that I have received his little boat and that it is beautifully carved. When I read which boat it was supposed to be, I laughed aloud with delight. It is perfect and my new greatest possession—above my blanket and musket, even. I will carry it wherever I go.

I hope the worst is behind us and the tide of this war is finally turning. I am sure by now you have heard of the victory at Vicksburg, too.

There is one more thing I need to tell you, but you must keep it to yourself for now. Quinn has been injured. It seems he will surely survive his injuries. We will be marching soon and leaving Quinn behind, so please tell me how he is when he arrives home in Lowell. He looked to be in good enough spirits when last I saw him in the hospital here, but these wounds can take a turn for the worse.

Take heart, my love. This war may be nearly over.

Your loving husband,

Emmett

I wanted to reach into the letter and touch my husband's words. I wanted to feel him in some way. I needed him. I needed his presence. His body next to mine. But the letter sounded so flat. Emmett was the opposite. He was strong and lively and compassionate. I missed that person with every breath I took. Especially now. The letters were crumbs to me.

Thinking of anything but my own pain was so difficult. But I forced myself to understand the words he'd written. Quinn was injured. Quinn was coming home. Would he recover or be forever unable to chase his daughter or swing her high into the air?

Cocoa growled in her dream, drawing my attention. I quietly prayed every day that I wouldn't lose her, too. She seemed to be in fine health still, but she was clearly aging. I sighed and went to fetch myself a cup of tea. I would write Emmett back now. I needed to tell him about Ronan.

I gazed out the window as I steeled myself to write. The leaves on the trees swayed slightly in the breeze. I thought of Ronan and Steven climbing the tree at the Independence Day celebration. How Ronan had clasped his hands together to boost Steven into the tree. I thought of their smiles, their laughs. How Ronan had watched Steven wobble on his way up. How he'd moved quickly under him, so he could catch my son if he needed to.

Who would catch *me* now? Emmett was not here. Ronan was not here. I felt I was falling into the abyss. I steadied myself and wrote. I tried not to dwell on my pain, because it would hurt Emmett that he could not be with me. And anyway, he would know exactly how I felt. He had been there from the beginning, too. He loved Ronan as I did. And he knew my heart as he knew his own. He would feel it breaking through my words.

The next morning, just as I was cleaning up breakfast, I heard a tap on the door.

"Coming!" I called. Cocoa lifted her head, her eyes barely open.

I opened the door to find Nessa holding Grace in her arms. Nessa's face was red and streaked with tears.

"Quinn has been injured," she said. I tried to look surprised.

"Oh, Nessa," I said. "How terrible. Please come in." I

took Grace from her. Nessa stood in the foyer, looking utterly lost and afraid.

"Sit down," I said. "I'll fetch some tea."

"Dog!" Grace said, reaching for Cocoa.

"Yes," I said to her, quietly. "Would you like to see the dog?"

"Dog!" she said again.

"Help me get your ma some tea first," I said, carrying her to the kitchen. I glanced back at Nessa once more. She was staring at nothing.

"Ma," Grace repeated, staring at me now. Her little face was scrunched with concern.

"We'll take care of your ma," I assured her, kissing her forehead.

I brought Nessa a cup of tea, and then, I took Grace over to Cocoa, who had fallen back asleep. Grace touched her softly.

"Ohhhh," she said.

"Gentle," I said.

She nodded and patted Cocoa not gently at all. But Cocoa didn't stir; she just kept on snoring. I stood and took Grace's hand and helped her stumble back toward Nessa.

"What did his letter say?" I asked, as I slowly sat down beside her.

"He was shot in the leg," she said, so quietly I had to lean forward to hear. Grace had wandered a bit and was playing with the fringe of the rug.

"He said . . ." she started. Finally, she turned to face me. "He's lost it. He's lost his leg. But he ought to be just fine otherwise."

My breath hitched.

"I'm so sorry," I said.

"He begged them to let him keep it," she went on. "But they said he couldn't. The bone was completely shattered. They told him inflammation would set in. And then he would die. So, they cut it right off."

"I suppose they know best," I muttered.

"What will he do without a leg?" she asked. Her eyes were round with terror.

"Well, I've read about these replacement limbs—"

Nessa winced, and I stopped talking. I took her hands in mine.

"You will both get through this," I said. "That's what's important. Grace will still grow up with her da."

Nessa looked at Grace and tears sprang to her eyes again.

"But will he be able to dance with her on her wedding day?" she sobbed. "And surely he can no longer be city marshal. He loved his job."

"Perhaps he can," I said. "A city marshal doesn't have to patrol."

Nessa shook her head.

"That isn't the type of city marshal Quinn was."

"I know," I said. "But things will be different after the war. We'll all be different."

"I should be grateful that he's alive, shouldn't I?" she asked.

"Yes," I said. "But not today. Today, you must be sad. Grieve the man that Quinn was, and then tomorrow, love and accept the man he will be. He will need your strength and support when he comes home."

She looked at our fingers intertwined and nodded. Grace hobbled over to us and gripped our hands, too.

"Ma," she said.

Nessa kissed the top of her head and whispered to her, "Da is coming home, little one."

Chapter Twenty-Six

AUGUST 1863

I arrived at the docks early on the day of Lydia's departure. Earlier than Phillips, even. I sat on a bench and let the sea breeze play with my hair, though it did not cool me. The air was sticky and thick. Dock workers bustled about, and seagulls squawked as they soared above.

I knew I ought to be thinking of my next Paddy letter, but what I was actually doing when Phillips sat down next to me, was talking to Ronan in my head. Telling him about the supper Mr. Joyce had cooked the night before, about the stories Steven had told me from school. About Cocoa and how she missed him so.

"South Carolina will be even more stifling," Phillips said. He adjusted his red necktie.

"But you'll get your cotton now," I said, more bitterly than I'd intended. "For certain."

"Yes," he agreed. "I'll get my cotton now. It's a good thing, too. The way Chase is handling these commerce licenses is making us all look like fools. There are grumblings that change is coming to the cotton markets of Union-occupied cities."

"What do you mean?" I asked. "Commerce licenses?"

"Permission to purchase cotton in occupied Southern cities," he said.

"You buy cotton from Southern cities?" I asked.

"Yes," he replied. "Who did you think was purchasing all of the cotton coming through Union lines?"

"I . . . I don't know," I stuttered. "But what about the Port Royal cotton?"

"Well, the two thousand acres certainly isn't enough. Not that it isn't important. The quality of the cotton grown there is unmatched. We must have it. But it isn't enough. I have licensed buyers in Memphis and New Orleans who purchase cotton, as well."

"And who is selling that cotton?" I asked. "Slave owners?"

"Sometimes," he said. "Widows. Anyone who is left at the plantations. The slaves must eat, too, you know. They have no fault in this war, but they are suffering. People are starving. Women and children and slaves are starving. Selling the cotton keeps them all alive."

I regarded him suspiciously.

"My buyers are not purchasing cotton from the Confederate Army, if that's what you're thinking," he said. "It is imperative that we control the cotton trade. The only other buyer is England, and England will be glad to trade in weapons."

Phillips could sense I was flustered.

"Besides," he went on. "What can your husband—or any of the soldiers—do without cotton? Certainly not bleed."

"I am too hot to think," I said. "But it seems wrong. Buying cotton from slaveholders? This war is their fault."

"I needn't remind you that we have always purchased cotton from slaveholders," he said.

We fell quiet.

"And who are your licensed buyers?" I finally asked.

"Are you interested in becoming one?"

I was flabbergasted.

"No, I am not!"

"Private citizens," he said, chuckling. "The president approves the licenses."

I spotted Lydia walking toward us, trailed by Zeke and Marie and the children.

"Speaking of the president," Phillips went on, lowering his voice. "Seems he is a fan of Paddy."

My head snapped toward him. His eyes twinkled with delight.

"He is?" I asked.

"Reads every letter," he said. "Told me so himself."

As he stood up to greet Lydia, he whispered to me, "Don't forget that."

Emmett

Chapter Twenty-Seven

DECEMBER 1863

M alone stumbled a bit as he sat in the chair next to me. He hadn't shaved in some time, and his strawberry-blond facial hair covered his chin all the way up to his ears and above his lip.

"Well, I suppose we know now that Meade isn't quite the arsehole that Burnside is," he said, taking another swig of whiskey. I sat with my head thrown back, staring at the stars, my coat unbuttoned. He passed the bottle to me, and I took it without looking at him.

"Small comfort," I said, drinking.

Now that Malone and I were sergeants, whiskey was easier to come by. After Fredericksburg, we had both been promoted—supposedly on account of the bravery we had shown transporting wounded men from that farmhouse. More likely, they simply needed more sergeants, since so many had been killed that day. We earned it enough at Gettysburg, though, and hadn't indulged in many of the gratuities of the job until now.

"Can you imagine storming those entrenchments?" Malone asked.

"It would have been Fredericksburg all over again," I said.

I passed the bottle back to Malone and looked at him. He shook his head.

"And like a couple of half-wits, we reenlisted," he said.

I laughed, already feeling the effects of the whiskey.

"I suppose we ought to see this thing through," I said.

"When will you take your furlough?" Malone asked.

"I've asked to be home for Christmas," I said.

"You excited to see your boy?" he asked. He handed me the whiskey again. I took another swig and tried to swallow the tears while the whiskey tried to free them.

"You're bloody right I am," I said. I cleared my throat. "Haven't seen him in two years. They change so much. How different will he be?"

"He'll still be your boy," Malone said.

"What will your ma do when she sees you?" I asked, passing the bottle back once more. Sometimes I forgot Malone was still a bachelor and a good deal younger than I.

"Scold me, most likely." He grinned. "I left a heap of things for my younger brother to do while I was gone. She's probably still holding a grudge."

I chuckled. "She can't stay mad for long," I said. "You're a hero now."

"You don't know my ma."

A shout rose up in the night. It was after taps, and so the men were expected to be quiet. I groaned, still not quite used to the fact that I had to deal with this sort of thing now.

"Let Collins handle it," Malone said. I lay my head back down, waiting for evidence that another noncom was on it.

"You know?" I said. "I *will* let Collins handle it."

The new draftees were angry and bitter and resentful. They had performed well enough in the autumn campaigns and would turn out to be good soldiers, I knew, if given time and experience. But they made me think of the riots and of Ronan. Had these men been there, at the riots? Had their lives been spared while his was not? The riots hadn't made one bit of difference, anyway. They were here, now, fighting, and Ronan was gone. When Rose told me of his death, I had felt only deep remorse. Another good Irish lad taken too soon. And for what? I wrote back to Rose with my deepest sympathies, but I longed to hold her, to help her through her pain.

Another loud clang rang out. Fights broke out among the draftees often enough, and I was in no mood to break one up tonight. I wanted to drink whiskey and look at the stars and think of seeing my family.

We waited to hear Collins's booming voice and evidence of the ruckus dying down before speaking again.

"Will you visit Pat's ma when you're home?" Malone asked.

My throat tightened, but I nodded.

"She's a good woman," I said. "She ought to know how her son stood next to his mates and marched shoulder to shoulder with us before he died. How he made good on Meagher's words about the bravery of the Irish."

"I'll drink to that," Malone declared, raising the whiskey bottle up high.

I closed my eyes and let myself see Steven's shy smile.

His black hair in disarray. Rose's lips. I would be home soon. Home. If only for a bit.

I had decided to surprise my family and so had kept my letters short and vague.

I arrived at the Lowell train depot late in the morning of December 20, 1863. The cold wind nearly blew my hat off as I stepped onto the street. It felt so strange to be back in Lowell. To see the scenes of my old life—a life that was entirely foreign to me now. My boots felt strange on the cobblestones. The sound of women laughing was unfamiliar. I was stopped twice on my way home for a handshake and told, "Thank you, sir."

As I approached the house, my heart beat rapidly. Was Steven out of school yet? Would Rose be home? Would Mr. Joyce be hammering away out back? I put my things down beside the door. I breathed deeply, and when I finally knocked, I heard Rose call from somewhere inside, "Just one moment!"

The sound of her voice stirred something inside of me. I felt lightheaded. I had not intended to cry, but already, before I even saw her face, I felt my cheeks grow wet.

She opened the door only halfway at first. At sight of me, she yelped and brought both hands to her mouth. I reached for her, pushing the door open wide, and caught her before her knees gave out. She fell into my arms, sobbing uncontrollably. I breathed in her hair, dampening it with my tears.

"It's all right, Rose." My voice cracked. "I'm all right."

She stood straight again after a minute and hugged me back so fiercely. The feel of her body pressed against mine filled me with a ravenous heat. She was here. I was here. Her body was on mine.

She pulled away only far enough to look at me. Her hands cupped my face.

"It's truly you," she said. Had I forgotten how beautiful she was? I didn't have words. She looked heavenly. Even better than in my dreams. When I thought of her, her curves were blurred. Her features hazy. But here, in front of me, she was perfect.

I kissed her quickly, our tears falling on our lips. She pulled me inside and stripped me of my uniform. Our hands grabbed at one another. I gently pushed her toward the stairs, not taking a moment to breathe. She gripped my shoulders, and I picked her up. A surprised laugh escaped her as I stumbled to our bedroom with her in my arms.

I laid her on the bed. I wanted to kiss her all over. I wanted my lips on every part of her body. But there was no time. We were both desperate, starved.

Her moans of pleasure were unmuffled. She tugged at my ear with her teeth, panting, "Oh Emmett." It was too much. I finished soon and rolled beside her, out of breath and without question the happiest man in all the North. She stared at me with a silly, satisfied smile, her cheeks flushed with contentment.

"Where am I?" I said, grinning wildly. "Is this heaven?"

She laughed loudly now.

"You're home," she said, rolling onto her side to face me. She lay her hand on my chest and her head on my shoulder.

I put my finger under her chin and lifted her face to mine. I kissed her softly.

"Mmmm," I said. "Home. Heaven. Feels the same."

"It does when you're here," she said. "Are you truly here?"

I patted myself. My face, my stomach, my legs.

"I think so," I said. "Seems to be true."

She giggled. It made my brain tingle. How I'd missed that sound. Nothing was better than making Rose laugh.

"I surely hope Steven is at school," I said. "Otherwise, he will certainly have some questions."

"Oh yes," Rose said, quickly. "Tomorrow is his last day before the holiday. "Shall I keep him home? Or shall we have the house to ourselves?"

She looked at me with desire and bit her lip. I groaned in response and pounced on her again as she laughed.

"House to ourselves, then," she giggled.

Chapter Twenty-Eight

Two days before Christmas, I took Steven to the shops to buy him a gift. Rose was writing, and Mr. Joyce whittled away in his workshop.

At first, Steven was quiet, which I didn't find strange. He had always been a quiet child, and he hadn't seen me in two years. And his Uncle Ronan, his best friend, had died earlier that year. He had plenty to be somber about. He had cut his hair short, too.

"Ma doesn't fool with it so much now," he said, when I asked him about it.

Still, he wore a pleased grin on his face and shot me small glances now and then that I pretended not to notice. I felt the same. Eager to make sure I was truly here. None of us could seem to believe it.

We spent most of the day idly walking around Lowell, enjoying being next to one another, only speaking when we had something to say.

He told me about school, his friends, woodworking, a one-armed man who had made Rose cry at the Fourth of

July celebration. I understood. She wasn't around the gore and horror of battle, and the sight of an amputee up close could certainly be jarring. He told me about what he had heard of the draft riot. Of Ronan's death.

"Ma said he was shot," Steven said. "By a soldier. Why would a soldier shoot Uncle Ronan? I want to ask Ma, but she gets so sad when I talk about it, and I don't want to make her sad."

"Well," I started, trying to think of where to begin. "The soldiers were called in by the mayor. The mayor was afraid that people were going to get hurt during the riot. That people would be killed. There was another one like it in New York City only a day before. Lots of people were killed there."

"But I don't understand why the soldiers killed Uncle Ronan if they were supposed to keep people from getting hurt."

I nodded. Steven was concentrating hard on a hat in front of us. He wouldn't look at me.

"There was a group of people . . ." I said.

"Irish people," Steven interrupted. "Like us."

"Yes," I said. "Like us. Except, perhaps people who weren't given the same opportunities as we were. People who are angry at what they have and, more importantly, what they don't have. They've been upset for a long time. And when they found out the Union Army was going to make them become soldiers, they got even more angry. They don't want to fight in the war."

Steven finally looked up at me.

"These people were trying to break into the armory," I said. "Where the army stores weapons. Lots of weapons.

The soldiers were trying to keep them from stealing those weapons and hurting people." I took a deep breath. "People like Miss Marie and Miss Lydia."

Steven nodded, deep in thought.

"Is it because they have black and brown skin? Like Ma talks about?" he asked.

"That's right," I said.

Steven's face twisted into a scowl.

"Uncle Ronan would never have hurt Miss Marie," he said, quietly.

I crouched so that I could look him in the eye.

"No," I said. "I don't believe he would have, either. Uncle Ronan was trying to help people. But the soldiers didn't know that."

"Why did they have to do that?" Steven asked, his eyes filling with tears. "Why did they have to try to break into the armory? Why were they so mad about becoming soldiers? You're a soldier! It's noble to be a soldier!"

I sighed. "It's difficult being a soldier," I said. "And dangerous."

"I know why it's dangerous," Steven said. "But why is it difficult?"

"Well, no one ever gives me hugs out there," I said, grinning. Steven didn't smile back. "We have to live in tents. It can be cold and wet, for many days at a time. And muddy. The food isn't very good. You have to drill, and that's quite boring. But most of all, it's lonely. I miss you and your ma fiercely."

"Ma says you're brave, too," Steven said. "That you must do things that you're afraid to."

"I suppose she's right," I said. "But when you and all your best mates are doing it together, it's not as hard."

We walked out of the hat store and into a toy shop.

"Is it hard . . ." Steven started. He swallowed and looked around to make sure no one could hear. "To kill other men?"

I stopped walking. It was a big question for a small boy. His eyes were wide. I didn't want to lie to him.

"During the battle, it's not hard. Because those men are trying to kill me. But after the battle, when I see all of the men who have died on both sides, it's very hard."

Steven's eyebrows furrowed in concentration. He nodded slowly.

"Enough of that, though," I said. "Let's buy something here, from this store." I put my hand on his shoulder. "Anything you'd like."

Chapter Twenty-Nine

"Are we going to Boston again for Christmas?" Steven asked, excitedly, the next day.

"No, darling," Rose said, her voice heavy.

"What about Miss Marie? And Levi? And Eliza?"

Rose pursed her lips as she put the breakfast dishes away.

"With Miss Lydia and Mr. Gil both gone this year, they've decided to have a small, quiet family dinner," she said.

She had written to me about Lydia going to Port Royal and about Marie's objections.

"How is Marie?" I asked.

"Still a bit distant," she said.

"So, it will only be us?" Steven asked, clearly disappointed.

"Yes, only us," Rose said. "But your da is here. And that's special enough for me."

Steven sighed, but said, "For me as well."

Mr. Joyce sat in front of the fireplace, reading the newspaper with Cocoa at his feet.

"I must go see Quinn soon," I said.

"Are you sure that's wise?" Rose asked. "I invited them for Christmas, but Nessa said he was still settling in. It didn't sound as if they would welcome visitors."

"Trust me," I said. "If there's anyone he'd be happy to see, it's me."

Rose chuckled. "So humble."

"He'll want to know news of the regiment," I said.

She shrugged and moved on to sweeping. A light snow had started last night and continued steadily into the morning. I watched it come down quickly now, piling up on the trees outside. I thought of the men in their winter log huts and homemade fireplaces that produced more smoke than heat. Poor bastards. I was glad to be home.

"Steven, should we play your new game today?" I asked.

"Yes!" He rushed to get it.

"Will you two join us?" I asked.

Rose looked at Mr. Joyce. He put down his paper.

"Why not?" he said. Rose smiled and sat next to him. Steven retrieved a large poster, which we spread across the table and studied. It looked like a long, winding snake chopped into small bits. We all chose something for our piece—a coin, a thimble, a button—and rolled the dice to move across the snake. We had to obey what was written on the spot. Skip a turn. Move ahead. Go back. Soon, when we all seemed to know what to do, I started to focus on my roll. Tried to make the dice land on the number I wanted. Made sure it was sitting in my hand on the opposite number.

Steven started to eye me suspiciously. I couldn't help but allow a small smile to creep onto my face. He narrowed his eyes even more during my next turn.

"Are you cheating?" he finally asked. Mr. Joyce laughed. I threw my hands up.

"I haven't a clue what you mean," I said. Now Steven started to smile.

"Yes, you do!" he cried. "You're tossing the dice funny. I caught you."

Rose giggled.

"Well, he isn't all that good at it," she said.

"I'm doing a very fine job of cheating!" I said.

Steven laughed now.

"So, you admit it! Ma is right. You're rotten at it. Your last two rolls have landed you on ill-fated spots."

"The two of you are just jealous that you don't have such skill. It's all in the wrist, you know."

Steven rolled his eyes.

"Well, none of you have noticed that I've been moving an extra space on each of my turns!" Mr. Joyce declared.

Steven's mouth fell open, and Rose laughed heartily.

"Grandda!" Steven exclaimed. "Well, that's just dishonest!"

Mr. Joyce winked and elbowed him. "I would never."

We played three more times after that, trying to see who could get away with the most cheating. It turned out that none of us were very good at it, and there was a lot of shouting and laughing and resetting pieces and rolling again.

When we stopped for dinner, Steven, my honest, rule-abiding son, said, "That was fun."

I grinned and pulled him in for a hug.

Our Christmas celebration was intimate and so full of love. I felt blessed that I could have it. It was a gift, and I wondered what I had done to deserve it.

The rest of the thirty days were just as idyllic. We celebrated birthdays that I had missed. We went on picnics. I cooked breakfast. We played in the park with a much slower but still healthy and happy Cocoa. I held Rose at night. Comforted her when she still found tears for Ronan. Made love to her like we were newlyweds.

Steven and Mr. Joyce showed me their shop. They taught me how to shave and sculpt wood as best as they could. I didn't have the knack for it like Steven did, but I loved to watch him work.

I visited Quinn. He gazed longingly at my healthy gait. He didn't try to hide it. He sat in a chair in the parlor with his jaw set. He was quiet at first, somber. I spoke of the regiment, of the Mine Run campaign. He finally grunted a smile when I told him the story of a draftee who'd nearly shot off his own foot.

Grace toddled over to him while we talked. She groped at his leg, reaching her small arms up toward him.

"Up," she said. "Up, Da."

Finally, a genuine smile pulled at the corner of his mouth. He reached toward her and pulled her onto his lap. She tugged at the beard he had let grow.

"I'm not sure what I would do without her," he said. She

giggled as he nuzzled his head into her small neck. "She still has her da. That's what matters."

Another day, I visited Pat's ma. She looked small, fragile. Nothing like the hearty woman I remembered. She wept and laughed as I told her stories of Pat. I wept too. I missed Pat. Being in his home, knowing he would never return. It hurt. When the stories dried up, we sat in silence for a bit before I left. I spent the rest of the day alone. I had a drink at the tavern for Pat and thought of him sitting next to me like he had so many times before.

When it was time for me to leave—to return to my regiment, to camp—Rose and Steven became strangers again. We didn't know how to say goodbye. We couldn't. It was far worse than the first time I'd left. We all knew now what we hadn't known then.

At the train station, Rose's hands shook. I bit the inside of my cheek so hard I tasted blood. Steven cried openly. I knelt down and held him.

"Don't die, Da," he said, between sobs. "Please don't die."

What was I to say? Was I to lie to my boy?

"Do you remember how your ma told you I was brave?" I asked. He nodded.

"You're brave, too," I said. "You continue to love me even when I go. That's brave. And you're kind. You're smart. You work hard. I am so proud to be your da. And I am going to try my hardest to come home to you again."

He sniffled and tried to hold his head high.

"I'm proud to be your son, Da," he said.

I felt my own cheeks grow slick with tears. I stood and grabbed Rose's shaking hands. Her bottom lip trembled, too.

"I can't do this," she said, softly. "I can't say goodbye to you, too."

I released one of her hands and held her face.

"You make me who I am," I said. "And I will see you again."

In this life or the next, I thought.

She kissed me fiercely. In front of our son. In front of all the people waiting and leaving and arriving.

"My heart and my soul are yours," she whispered. "They always have been."

I hugged her one last time before stepping onto the train. This time, I did watch them from the window as the train pulled away. I watched my family hold each other as I left them.

It would have been easy to desert, then. No one was there to lead me back. To make sure I switched trains at the correct station. To march me back to camp. I felt as though some vital organ had been ripped from my body, but I went anyway.

As I dragged myself from one railway station in Boston to another many blocks away, I heard a group of gathered men shouting. I might have simply walked on by if I hadn't recognized a voice.

"I won that last round, fair and square. You owe me," it was saying. I elbowed my way through the crowd, trying to push past the young men swarming toward the sounds of an impending fight. Those sounds made the hairs on the backs of their necks stand on end, and they couldn't

LISA BOYLE

help but watch and hope for the opportunity to hit someone.

"And how 'bout the round before that?" a different voice replied. "You've been cheatin' me this whole time."

Then, a chuckle from the man with his back to me. I would know that chuckle anywhere, because—like the sound of an impending fight—the sound of that chuckle made blood rush to my face. Formed my hands into fists. And now I could see his giant back, his enormous shadow. I should've killed him when I had the chance.

"Prove it," he said.

"McDermott!" I shouted, cutting him off. He whirled around. "We've missed you down in Virginia." His red face paled. At first, he just stared stupidly at me.

"Why don't you go back there, then?" he finally replied. "Where you can miss me properly."

"You should come, too," I said, stepping closer. "We've got a firing squad and a giant feckin' box with your name on it."

He snarled. "And I've got letters with your pretty *wife's* name on 'em."

I didn't hesitate. I grabbed him by the shirt and punched him in the nose. He took only a moment to recover, wiping the dripping blood before coming at me. I tried to dodge and at first succeeded. But he turned, and his elbow met my jaw, knocking me off-center, causing my vision to spin. Just then, a couple of police officers came barging into the crowd.

"Break it up, men!" One of them grabbed McDermott's arm and the other mine.

"This man is a deserter!" I shouted as loud as I could. I

spat blood on the ground beside me. Now people stared from the sidewalks. From windows. "You ought to be dead right now," I shouted at McDermott. "You ought to be shot for being such a bloody coward. You snuck away like a damned snake. After your comrades died beside you!"

"Get the fuck out my face, Doherty!" he screamed.

The police officer started to drag me away. I smiled at McDermott and tried to shrug the officer off of me.

"You need to calm down, soldier," he said. "Take it up with Governor Andrew."

I put my hands up.

"All right," I said. "All right."

He let go of me. The crowd still stared at me—as if *I* were the monster. I adjusted my jacket and walked to the train station, rage still boiling inside of me.

Chapter Thirty

MARCH 1864

M alone came back from furlough in nearly as foul a mood as I had. The time away had not renewed our desire to fight, but rather, made us resentful. My news of McDermott did not help matters.

"I got one good hit in. But the traitor was walkin' around Boston, free as a bird," I told him.

"I hope he gets the clap," he grumbled. "Can't we finish this bloody war already?"

We were getting dressed for the day, Malone wrestling with a rolled-up sock while I buttoned my shirt.

"I intend to," I said.

Malone raised his eyebrows. "How's that?" he asked.

"We're leaders now, aren't we?" I asked. "Isn't it our job to make those men into soldiers?"

Malone chuckled. "Only so much you can do with this sorry bunch."

"They may not like that they're here, but they're here. None of us like it. But we're here to win. I'm not doing another three years, Malone. I know I signed up for it, but

this war needs to end. I'm not gonna watch these boys bumble around any longer."

He grinned at me as he shoved his foot into his boot.

"Let's see what you've got, Sergeant," he said.

We marched ourselves to roll call, and I watched the draftees roll out of their tents, sniffing and yawning and scratching themselves.

Malone and I were waiting when the bugle played for the second time that morning, and most of the soldiers meandered over with sour faces. If they were looking for a fight, I was going to give it to them.

All who were late or absent for roll call got put on the blacklist for the day's most terrible tasks. After breakfast, when it was time for drilling, I looked out at the men. A noncom like myself didn't normally make big speeches. Noncoms did what the commissioned officers told them to do, which was to shout commands at the enlisted men. But I had something to say.

"Some of you were forced to be here," I started. "Others were paid handsomely. Plenty of your friends have already crept away, deserted at the earliest opportunity. The fact that you're still here makes you better men. But it doesn't make you soldiers. I'm not going to wait until a battle to find out which of you are cowards and shirks. I'm going to find out now. Today, there will be punishments. If you're out of step, you'll do double guard duty. If you fumble your weapon, you'll spend the afternoon bucked and gagged. Do you men understand?"

The lieutenant eyed me with interest but didn't intervene. The soldiers glared ahead, or spat on the ground, or shuffled their feet in protest. I didn't care.

That afternoon, I shouted at them until I was hoarse. I meted out punishments as promised, and as the men limped away at the end of the day, grumbling under their breath, I didn't feel one bit of regret. Perhaps they would hate me. But I would do everything in my power to make sure this was the last season of fighting.

The leaders at the top were good men at this point in the war. General Barlow, the head of the division, and Colonel Smyth, the head of the brigade, were highly respected leaders. Still, they weren't in charge of training these men. I was.

Though Malone mocked me that night, he admitted it would do the new recruits some good.

"Rascals they are," he said. "Let's see how many leave tonight, huh?"

"I hope they do," I said. "I would rather have one hundred brave men than a thousand poltroons."

Malone nodded and chewed his beefsteak. We had fried it in pork fat that night, and it was quite good.

General Ulysses S. Grant arrived that week.

"He's a wee fella," Malone said, trying to hold in his laughter.

He rode by us so quickly I could barely see enough of him to agree. He lacked the usual pomp that typically accompanied our commanders.

When I saw him again, though, his horse stood still, and the general puffed on a cigar, studying us carefully. No one would guess by his attire or attitude that he was now in command of the entire Union Army.

Things began to change after that, and not in a way they had ever changed before. It seemed as though General Grant was of the same mind as I was. He was a man who wanted to win. The first thing he did was set new rules for training. Pat and Malone and I had learned most of our technique from Quinn. Now, all the new recruits were taught to fire in the presence of officers. We drilled so often, I sometimes heard myself shouting the nine counts of the loading procedure in my dreams.

By late April, our heavy rations and boredom no longer comforted us, so those in charge set up baseball games.

"I like him," Malone announced, as we sat on the ground, watching the games. "I'd like to have a drink with him."

"Who?" I asked.

"General Grant."

"Does he look like a fun lad to you?" I asked.

Malone chuckled.

"Not at all. But he looks like he knows just what we've been through. Like he's experienced it, too. Not just the war, either. Regular struggles. He's a man like us. He knows a hard day's work."

"He doesn't know just what we've been through," I said. "Not as Irishmen and not in this war, either. He hasn't been fighting Lee."

"You're difficult to impress, Doherty," Malone said, shaking his head. "Most of the men who don't like the looks of Grant were McClellan men. But not you. You despise them all equally."

"I don't despise him. In fact, I like the changes he's made. But is it enough? I'm only worried he doesn't have any idea what he's up against over here. This is Lee we're fighting."

"And Lee is a man, just like the rest of us," Malone replied, turning to me. "Do you know why you're still here, fighting?" he asked.

"To win the war," I said. "It's up to us now to do it."

Malone sighed. "And do you know why you stayed in the beginning? Was it because some smug bastard tied you to a wooden horse when you stepped out of line during drill?"

"I stayed because I'm not a deserter," I said.

Malone shook his head. "What makes you *fight*, Doherty? What lights up that fire inside you? What makes you stand tall during battle?"

I was quiet.

"We fight for Clifford and Banks. Our brothers. The men standing by our sides. That's what we all fight for. Each other."

I looked at the other soldiers across the field. Lounging, laughing with their mates.

"These new men are different, sure," Malone went on. "They're here reluctantly. They aren't volunteers, like we were. But if you can show them what it means to be a leader, to be their brother, we'll win. Bobby Lee's gettin' tired out there. We're wearin' him down."

He was chewing a blade of grass. He took it from his mouth and looked at it, before stomping it into the ground with his boot.

"I'm just sayin'. Discipline is all well and good, but you

can't beat men into submission. You can't yell them into carin'."

"I'll make them care," I said.

"You can't, really," he said. "You can only prepare them. Make them see that *you* care about *them*. That you're on their team at the end of the day. Right there. Next to them. Dealing with all this shite, too."

Finally, I stood, shaking my tingling legs. The winning team of soldiers were leaping into the air, huddled together in a group. The losing team had already wandered off. I squinted into the sun at them. I hated these games. I would have loved them in the beginning, but now, I only wanted to fight and go home.

"I am here, Malone," I said.

"You're here, but do you believe in them? Do you believe in General Grant? Or are you bitter that no one seems to care as much as you do?"

I looked at him hard, but I knew he was right.

I spent half the night thinking about Malone's words and, after roll call the next morning, sat down with the men to eat breakfast. They sat up straighter and looked into their food and stayed quiet. We ate in silence that first day. And the day after. Finally, on the third day, when they realized I was making it a habit, they began to talk quietly to one another. Snickering under their breath.

On the fourth day, one of them spoke to me.

"Sir, is it true about the whiskey?" he asked. "At Antietam? At the bridge?"

I smiled and thought of Pat.

"Sure is," I said. "We stood in those woods for hours waiting to cross that bridge. We all knew General Burnside was in a tricky position. The man was embarrassed. We had some leverage, and the 51st used it."

The soldier smiled, and I realized they were all listening. I cleared my throat.

"Another time," I said, a little louder, "back when General Meagher was still here, General Burnside forbade fires on a night when it was snowing . . ."

"Was this in Fredericksburg?" another soldier asked. ". . . Sir?"

For a moment, I was annoyed by the interruption. But then, I realized they all knew these stories. Maybe they didn't want to fight, but these stories had become legends. There was something inside these men that wanted to be a part of that.

"It was," I said. "The night before we marched on Marye's Heights."

A few of them smiled encouragingly. They probably knew the rest but still wanted to hear it.

"We were all freezing," I went on. "And had been shelled all day in that stinking city. It smelled terrible. Meagher was furious. He stomped through the brigade, telling us all to start a fire. 'It's too bloody cold for these foolish games,' he said. Defied orders right there. It's a good thing, too. We would all have woken with frostbite the next day, otherwise."

Just then, a group of men marched past with pressed uniforms, straight hats, clean faces, and worry in their eyes. Row after row after row. My men looked at me in confusion. I stood up and watched the fresh soldiers—in awe, at first. Then, I began to laugh hysterically, suspecting I knew exactly who these men were.

"Malone!" I shouted at him across the tents. His wily smile popped into view. "Are you seeing this?"

"It's Washington's heavy artillery!" he hollered back. The fresh men marched between our shouts, looking bewildered. These were the men who had spent the war behind Washington's fortifications, manning the guns and keeping pigs for fresh meat. They had never fought. Never fired their musket at the enemy, despite being trained as infantrymen like us. I turned to the enlisted men still seated around me. Dirty faces, worn uniforms, eating slop.

"Looks like your luck has run out, heavies!" Malone shouted.

A few of them looked truly incensed as they watched Malone and I laugh at them.

"No fort down here in Virginia to hide behind," I shouted back. One of the soldiers from the heavy artillery unit dropped his musket and tripped up the entire formation.

"Guess it's the buck and gag for him, huh, Sergeant?" the private beside me asked. I winked at him, and he laughed openly.

Malone whistled across the way.

"Lookin' sharp!" he shouted.

"It's a late Christmas present." I clapped my hands. "But we'll take it! Bobby Lee better watch his arse."

Our soldiers grinned at each other. They were excited. They were finally excited.

Chapter Thirty-One

MAY 1864

W e broke camp on a beautiful morning. Sunny with a cool, steady breeze. I was neither sweating nor chilled. We ate a large breakfast, and I savored my coffee with a pinch of sugar. The birds tweeted loudly, and the spring flowers swayed in the wind. It all felt like an omen. The men were calm. Ready. I said a prayer of thanks.

As we marched, we gazed over our shoulders, watching our camp fade into the distance. We marched away from the promise of spring. Of new life. We did it willingly and not so willingly. Each of us had reasons of our own buried deep within that propelled us forward, every step. We had a feeling this war was about to turn. That things would be different from here on out. But how, we weren't sure.

We marched to the Rapidan. By then, the new recruits had shed all the extra equipment they'd foolishly thought they would need. The artillery men would pick at it greedily when they came along, grabbing the best of the spoils and hanging it on their guns.

There was still daylight when we reached the old Chancellor House. A year before, we had buried our dead here. Our peaceful morning march turned into an eerie night's rest, sleeping atop the bones of our comrades. We got an early start, before even a hint of dawn was upon us, and we marched south and east until we finally halted.

We stood, letting the sun bake us, waiting for orders. I pulled off my cap and wiped my brow. Finally, we were told to change direction and the pace quickened. I urged the men to drink water.

We kicked up dust on the road, and soon, the sprawling fields grew into a wilderness, choking our path. We squeezed behind one another, the vines and brush and burweed reaching for us, the treetops closing in above. I thought about what it would be like to march through these woods to meet the rebels. How would we find the enemy in there? It would be like fighting a battle blind.

But the sounds from up ahead told me this was exactly what we would be doing. General Hancock directed men out of the column and into battle lines, putting others to work felling trees and building breastworks along the narrow road. But there wasn't room for us all. Confusion reigned as cavalry tried to pass and men dragged logs across the narrow road and others loaded their muskets.

I directed some men from our regiment to help with the breastworks, and then Malone and I and a few others began stacking logs. It was hours past noon when General Hancock ordered the first three brigades of the second corps—our corps—into the woods after the rebels. A different division had been holding them off, smashing into rebel lines and setting the woods on fire with sparks from their muskets. It was a terrible sight, and the sounds and smells drifting toward us were those of hell itself.

Colonel Smyth got the Irish Brigade into formation next. I stood at the end of the line of battle, looking to my left to make sure my men were ready. Behind us, Malone shouted at the men to stay close. The soldiers ahead of us disappeared into the tangled, choked brush. At the last minute, I swung my musket over my shoulder and grabbed the ax I had been using to fell the trees. We would need it in there.

Somewhere up ahead in the woods, thousands of muskets fired and echoed and fired again, their pops turning into a roar. The sounds of my men's stomping boots and clattering metal disappeared, muffled by the terrain. My own breath seemed loud. My heartbeat deafening. When I called for the men to ready their muskets, I felt as though I were shouting at ghosts. They had been swallowed up by the density of the growth. Branches, roots, bushes. With my sword in one hand and my ax in the other, I hacked at the weeds and vines threatening to trip me. Still, they tore my pants open at both knees.

I could smell the fire right away. It was close. The smoke snaked in and out of the trees. Ahead, I could see the flash of a musket, and the burst of smoke seeped into the hovering cloud from the brushfire. Puddles of mud began to appear—the overflow from a creek winding just around the edge of my field of vision. I stepped in one unwittingly and fought to keep my boot.

"Keep moving!" I shouted to the men I could only trust were still there, still fighting with the wilderness.

My hands were sweaty and bloody from the burweed, and slippery against my weapons. I strained to listen. Tried to parse if I was hearing sounds of victory or defeat—if they came from our men or the enemy. The cries of pain or elation, the thump of a body. My ears rang from the effort.

To my right, a soldier tried to run past me to the rear, stumbling and tripping and wiping his hands on his pants as he righted himself.

"Soldier!" I shouted at him. "We are not in retreat!"

He only stared at me, blinking for a few seconds, before continuing on his way. I cursed under my breath.

Malone emerged from a giant tangle of vines.

"What is this shite?" he shouted, huffing as he cut his way free. A minié ball whizzed into the branches above me, raining down leaves.

"Close ranks!" he shouted, looking around. "Where in the bloody hell are they?"

"Who?" I asked. "Our men or theirs?"

"Anyone!"

I wheezed, the smoke invading my lungs, and reached for my canteen. I took cover behind a tree as I drank, watching Malone hack at a branch.

I could see the fire now. About thirty paces ahead of us. It blazed, catching on branches and leaves and oozing through the woods, as if poured from the heavens. Figures, outlines of men, ran around it on each side, dropping every so often with a cry of pain. Then, I noticed a large, jagged rock, taller than I at the edge of the fire.

I grabbed Malone's sleeve and pointed at it.

"How about fishin' for some rebs?" I asked. He looked confused, but we picked up our boots and hacked our way over to it.

"It's bloody hot over here, Doherty," he said, eyeing the growing fire beside us with a bit of panic.

I sheathed my sword and gripped the ax with two hands, as if about to chop down a tree. I stood with my back against the rock.

"Fix your bayonet," I said, real quiet. He grinned at me now that he understood.

"You're a madman," he said.

"They're coming right around the edge of this," I said. "It's no good trying to shoot at them in this smoke. We'll miss every time. We'll be right here waiting instead."

Malone fixed his bayonet, chuckling and shaking his head. Still, he said, "For Meagher."

"For Meagher," I said.

We waited until we heard boots crunching through the woods and the yells of the rebels. It wasn't until we saw their gray coats and watched their bodies stiffen as they realized we were there, that we swung and thrust at them. They dropped to the ground, and we pulled our weapons out of their bodies before saying a short prayer. We spent the evening this way, waiting at the edges of fires, behind rocks, trying not to fall into streams and swamps. Sweating. Killing. Praying.

Sometime during the night, we tried to find our way back to the breastworks, stumbling and crashing through the darkness. When we finally reached Brock Road, it was nearly morning. I dropped my bloody ax to the ground and fell into a deep sleep.

We thought we were safe the next day when we were ordered to hold the entrenchments. Other brigades were sent back into the woods, but we were not. The generals thought we were winning until our troops came running back, leaping over the breastworks, desperately reloading their muskets.

The fire came, too. The long arms of tree branches, red and orange and angry, collapsing in the heat, reaching out as if to grab us. The breastworks caught fire, making the men leap backward. And still the Confederates came bursting in like demons. We fired through the flames, at the rebels, at their flag. Next to me, a private bayoneted a man. Finally, our reinforcements came, and we drove the Confederates away, leaving only smoldering bodies at our feet.

That night, Malone walked down the entrenchments, sitting at fires and nodding along as men told stories of the past two days. We always took turns at this after a battle. But tonight was not my night. When he came back, he let out a whistle.

"Those boys to the north of us had a hell of a time today, too," he said, sitting beside me.

"General Grant sure got a taste of Bobby Lee, didn't he?" I asked, rubbing the back of my neck.

"Think we'll be going back the way we came tomorrow?" Malone asked.

"Would be a shame, wouldn't it?" I replied. "All that to be sittin' exactly where we started."

"That's how it goes in Virginia, though, isn't it?"

LISA BOYLE

"Should we keep answering our questions with more questions?" I quipped, and Malone laughed. A new recruit sat near us, a dazed look in his eyes.

"You all right, lad?" Malone asked him.

The young man focused on him.

"Yes, sir," he said. "Just thinkin' of home."

"That was one hell of a first battle," Malone said. "They aren't usually like that. Typically, we can see each other and the rebels, too—long before we stumble right into them. That in there was some sort of sick joke dreamed up by the devil himself."

"Huh," the soldier said. I wondered if he was trying to laugh. "You've got that right, Sergeant."

Malone slapped him on the back.

"Just think of how proud that lady friend of yours will be when she hears of your bravery, huh?"

Finally, a small smile.

Malone started a fire, and we made coffee and ate our pork and told stories of battles from early in the war. Ones to make the new recruit laugh. He seemed to calm down a bit. He told us his name—Private Campbell—and a little of his family, too.

Then, we heard a band playing, and we all quieted to listen. Only the agony of the soldiers lost to the wilderness could still be heard. It was "The Star-Spangled Banner." Malone, of course, began to sing along.

I nudged Private Campbell and whispered to him, "This war is terrible. What we have to do, what we have to see. But this is about *us* now. The story Sergeant Malone is singing. About the flag. We're part of it. This flag, this country. It's ours. We've earned it."

He looked at me intently.

"*You've* earned it," I said. His jaw set as he nodded. He was starting to understand. There was pride in what we were doing. It was dirty, torn-apart, ugly pride. But it was pride all the same, and wearing it was the only thing we could do.

We had only a moment of relative quiet after the song ended before the Confederate band struck up "The Bonnie Blue Flag" in response.

"Northern treachery my arse!" Malone shouted. Private Campbell laughed a little.

"Go ahead," Malone said. "Shout at 'em! They'll try to kill us either way."

Campbell laughed again.

"I'll piss on that Bonnie Blue!" Malone yelled.

"Traitorous cowards!" Campbell said, loudly.

"Yah!" Malone cried in encouragement.

"Gray-back bastards!" Campbell shouted.

"That's right!" Malone added. "We don't give two shites about your heritage!"

I grinned, watching the two of them.

"Come on, Doherty." Malone pulled me to my feet. "Get in on this!"

"You'll rot in hell, you treasonous pigs!" I shouted.

Malone laughed. Campbell looked giddy. The rest of our company started in on it, too. We were like drunk men, delirious with exhaustion and pain and frustration. We mocked the rebels into the night. It felt like absolution.

Chapter Thirty-Two

Nothing happened the next morning. Malone winked at me.

"Guess it's back across the Rapidan, eh?" he said.

I shook my head.

"More of the same."

Our breastworks looked strong again. For nothing, I supposed. By late afternoon, we knew we would be moving soon. We waited in the heat for our orders. Finally, just as dusk was setting in, we heard commotion along the Plank Road. General Grant was riding toward us. I expected him to turn north onto the Brock Road. We all did. I caught his eye as he approached. He wore the look of a determined man. He took a hard right, south, and did not glance back over his shoulder. The men erupted into cheers around me. I looked at Malone as a smile spread across his face.

"You were wrong, Doherty!" he shouted. I laughed.

"On to Richmond!" I shouted.

"On to Richmond!" the men responded.

A lieutenant tried to restore order, hissing, "You'll alert the enemy, you fools!"

We tried to quiet ourselves. But us veterans had never seen anything like it. We could hardly believe our own eyes. A general who didn't pull back and lick his wounds after a battle. I took a swig from my canteen and noticed it was nearly empty. I hoped more provisions were coming. We would be on our way again.

Our corps—the second corps—was ordered to stay in place and protect the rear as the fifth corps followed Grant, marching toward the Spotsylvania Courthouse. As we watched them march past, we all wore stupid grins.

When we finally moved out deep in the night, we marched in an exhausted cluster, falling asleep as we walked, bumping into each other in the dark. We stopped at a tavern for a bit and then marched some more. When we finally reached the Po River, we were all nearly delirious. Thoughts came and slipped away as easily as breathing. We crossed the river and quickly back again, firing at rebels in the distance as we went.

As soon as we set up along the breastworks another division had dug, I made coffee for myself and the men I'd assigned to stay awake. The others were told to rest, and they stumbled only a few yards into the woods before falling asleep under the shade of a tree.

"The hell was that?" Malone asked.

"I think we were bait," I said.

"I'm too bloody tired to be bait."

"Johnny Reb hasn't slept either," I reminded him.

"Do you suppose it's a blessing to be killed when you haven't got your wits about you?" he asked.

I watched the men to our left lining up for battle, being sent in to support those who had gone in earlier that day. They tucked their heads down and read over their last letters. Or looked to the sky and silently prayed. I watched the stretcher-bearers carting off some of the wounded, while other injured men limped by on their own, barely able to drag themselves along, the pain likely the only thing keeping them awake. I didn't answer Malone. I didn't know when it was best to be killed.

We took turns eating, sleeping, and watching for the enemy. The next day was much of the same.

There were whispers of a large attack being planned. My head was a bit clearer, and I wrote to Rose and Steven when I was able. But by now, mail had been halted. Nothing was to come in or out, and I ached to send them word of my well-being. I wrote anyway and imagined it reaching them.

Just as I was signing my letter, rain began to fall. Though it was only a light drizzle, the clouds brought cooler weather, and by nightfall, fires blazed among our troops. Campbell came to me while I was nibbling on my hardtack.

"Is it true, sir?" he asked. "Will we be going into battle in such large numbers?"

The pop of muskets rang out to our left. We barely glanced their way.

"They say the whole corps will go in at once, don't they?" I asked. "Each regiment behind the next."

Campbell nodded.

"I've never seen anything like that before," I said.

"Perhaps it will work," Campbell said.

"Perhaps it will," I said. "This could really take those rebs by surprise."

Campbell nodded enthusiastically, glad that I agreed with him.

The wind whipped around now, causing the fire to shrink and grow. A lieutenant appeared before me.

"Rouse the men," was all he said.

Campbell and I stood and saluted him.

"Yes, sir," I said.

I winked at Campbell.

"A nighttime march in the mud," I whispered to him. "A real treat."

I hollered at the men to come to attention. They put their fires out before gathering around the lieutenant. We weren't told much but were shuffled into position—one regiment behind the next, just as we had heard, our elbows touching the man's beside us, rain pounding on our heads. Malone and I were positioned at the end to keep the men in line. The night was cloudy, darker than usual without the light of the moon. We were to be nearly silent. No yelling. No firing our weapons until we reached the enemy.

We swore and stumbled and tripped on the heels of the man before us throughout the night. The wind was bitter and unrelenting, and we shook violently.

"Do you suppose we're walking in circles?" Malone whispered. "I'm certain we started at the tree we just passed."

"I'm certain all of these trees look the same when it's this dark," I answered.

Sometimes our legs sank in the mud—all the way up to our knees. We tried not to fall as we pulled ourselves free. We gripped each other for balance and helped each other across rushing streams. Finally, the rain let up just as the light hue of morning began to outline the objects around us. We halted. I rubbed my eyes and glanced around. The rain seemed to have settled just above the ground in patches of heavy fog. My teeth chattered. We moved again and soon heard muffled cheers ahead of us. We had come upon the rebels' picket line so quietly that they'd had no time to run or alert their troops and were now being sent to the rear as prisoners, passing each regiment with their heads hung low.

"Cheer up, Johnny Reb! We've got food behind the lines," a soldier from the 88th said, to snickers. The Confederates were always hungry.

We marched quicker now, into an open field. Then we ran, sopping wet and feeling like heroes. Messengers of death charging silently into the dawn.

Chapter Thirty-Three

A head of us, the 66th New York celebrated our victory too soon. The first ravine they came upon was not, in fact, the Confederate's entrenchments, and their whoops and hollers only stripped away our veil of secrecy. The rebels knew we were coming now.

We pulled apart their abatis, throwing aside sharp-tipped branches as we climbed toward the enemy, praying their musket fire would continue to miss us. Finally, a few rounds fired into the men beside me, but it was too late. We reached their entrenchments, bayonets fixed. Most of the rebels ran into the woods behind them. A few swung the butts of their muskets at us wildly. We knocked them down, stabbed them, while the rest of us chased down the fleeing men, firing at their backs, into the trees. The rebels stopped running. They put their muskets down and their hands into the air, turning slowly, heads ducked low.

"Cease fire!" I yelled.

We hurried over to them, wild with excitement at the

number of men and flags and guns we were taking. While Malone and I helped to gather the prisoners, some of our men took off in search of more Confederates. Malone cawed like a maniac and then started to sing at them.

> Then o what fun to see them run
> And to leave a name in story, o!
> With my father's gun, I'll follow the drum
> And fight my way to glory, o!

"What, did they send the band in after us?" a Confederate scoffed, as I patted him down, searching for knives and other spoils.

"That's right," Malone said. "You were beaten and captured by the regimental band. How do ya feel about that, Johnny Reb?"

"Why is it that some of you Irish got yourself some brains and others of you fight for the Union?" the prisoner retorted.

"How is it that every single one of you secesh haven't got any brains at all?" I asked before shoving him hard. "Get to the rear."

With the men and guns secured, Malone and I pressed forward, looking for our regiment's battle line. What we found was chaos. Men running this way and that, shooting at anything and everything that moved. Union soldiers turned Confederate artillery around to face the enemy and then fumbled over it.

"Fall in rank!" I shouted. A few turned to look at us, as if startled from a dream. Others simply kept plowing ahead.

Then, something appeared out of the woods. A solid

gray wall of men. Minié balls instantly began to whistle at us, pinging off the trees and the ground around our feet. I watched a few of our men fall, hit.

"Fall in rank!" Malone shouted, desperately.

The men finally began to see the seriousness of it all, but they were so turned around, so confused, that they just sort of stared in horror. Malone ran ahead, grabbing some of the men and throwing them back into formation.

Then, he fell. I waited for him to get up again. He didn't. He rolled over in pain. I ran to him, my unloaded musket bumping against my leg. He was cussing and moaning.

The blood came from his arm, but I didn't stop to look at it too closely. I hooked my arms under his and started to drag him back. He was light, and so I went quickly—until something caught my foot. I fell back before I had time to catch myself, smacking my head so hard that everything went black.

When I opened my eyes again, I could hear someone shouting for me in the distance. It took me a moment to focus. Malone had rolled to his side, and was clutching his hand, which was pouring blood. I got to my feet as quickly as I could, but when I looked up, the rebels were so close. The minié balls were flying all around us now. I crouched back down.

Damn it, I thought. I tried to boost Malone up again on his good side, but when I looked to our men, I could barely see them. They were falling back. Probably to the entrenchments. We wouldn't make it. We would die first. The musket fire was too heavy. I turned back toward the gray coats marching closer.

Don't die, Da, I heard Steven's voice in my head. I tried

to think. Tried to slow my breathing. I couldn't leave Malone. Not after everything we had been through. And besides, the rebels were only yards away. I could see the CSAs on their belt buckles. Slowly, I lifted my hands into the air, one at a time.

Rosaleen

Chapter Thirty-Four

JULY 1864

I had stewed for days over what Donahoe had written.

Certain misguided voices among us have suggested that slavery caused high taxes. What of now? Taxes are the highest they have ever been. This can't be blamed on the South. These soaring taxes are the doing of THEIR president. He seeks to empty your pockets now that he has already taken your sons. Perhaps it is time for peace without victory. Before he leaves you with nothing at all.

He had all but printed Paddy's name. I needed to respond. President Lincoln wasn't the only man taking the lives of loved ones.

It had been three months since I last heard from Emmett. Though I tried to tell myself that it was only because mail had been halted for so long, I was no longer convinced of it. I reluctantly and desperately scanned the names in the newspapers every day, horrified by the growing number of dead men. The lists had never been this long. My sleep suffered as I imagined all the possibilities. And so, to occupy my mind in the early morning hours after a night of little sleep, I went to my desk and wrote.

To the sons and daughters of Erin,

The Boston Pilot is promoting "peace without victory."

Do not be fooled into thinking Donahoe wants peace. The Copperhead has shown that he will accept Irish blood as long as it's on HIS terms, to HIS benefit.

He believes an Irish life is better sacrificed to the streets. Cut down like a wild dog, in riots that he causes. But we Irish are noble and honor-bound warriors, not fooled so easily. We have bled and toiled for our new nation, and we will not hand it over to tyrants.

He does not speak for the Irish and has not for some time now. He said we would not fight after emancipation, and we did. He said we would not fight next to Black troops, and we do.

Good Irish lads did not die so heroically for us to betray them in defeat. Stand with me and our soldiers in saying: Peace will come ONLY with victory!

Signed,

A Paddy

I stood to make coffee. I would take it to Phillips at daylight. It could not wait.

～

Phillips looked tired in a way I had rarely seen. He was still polished. Still dressed in only the best. But he had dark circles under his eyes. New creases at the corners of his down-turned mouth.

"What's bothering you?" I asked, as we sat across from each other. He rapped his fingers on his desk and gazed past me.

"Are you also angry that the Thirteenth Amendment failed to pass?" I asked, with only a touch of sarcasm. "Surely it's a loss for wage labor advocates."

He rubbed his temples. "That, yes," he said. "And other political foolishness."

I raised my eyebrows.

He sat back and propped one leg atop the other, resting his ankle on his knee. He folded his hands together.

"The Purchasing Act," he said. "It stipulates that only government treasury agents are allowed to purchase cotton in Union-occupied territories."

"Your citizen buyers can no longer operate," I said.

"Correct."

"Don't you have men everywhere?" I asked. "You must have someone in the Treasury Department."

"I'll have to come up with one, won't I?" he said. "I certainly won't be bidding for cotton at auction. It's too expensive. I can buy myself a treasury agent for less money and headache."

"How do you stomach it?" I asked.

"The corruption and bribery? I like to chase it with my finest whiskey," he said, smirking. I rolled my eyes.

"No," I said. "Giving money to those traitors. Do you still believe it is a humanitarian effort?"

"More than ever," he said. "The inflation and starvation have certainly not lessened. And," he went on, straightening a bit in his chair, "it's my patriotic duty."

I snorted. "I wasn't aware you were a citizen of the Confederate States of America."

He ignored that. "Your husband uses a musket. You use a pen. I use . . . diplomacy." The mention of Emmett made me wince.

"You truly believe so?" I asked.

"These Southerners," he went on. "They thought they could do it without us. But they learned quickly that they cannot. They have their cotton, but they cannot eat it. We are intertwined in a way that cannot be unraveled. They can starve. Or they can take the Oath of Allegiance and sell us their cotton."

He sighed. "Were it up to me, I would only purchase from Negro-owned land. Those plantations produce more cotton, more consistently, than white-owned plantations. It is no secret that men work hardest for themselves. But there are simply not enough Negro-owned plantations to purchase from."

I wanted to believe him. I gazed around the ornate room. The gold-plated frames. There were surprisingly few images of his family hanging on the walls. I wondered why. Though he was unmarried, he must have had parents, brothers, sisters. There was none of that.

"I responded to Donahoe," I said, handing him my letter. I watched him read it, and he chuckled when he finished.

"You want to punish the man, I see. Humiliate him."

"He deserves it," I said. "He believes this is all a game. That we can simply cast aside the past three years and the deaths that have come with it and make some sort of deal with the Confederacy. It's sickening."

My eyes filled with tears. I tried to swallow them. I bit my lip, but the sobs still came. I knew Phillips felt uncomfortable, but I could not hide my grief and fear. He cleared his throat.

"Is it your husband?" he asked. I nodded and tried to calm myself.

"I haven't received a letter since April," I said. "This ongoing campaign has been so bloody . . ."

I trailed off, afraid I might start sobbing again.

"Well . . ." Phillips shifted. "We'll have to find him, then."

I looked up, a bit surprised.

"That doesn't exactly fall under our typical agreement," I said.

He smiled.

"I can't very well have you become too distracted now, can I? Not at this point in the war."

Over the next few weeks, I tried to stay abreast of congressional news while I waited for a letter from Emmett, for news from Phillips. But nothing came. I worked long hours for Calvin. I helped Steven study. I became such an intense, anxious presence that I eventually drove Steven back into the workshop with Mr. Joyce. It was probably for the best. I cleaned the house until I eradicated every crumb and speck of dust. At night, I cried and let my imagination haunt me.

And then, one evening, I received an invitation to dine with Mrs. Sarah Butler. The idea of spending an evening with a member of high society exhausted me, but I knew I couldn't pass it up. The Butlers were too important. Besides, she might be good company. She must have also worried after her own husband sometimes.

For the occasion, I chose a rose-tinted gold dress with a brown sash tied around my waist and a crinoline underneath that trailed far behind me like an ocean wave. I swept my hair into a cascading knot at the top of my head.

I sighed as I gazed at my appearance in the mirror. I could do this for a few hours. It would only be one evening. Time I would probably otherwise spend annoying Steven and Mr. Joyce with my constant commotion. I kissed them both before leaving.

The Butlers' house was enormous. I had long thought Phillips's house too grand, and theirs rivaled it in size. The Butlers had children, though, while Phillips had only himself and his staff.

Mrs. Butler greeted me cordially with a warm smile and a hug.

"It is so lovely to meet you," she said. "My children are at the theater tonight, and so, I thought I would call on the woman who Ben had spoken of so highly. Please, come sit."

Our steps echoed through the empty house as she led me to the parlor for tea.

"I understand your husband has been off fighting this war for some time, as well," she said, once we were seated. I nodded.

"Yes," I said. "He joined late in '61. He is a sergeant in the 28th Massachusetts Infantry."

Mrs. Butler pursed her lips and touched my arm in sympathy.

"I miss Ben greatly when we must be apart, which is far less frequently than most. I cannot imagine how difficult it must be. Do you have children?"

"Yes," I said. "One son, Steven. He will be turning nine years old next month."

Sarah's face broke into a wide smile.

"How delightful," she said. "He is the same age as our Bennie, then. Perhaps they can meet sometime."

I smiled back.

"That would be lovely," I said. "Steven struggles with missing his father. It would be nice for him to have a companion who understands."

"It is so hard on all of us," she said. "There was much activity at Fortress Monroe this spring, and I'd hoped it would mean the end of the war. I'm so weary of it all."

"Yes," I said, in a quiet voice. "As am I."

I glanced down at the teacup in my lap and tried to hold back my tears. They always threatened to gush out at the most inconvenient times. I took a deep breath and looked back up at the woman. Her black eyebrows were thick and animated, and her lips were full. She had been an actress when she was younger, and I could see how her bold features had most likely been an asset onstage.

"I read your husband's letter about prisoner exchanges," I said. Prisoner exchanges had officially ceased in December of the previous year, but when the Confederacy allowed a handful of the sickest prisoners to return home in the spring, public outcry demanded to know why others could not do the same. In a letter published yesterday, General Butler had finally responded.

"Ah, yes," Sarah said, setting down her teacup. "Ben has been vital when it comes to the exchange of prisoners. He has been able to be flexible and diplomatic where others only use those poor men as pawns. Benjamin has always had a heart for the discarded. Which is why he cannot budge on the Negro question."

"I certainly understand," I said. "I would not expect us to turn our backs on any of the Black soldiers after what they've done for the cause. It's a travesty that Congress took so long to pay them equally."

"Precisely," Sarah said. "Until the Confederacy can recognize Negro soldiers as legitimate prisoners of war, able to be exchanged just as their white counterparts are, we cannot resume prisoner exchanges."

"I do wish the Confederacy would agree to accept our terms quickly," I said. "Those men who returned this spring were in the most wretched state."

"Indeed." Sarah shook her head. "This war has become a terrible thing. I hope my husband can help bring about the end of it soon."

I gripped my hands together to stop them from shaking. I tried to truly listen to her, to speak with Sarah Butler as if our husbands were the same. As if I knew that my husband was safe and alive, just as she did. But I did not. We were not the same at all.

Chapter Thirty-Five

AUGUST 1864

Phillips and I sat in the corner of a hotel dining room on Merrimack Street. We sipped whiskey and watched the local politicians and businessmen carrying on as if other men weren't off dying. I scanned the room for Calvin but couldn't find him. I was the only woman there.

"Paddy's latest letter has created quite a stir," Phillips said.

"Amongst whom?" I asked.

"My editors," he said. "They think it's a bit provocative to call out Donahoe by name."

I raised my eyebrows. "You must have known they wouldn't like it," I said. "Yet, you published it anyway."

With a flick of his wrist, he swirled his whiskey.

"I wanted to see their reaction," he said. "I wanted to see how far was too far for them. I think we've nearly found it. As for myself, I quite enjoy the personal attacks."

He threw his whiskey back and excused himself to get another. When he returned with a new, full drink, he took a deep breath.

"That's not all," he went on, as if he had never left. "I have news of your husband."

My breath caught in my throat.

"Is he dead?" I asked. The room began to spin. I gripped my legs under the table, trying to steady myself.

"No," Phillips said. "He is a prisoner. Barlow found a Private Campbell who believes Emmett was captured at the Battle of Spotsylvania Court House. Your husband stayed behind to help an injured comrade during a retreat. Private Campbell looked for his body the next day but found nothing. I didn't want to tell you until I received confirmation. So, I contacted a friend down in Richmond. There is record of a captured Sergeant Emmett Doherty being transported through Richmond in June. Headed further south to a prison. Though I'm not sure which prison yet."

At first, all I could feel was relief. He was alive. I looked around the dining room, watching the figures blur as I cried silent tears. But then, I thought of the gaunt prisoners from the spring, and my head spun. Phillips took another long drink.

"So, that's it, then," I said, my voice shaking. "He'll languish there. Starve. Get some horrific disease. Suffer terribly. He'll be dead before winter is over."

Phillips stared into his whiskey. His jaw clenched. His Adam's apple bobbed up and down as he swallowed.

"I have a proposition," he said. "It could be foolish on both our parts, but I know you. I know that if you do nothing—if you wait for these horrors to befall your husband—you will very well go mad. I would rather not see it."

"Go on."

"The president knows he needs to keep the New England states happy. For this, we need cotton. The new rules—the ones he has written—are set to be announced later this month. They stipulate that anyone who owns or 'controls' cotton outside of Union-occupied territory is permitted to bring it into Union-occupied territory where he or she can sell it to a treasury agent. Which means, my buyers are now permitted to go into enemy territory to purchase cotton."

"Please get to the point," I said.

"How would you like to work for me as a cotton buyer?" he asked.

He must have read the confusion on my face, because he hurried on.

"If you can transport bales of cotton from enemy territory, you can transport a man."

When I fell asleep that night, I dreamt our house was in flames, and I stood in the kitchen, watching it burn. The couches, the chairs, the tables. The fire crept closer to me. I heard Steven calling my name in the distance. Then Mr. Joyce. But I didn't move. I couldn't.

I woke up gasping for air, feeling as though I had truly inhaled smoke. When I stood, I knew I could waste no more time.

I would need to write to Mrs. Butler. Surely her husband could track down Emmett quicker than Phillips could. As the former prisoner exchange negotiator, the general would have important contacts. I scribbled her a note.

Mrs. Sarah Butler,

I wanted to thank you again for your hospitality this summer. It was a pleasure dining with you. I have recently learned some disconcerting information regarding my husband's whereabouts. He has been captured and taken prisoner. There is record of him passing through Richmond, but none regarding his final destination. If there is any way General Butler could find out where he is now, I would be eternally grateful. Please send your response to the address below.

Deepest regards,
Rosaleen Doherty

I wrote Phillips's address at the bottom, folded it, and tucked it into my purse.

Mr. Joyce would be the first to know. He would need to look after Steven. I was asking a lot of him, but he knew my love for Emmett. He had been there before we were married, and he had loved him like a son even then.

I found him in his workshop sanding a small, wooden box. He smiled when I walked in but didn't look up from his work.

"Mrs. O'Brien wanted a jewelry box for her daughter's fourteenth birthday," he said. "I didn't have the heart to tell her the real reason Beth misplaces her jewelry. It isn't because she doesn't have a box. It's because she loses it in the river when she sneaks off to play with the neighborhood boys."

"I suppose we all need to be in denial sometimes," I said quietly. "It's no secret that Beth spends all her time with them and would rather get swept away in the river than wear jewelry."

Mr. Joyce chuckled. "I suppose we like to see ourselves in our children. Even when we aren't really there."

I sat down in the seat across from him where Steven usually sat. I crossed my legs and looked at my folded hands in my lap. Mr. Joyce stopped sanding and put the box down. He looked at me carefully.

"You've heard news of Emmett, haven't you?" he asked.

I nodded. "He's been captured."

Mr. Joyce inhaled sharply. The wrinkles in his forehead deepened. He reached out and grabbed my hands. I looked down at them.

"He's alive then," he said. "We must pray that he makes it through this."

"Yes," I said. "We must pray." I looked back up at him. "But I can do more than that and I intend to."

I took a deep breath. "I will need you to take good care of Steven while I'm gone."

"Rosaleen," he said, shaking his head. "Don't do something foolish."

"You know how special Emmett is," I said. "He would go

to the end of the earth for me. For anyone he loves. I've seen how those prisoners suffer and I cannot let it happen to him."

"What do you intend to do?" he asked.

"I intend to save him," I said. "My acquaintance—the one who publishes my letters—he does business in Union-occupied territories in the South. He's sending me to New Orleans to become a cotton buyer. I'll put a plan together once I'm there."

He pulled away and straightened up. "A cotton buyer? How does that help Emmett?"

"Cotton buyers go behind enemy lines." My voice was small. Not at all reassuring. I cleared my throat and spoke again. "I will go behind enemy lines and I will rescue him from that hell."

"But how?" he asked, his hands animated now, reaching for answers. "What will you do? Storm the prison? What weapons have you at your disposal? What army?"

"I am a woman," I said. "I can be discreet. I can be unassuming. I can blend in or stand out. I can be whoever I need to be. Whoever Emmett needs me to be. I just need to get closer to him. I will find a way to get him out."

"And where is he?" Mr. Joyce demanded. "Do you know?"

"He's not in Richmond," I said. "I know he passed through to a prison further south."

"Oughtn't you wait for more information?" he asked. He folded his hands together and leaned his elbows on his thighs, dropping his head for a moment before looking back up at me. "You know how much I love you, Rosaleen, but you can be rash. Perhaps it's prudent to be patient right now. You have no plan."

"Emmett can't afford for me to wait," I said. "I'll go down there and establish my cover. I can do that much until I have more information."

"Who told you he has been captured? How do you know it's true?"

"My source's information is always correct," I said. "Always."

Mr. Joyce sighed. "Your boy needs you here."

I shook my head. "My boy needs his father. I'll come back. And I'll bring his da home, too."

"And what if you don't?" he asked. "What if he loses both parents?"

I bit my lip. "Pray that he won't." I stood, leaned down, and kissed Mr. Joyce's cheek. "Thank you for loving us all. I wouldn't trust Steven with anyone else."

Once I had told Mr. Joyce about my plans, I went directly to Nessa's. She was relieved when I asked her to fill in for me as Calvin's clerk while I was gone. Relieved to have some time away from the house. Relieved to work again.

"Will Maeve be able to handle Grace all day by herself?" I asked, realizing my error too late and amending, "With Quinn's help, I mean."

"My ma will help, too," she said. "I love my time with Grace. And Quinn, too, now that he's home. But I've been aching to make myself useful to society."

"Should you ask Quinn first?" I asked. "Doesn't he need . . . help, as well?"

Nessa bit her lip.

"He doesn't like to admit that he needs any help" she said. "He's been trying to learn to do things for himself. I finally talked him into a replacement leg. A man is coming to the house to have him fitted."

"That's fabulous!" I said.

"And costly," she said.

"Calvin will pay you the same wages I make."

"And it will help," she said.

Two days later, I performed my last duties for Calvin before leaving for New Orleans. It was time to say goodbye to Marie.

I took off my hat as I entered the inn. With my handkerchief, I wiped the sweat from my hairline. Marie and Miss Susan stopped sweeping the dining room to greet me.

"Marie," I said. "Could I speak with you? Perhaps we could take a walk?"

Fear flashed in her eyes. She stiffened.

"Is this about Lydia?" she asked.

"No," I said. "No, it's not."

She glanced at Miss Susan, who shrugged.

"Well, all right," Marie said. "Let me put this broom away and wash up real quick."

"I'll be going away for a bit, Miss Susan," I said, once Marie had left.

"Where are you going?" she asked.

I looked out the window for a moment.

"To do something that needs to be done," I finally said. I

walked to her and hugged her tight. "I hope to be back soon."

She hugged me back.

"Be careful," she said, as I pulled away. "Whatever it is. This world is dangerous right now."

I nodded as Marie returned.

"Let's get going," Marie said. "I've still got dinner to cook."

I looked at my friend. She seemed to have aged so much in these past four years. But so had I. Evidence of my own fear was fixed into my face, too.

We walked south, toward the Common, and I left my head uncovered, letting the breeze whip my hair around my face.

"How is Gil?" I asked. "Have you heard from him?"

"He's back at camp at Hilton Head in South Carolina," she said. "That battle back in February in Florida unnerved him. He had to leave behind a fellow soldier who fell wounded. He said that when he looked over his shoulder in retreat, he saw Confederates shooting the Black soldiers left behind. He saw it with his own eyes, and he was afraid no one else would ever know. That no one would ever believe him. But then Fort Pillow happened, and now we all know."

Emmett was helping a wounded comrade, I thought. But that was because he expected to be treated as a prisoner, not murdered. I was quiet for a while, thinking of what to say. Nothing felt adequate.

"It's sickening," I finally said. "The way they're treated. Not like soldiers. Or even men."

Marie didn't say anything. She seemed to be lost in

thought.

"And Emmett?" she finally asked. "Have you heard from him?"

"He's . . ." I started. My voice quavered. I took a deep breath. "He's been captured."

Marie stopped walking and touched my arm.

"Oh, Rosaleen," she said. There was such concern in her eyes, such sympathy.

"I'm desperate, Marie," I choked out. "I can't lose him. I can't leave him to suffer in that way."

She rubbed my arm.

"We'll talk to the church," she said. "I've heard you can send the prisoners things. Though, I'm not sure how often it reaches them. They're thieves, too, down there."

I shook my head.

"I've already done something, Marie," I said. "It's a bit like a deal with the devil. I hate that I've got to do it, but I've *got* to do it."

Marie's eyebrows furrowed in confusion.

"Honey," she said. "As long as you haven't made a deal with Jeff Davis himself, I doubt it's that awful."

I closed my eyes.

"How about a deal with your least favorite person in the North?"

"Phillips," she said, immediately. She gave a wry chuckle. "Should have known."

I opened my eyes again. She shook her head.

"Just like him to take advantage of you at a time like this. What does he want from you?"

I took a deep breath. "He's taking me down to New

Orleans where I'll be able to help find Emmett. And hopefully save him."

"And?" she asked, one eyebrow raised.

"And I'll be going behind enemy lines to buy cotton for him."

"Buy cotton?" she asked. "From *slaveholders?*"

I looked around at the bustling city. How did all these people just continue to go about their lives? How did they wake up every day and shop and laugh and drink tea? I tried to remind myself that I had done the same for most of the war. It was the only thing to do.

"Yes," I said. "From slaveholders. And hopefully, I'll smuggle Emmett out right along with that cotton."

She pursed her lips.

"You must be desperate," she said. "The Rosaleen I know would never aid the enemy."

A lump formed in my throat. Twice, I tried to swallow it.

"The Rosaleen you knew never had to choose between being morally perfect and saving her husband's life."

Marie sighed and crossed her arms.

"This Phillips man is using you during this trying time. Just as he's doing with my sister."

"Has he hurt Lydia, though? Has anything bad come of their arrangement?" I asked, desperately.

Marie scowled.

"That's just luck. She hasn't stumbled into a crisis yet."

"Marie, I know this is bad. I know it's worse than bad. It's something I spat at only months ago. But this is Emmett. And if it means I won't have to learn that he rotted away in a hell of a prison, his bones buried in

Southern soil where I'll never be able to find them, I'll do it. I'll do it to have the father of my child—my closest friend in this world—home and alive."

Marie uncrossed her arms and reached for my hand. She took it gently in hers.

"I would do anything for Gil, too. Anything. I understand it, even if I don't like it." She took a deep breath. "I'll pray for you," she continued. "That God saves Emmett. And that God saves your soul."

Chapter Thirty-Six

SEPTEMBER 1864

That evening, we heard the news that Atlanta had been captured. There was celebrating once again in the streets, though I was busy packing my things. Other than clothing and writing materials, I didn't know what else I would need. I stared stupidly at my open, full suitcase.

Steven crept in behind me and sat on my bed beside the suitcase.

"I suppose everyone's melancholy is cured now," he said. "We're to win the war again."

I gave him a weak half smile.

"Let's hope so," I said. "Perhaps the war will be won by the time I arrive in the South."

"Tell me again why you must go," he said. His lips were pursed. His eyes narrowed. I sighed.

"Because I love your da so fiercely that I cannot wait," I said.

"I'm afraid for you," he said. I sat next to him.

"You don't need to be afraid," I said. "My friends will help me. And I will look out for myself, too. I'll be careful."

"I thought Da was strong and brave," he said. He looked at me with anger in his eyes. "Why did he let them capture him?"

"Oh, darling," I said, cupping his face in my hand. "That's precisely why he was captured. Because he *is* strong and brave. He stayed to help an injured man. A coward would have fled."

Steven pulled his head away.

"Then why doesn't he save himself now?" he asked.

"I'm not sure he can," I said. "He's deep in the South. Even if he were to escape, he would have nowhere to go. No one who would help him. And he's been in prison for months now. He could be sick . . ."

"I know," Steven said, interrupting me. "I saw the photographs, too." He stood and began to pace.

"What if you get there and . . . and . . . it's too late?" Tears welled up in his eyes.

"Then I will be sad," I said. "But I will also be proud that he gave his life for a worthy cause and died because he tried to help a fellow soldier."

I went to him. He stopped pacing and stood with his back to me.

"But that is why I must go," I said, putting my hand on his shoulder. "I must try to reach him before it *is* too late. He would do the same for me. And for you."

Steven said nothing but turned around slowly. I pulled him close for a hug. When he pulled away, I shut the suitcase. I had packed enough.

I was up early the next morning. I would take the train

to Boston and then board the ship that would take me to New Orleans. Phillips would be coming, too.

Mr. Joyce and Steven walked me to the train depot before school started. Steven was still sullen, and I understood. My boy was frightened. I felt terrible for leaving him, for causing him so much distress. But I knew he would be safe and loved and that would be enough for now.

"Your da and I will be home before you know it," I said to him at the platform. "Please help Mr. Joyce while we are gone. I love you so much."

He looked at me coolly. Though he was still angry, he said, "I love you, too, Ma."

I hugged Mr. Joyce and whispered to him, "Thank you."

"Take care of yourself," he said. "We'll be waiting."

I boarded the train and sat at a window facing the platform. I blew Steven a kiss. The corner of his mouth slowly curled up as he pretended to catch it. The train pulled away, and my heart lurched right along with it.

The docks in Boston teemed with sweaty workers and impatient passengers. The war had not slowed commerce or travel, it seemed. Phillips was dressed lavishly, as usual —his hair, mustache, and eyebrows recently trimmed and groomed.

"You're going to love New Orleans," he said, smiling. He offered his arm to me, and I took it.

"Remind me again. Why New Orleans?"

"It is one of two union-held cities from which my

buyers—and my treasury agents—operate. The other is Memphis. New Orleans is the further south of the two, so it will be closest to Emmett. But it will still be quite the trek."

"And why can't we just hop off from the South Carolina island where Lydia is? Or from Washington, even?"

"Well, for one, you would just be an American citizen there. Not a cotton buyer. You would have no cover. And two, those coastal areas are blanketed with Confederate soldiers. They *are* fighting a war there, and they are a different country now—according to them. We can no longer simply come and go."

"And the area around New Orleans is not blanketed with Confederate soldiers?"

We walked along the dock, toward the ship at the end.

"They do not have nearly enough men to cover all that land. The Union Army took New Orleans early in the war, as you know, and has continued to hold the city. While the rest of the land down there is the Confederacy's until the Union Army takes it, most of it is not guarded in the same way that the coast is. The city of Mobile, for example, is held by the Confederates, but the fort at Mobile Bay is held by the Union. It is supposed to be a blockade. The Union prevents anything coming from and going to Mobile."

He paused to tip his hat at a group of passing businessmen.

"Which is why you will need a special permit to enter the city of Mobile. A special permit for *cotton buying* only. It will state that you 'control' cotton inside of Confederate territory and that you are there to get it. That is why your cover would not work in Virginia or South Carolina. I have no treasury agents there. In fact, the cotton buying business does not exist in these places to the extent it does along the Mississippi River. Cotton is primarily grown along the Mississippi River—from Memphis to New Orleans—as well as in Alabama and Georgia. South Carolina grows just enough cotton for your cover to still work there if need be, though it will be riskier. My cotton buyers typically have no reason to travel that far. The best cotton in South Carolina is, after all, on Port Royal, which we control."

"And what of North Carolina?"

"Even riskier. Though there are *some* cotton plantations in the state, there are not many. For now, let's hope Emmett isn't there and focus your efforts farther south."

"Any news on that? On which prison he's being held in?" I asked, stepping onto the ramp to the ship. I held tight to the railing with my other hand.

"Not yet," Phillips said. "But I am making inquiries."

"I left a note for Sarah Butler," I said. "I asked her to speak with the general about Emmett's whereabouts. Perhaps he can find him."

Phillips set his jaw. I could see his pride was a bit hurt, but I didn't have time for that.

"I asked her to write back to your address," I said, and his expression softened.

"Very well. I suppose we ought to use all our resources."

We stepped onto the deck, and Phillips led me away from the shuffling bodies. We stood at the rail, looking to the mouth of the harbor. Next to us was another passenger ship, and I watched a young girl peek over the side into the ocean. A boy came up behind her and knocked the hat off her head. It fell into the water and bobbed next to the boat. The girl rounded on him and started yelling. He laughed and ran away. Brothers and sisters, I assumed, though their parents were nowhere in sight. The girl looked forlornly back at her hat in the water, wiping her face with her sleeve.

"You will be staying at a boardinghouse," Phillips said, interrupting my thoughts. I wondered if he had been watching the children, too. "It's one of the better ones in the city. Still, you'll need protection. This—" he opened his coat to show me a pistol peeking out of his inner pocket, "—is for you."

He went on. "In order for this to be a success, everyone must know you only as my buyer. You are no longer Rosaleen the abolitionist, champion of the Union cause. You will be Miss Reilly. Unmarried. You do not care about the moral issues of the war. The Negro is only your friend when he or she is useful to you."

I hated this.

Behind the ship's mast, a man stared at us. He was too far away to hear us, but his intent seemed clear.

"There's a man watching us," I muttered, squinting back toward the water. The reflection of the bright sun was blinding.

"What does he look like?" Phillips asked.

"He's large," I said. "His clothes are those of a laborer."

"A dockhand?" he asked. "Or a crew member?" The ship began to rock more violently now. We were preparing to depart.

"I'm not sure," I said. I looked back, but the man was no longer there.

"I'll keep an eye out," Phillips said.

"I've never used a pistol before," I said.

"We'll switch ships at Fort Morgan at the mouth of Mobile Bay," he said. "I'll teach you there."

The ship pulled away from the dock, and I gripped the railing to steady myself. I felt close to my own da again. The ocean did that. The birds squawked overhead and the ship creaked, and I closed my eyes and smiled. My memory of him had faded, and I was left with only a feeling of the love he'd felt for me, buried deep in my soul. It was warm and comforting. *I wish you could have met your grandson, Da,* I thought. *You would have loved him.*

I opened my eyes again and watched as the ship righted itself on the outskirts of the harbor, preparing to sail into open waters. Boston grew smaller. The sounds of the city faded away. I breathed the ocean air in deeply.

The sleeping arrangements and meals were surprisingly good. Despite my worry for Emmett and my reluctance to be involved in the cotton trade, I began to feel excited about seeing a new city. A new part of the country. I had never seen the South before.

After seven days, we docked at Mobile Bay. I hadn't seen the suspicious man again. "He was probably a dock-hand," Phillips said.

When we disembarked at Fort Morgan, I stepped onto solid ground with shaky legs. The fort sat at the tip of the peninsula, overlooking the bay. The walkway was flanked by golden sand. Palm trees swayed in the wind.

"I detest travel by boat," Phillips said, clearly feeling the effects, as well. I laughed at his sour expression.

"What?" he asked.

"Just imagine you drank too much whiskey," I said.

"I did drink too much whiskey," he said. "It's making it worse. Come now, and let's teach you how to shoot a gun."

"Wouldn't you like to get rid of your sea legs first?" I asked.

"I will," Phillips grunted. "We've got to walk a ways to the place I have in mind."

Chapter Thirty-Seven

I had learned to never be surprised by Phillips, so when we walked through the fort and then out the other side —waiting only moments for the posted Union soldiers to check his papers—trekked miles across the peninsula, and strolled into an abandoned house, I didn't question any of it.

The air was hot and sticky, and my hair had turned puffy and wiry. It stuck to my sweaty neck and face, and I tried to smooth it back as we walked inside. The still air was no better than the air outside. I fanned myself. I followed Phillips down a short hallway to the dining room, where he pulled out the gun.

"This is a revolver," he said, placing it into my upturned palms. "It is not loaded. Take a good look at it."

I turned it over in my hands, feeling the cool steel, noticing the weight of it, the length of the barrel. It was no longer than my hand. Phillips pointed at the fat part above the trigger.

"It has six chambers," he said. "Do you see them?"

I nodded.

"That's where the ammunition goes," he said. He took it from me again and pulled back the lever at the top. "This is the hammer at half cock," he said. Then he pulled it back farther. "Full cock. Half cock to load. Full cock to fire."

He handed it back, and I tried it myself.

"You'll keep five of the six chambers loaded," he said. "Don't get it wet, and if you do, clean it and reload it."

I nodded again, and he set the gun on the table.

"I'll show you how to clean it later," he said. He pulled out a flask.

"This is where your gunpowder is stored." He pulled the hammer back and opened the flask. He poured the gunpowder directly into the chamber. Then, he held up a small lead ball. "And this is your bullet. It goes in next." He dropped it into the chamber and pulled another lever underneath the gun. "Loading lever," he said. It pushed the ball down even farther. "You do that in each of the five chambers first. Five, not six. There are safety locks between each chamber, but I want the sixth empty for now, since you're new at this. I would rather you not shoot yourself in the leg."

He loaded the other four chambers quickly and deftly. I hadn't supposed Phillips handled guns frequently, but now that I thought about it, it seemed obvious that he would need to protect himself.

"The caps are last," he said. "Do not put your fingers anywhere near the opening of the barrel when loading the caps. If the gun accidentally fires, you'll blow your fingers off."

I watched him put the caps on, holding my breath as he did so.

"And lastly," he said, raising the gun toward the next room. "You put the hammer at full cock and pull the trigger." He aimed at the mantel above the fireplace. The revolver fired one, two, three, four, five times as smoke ballooned from the barrel and three vases shattered into pieces, shards of glass flying across the room. My ears rang. He waited a minute before speaking again. His ears must have been ringing, too.

"Couldn't wait for them to take this bay," he said. "I hate the bastard who lives here. With the Union Army so close, I knew he would flee. I'll be back with his most valuable possessions, and you can blow them to bits."

He put the gun on the table, and I glanced at it, too afraid to touch it alone. But in just a few minutes, he was back, holding figurines and jewelry boxes and photographs in frames. He lined them up on the mantel, careful not to step on the shards of glass as he made his way back to me.

He grinned. "Your turn."

By the time our ship left for New Orleans that evening, I had learned to load, fire, and clean the revolver. I hit only two of the targets, but Phillips took out the rest.

My eyelids were heavy, and I wanted nothing but to sleep. My arms and fingers ached in a way that they hadn't since my time at the mills. We pulled into the mouth of the Mississippi River at dusk. Along the shores, I could see Black families still at work in the fields. The not-quite-enslaved-anymore, I thought bitterly, recalling General Nathaniel Banks's lessee policy that still treated them as though they were. The land was a furry green all around us, and large, looming oaks stretched from plantation to plantation, Spanish moss hanging from their branches.

Soon, the space between the houses narrowed. The ground became more dirt than grass. Piles of something wrapped in canvas lined the shores, suddenly stacked everywhere. As tall as a man on land and as high as the tip of the ship's stacks on the decks of the steamers being unloaded at the shipyard.

"Cotton," I breathed.

"More precious than gold," Phillips said.

Men worked in groups of four and five to heave the bales from cart to stack, stack to ramp. From there, the bales were rolled up the incline. Machines did the work, too—hooks attached to the bales and men pulling on a rope that looped through a pulley on the ship. The horses strapped to the carts waited patiently, flicking their tails at the mosquitoes and flies. Their day must have been nearly done. Darkness enshrouded us.

The city rose up in the wake of the cotton district. The streetlamps were being lit one by one as our ship pulled in. The smell of the river—fish and waste and sweaty men— mixed with the smoke from the steamships, making me cough. I tried to fan away the stench. Phillips led me to the shore, carrying our suitcases, until a man with light-brown skin took them from him. He and Phillips spoke to each other in a language I couldn't understand.

The three of us walked toward the city. With each step, I kicked up dust from the street, and the dirt clung to my sweaty legs and the backs of my arms. Ahead of us, a large church loomed, its three steeples reaching high into the sky, disappearing into the darkness. Below the church was a sprawling garden. Some people passed through it briskly, while others sat in conversation. We walked on.

The city grew around us. The streets changed from dirt to stone. Buildings lined the street, shoulder to shoulder. Despite the falling darkness, the city was very much alive. Union soldiers patrolled the streets. Ladies laughed behind their fans. Light-skinned Black men, dressed nearly as handsomely as Phillips, conversed under awnings. Horses waited on the street and in alleyways, carts still attached to their shoulders. Banners and signs jutted from stores and stretched across the street: Clothing, Furniture, Photography, Gloves, Coal Oil, Lamps, Jewelry.

We stopped in front of a four-story building, each level boasting a balcony with an ornate iron railing. Its sign announced: Boardinghouse. The man carrying our suitcases set them down in order to open the door for us, and we walked inside. It was dark on the first floor, and there were no windows. Behind a desk, a small, beady-eyed old white man glanced at us over his glasses. He waved us on without a word, and the man with our bags led us up the narrow stairs. At the third level, we went down a hallway and into an empty room. It was small but clean and neat. Two tall, narrow windows looked on to a balcony, and the lights from the street spilled into the room, across the floor, and almost touched the bed. The man put our bags down and lit the lamp on the wall. A desk, a bed table, and a washbasin had been hiding in the dark. He nodded and left us.

"I'll be staying in the room next to this one tonight," Phillips said.

"Shouldn't you be staying at some grand hotel?" I asked. He smiled.

"I'll show you the grand hotel tomorrow," he said. "It's the Union officers' headquarters and where you ought to go if you're in desperate need of help. My treasury agent stays there, and occasionally I do, too—depending on to whom I would like to make my presence known."

I looked around the room again, already longing for home. I missed Steven. But home was not home without Emmett. Finding him, saving him—that would take patience. I needed to settle in for now.

"We'll get started tomorrow," I said.

"I'll introduce you to the other buyers," he said. "Watch how they move. To whom they speak. Some will venture into Mississippi. Others will go to Alabama."

He crossed his arms and sighed.

"Establishing your cover is our priority until we know in which prison Emmett is being held. Since it's likely he is in Georgia or South Carolina, you will want to become familiar with the routes there. Take a ship to Mobile Bay again. This permit," he said, retrieving it from his pocket and extending it to me, "will get you past the fort at the mouth of the bay and into the city of Mobile. The only road out of Mobile goes north. Take that until you find the road that cuts east. I will obtain a map for you in the meantime."

I nodded and took the permit.

"I have money for your transportation once you're in Alabama—which I've already arranged—and to purchase the cotton. It should be more than enough. You'll take the cotton back to Mobile, have it put on a ship and brought back here to New Orleans, where you will sell it to my treasury agent. You won't start for another week. You can familiarize yourself with the city until then."

He had planned so much already.

"Thank you," I said.

He cleared his throat and looked down at his feet.

"I take care of my people," he said. He collected his suitcase. "I'll see you in the morning."

Chapter Thirty-Eight

Despite the heat, I slept soundly that night and woke to the rising sun bursting through the edges of the curtains. I pulled the curtains and unlatched the window. There was no breeze. Only the loud sounds of a lively city. Sellers hawking fruit and fish and hats and umbrellas. Friendly, happy greetings between neighbors. Conversations in unfamiliar languages. I washed my face and went to Phillips's room. Before I could knock, the door swung open.

"Ah, hello," he said. "You're right on time. The keeper just delivered breakfast. Come in."

I entered, bracing myself for some shockingly intimate glimpse into Phillips's personal life. But the bed was made so neatly it appeared to have never been slept in. His suitcase was shut tight. The chamber pot already emptied.

He crouched low and stepped out onto the balcony. I followed. There were two chairs in the corner and a table just large enough to fit our two steaming-hot breakfast plates. I sat and looked at my fried eggs and sausages. Phillips was already chewing.

"Andouille sausage," he said, once he swallowed. "It's French. Try it. You've never had anything like it."

I took a bite. A host of flavors overwhelmed my mouth. As I chewed, my tongue grew hot. I quickly sipped my tea.

"Why is my tongue on fire?" I asked.

Phillips chuckled.

"There are peppers in it," he said. "Do you like it?"

"Who, me? Raised on potatoes and boiled ham?" I smirked. "They don't serve this sort of thing at the Irish pub. I suppose it'll just take some getting used to." Beads of sweat already dripped down my spine, my face, in between my breasts. I fanned myself. "Just like this heat."

Phillips swallowed another bite.

"Have a look at the buyers. They pass through the corner here every morning before starting on their day's work. First—" he pointed with his fork to the street below, "—you'll see Reuben."

I looked where he was pointing.

"Large Jewish man," he said. "He's about my age." I saw him. Tall, strong, broad everything.

"The Jews are often blamed for this whole wartime cotton trading business," he went on. "Many Union generals despise them. Reuben's family has been in commerce—buying and selling—for many generations. He understands trade. He's a smart man. Not friendly, though. He'll barely utter two words to me."

Reuben walked with his head held high, but he only looked ahead. He was not distracted by anything he passed and did not stop to talk to anyone.

"Nicholas is next," Phillips said, pointing over his shoulder. "Irish. Short. Stocky. Young."

I spotted him. His face and arms were red, burnt from the sun. Unlike Reuben, Nicholas's gaze darted from side to side, taking in everyone and everything.

"He's lived in Louisiana since he was a small child," Phillips said. "Doesn't care about the Union or the Confederacy and has thrived in the chaos of war. I think he enjoys getting himself out of tricky situations. He knows quite a bit about the locals but has few friends."

"Next," he said, after taking another bite, "about ten paces behind Nicholas will be Jasper. He's a handsome man. Tanned skin. Blond hair to his shoulders, always falling into his face. He says hello to just about every lady he passes."

I watched him stop to tip his hat to a small group of women. They giggled and patted their hair behind their fans.

"His family has been in Louisiana for generations. They were some of the French Acadians who settled here in the 1700s. They are called Louisiana Creoles. He also has a bit of Spanish in his blood, and who knows what else." He caught my eye. "Do not find yourself alone with him." I nodded.

"There are others," he went on. "But those three are my best, most reliable buyers. Their loyalties lie with me, because I pay them well and I understand their motivations. I anticipate their needs. They are the ones that go the deepest into enemy territory. They have a system, and they have loyal sellers. If you want to evade suspicion, you'll study them. Try to be like them. As quickly as you can.

They are on their way now to meet with my treasury agent. Shall we follow?"

I swallowed another bite of my food, my throat burning.

"Yes," I said. "Let's go."

The St. Charles Hotel was imposing. We pushed our way down Canal Street, swollen with people, and past a statue of Henry Clay. Though St. Charles Avenue featured many beautiful buildings, the hotel eclipsed them all. It sat above street level—the first floor a collection of concrete and windows and doors. It looked as though there should be stairs leading from the street to an entrance on the second level, but there was not. Beginning on the second level, large Greek columns lined the façade, making it feel more like an official government building than a hotel. Horses and carriages and dignitaries and military men crowded the street in front of it.

We elbowed our way through, and Phillips led me through the crowded lobby, around marble beams and velvet couches, down a hallway, and finally, through a door that led to a small library or study of some sort. The buyers I had seen from the balcony looked up in surprise, and a man behind a desk broke into a wide grin. His teeth were incredibly crooked. He was dressed in a shabby suit and boasted an uneven haircut.

"Mr. Phillips," he said. "How wonderful for you to join us. This is the new buyer you were telling me about?"

"Yes, Mr. Blackburn, it is," Phillips said. He took me by the elbow. "This is Miss Reilly."

I forced a smile. "Hello," I said. Reuben ignored us, and Jasper gave me a friendly smile that was not at all like the ones he had given to the young women on the street. I had a sinking feeling that I might be too old for him. Nicholas raised an eyebrow.

"Miss Reilly," he said, reaching out a hand. "An Irish Yankee."

I shook his hand.

"Pleased to meet you," I said.

"Well." Mr. Blackburn closed the book on his desk. "That should be all for today."

The men shuffled out, Reuben first, Jasper last, Nicholas in between.

"Mr. Blackburn here purchases incoming cotton deliveries every Thursday," Phillips said, once the other buyers had left. "I expect one cotton delivery from you each week to start."

I kept my eyes on Mr. Blackburn, who was studying me. It had been quite some time since Phillips had spoken to me with such superiority, and I didn't trust myself not to roll my eyes. I wondered if he secretly enjoyed exerting such power over me, or if he preferred what our relationship had grown into instead.

"Yes, sir," I said.

"He will pay you by the pound," Phillips went on, "based upon the prices of the New York cotton exchange."

"I understand," I said.

"Very good," Phillips said. "I'll show you around the city, then."

I smiled at Mr. Blackburn.

"It's lovely to meet you, sir," I said. "I look forward to doing business with you."

"Yes," Mr. Blackburn said. "And I as well."

I followed Phillips back through the lobby and out to the busy streets.

"Another thing," Phillips said, as we walked briskly back toward the boardinghouse. "You'll offer the seller greenbacks first. If they refuse and you're desperate, give them specie. Their government prohibits them to trade in greenbacks. Ours requires it. One of you will have to break the rules."

"Do you truly expect cotton from me each week?" I asked.

"Yes," Phillips said, seriously.

"Don't you think I have better things to do?"

"Better than establishing a believable cover?" he asked. "No, I do not. Once we find Emmett and put together a plan, you can disappear. Until then, it's to your benefit and his for you to purchase cotton. You will need to know the land. You will need to be able to traverse the roads in the dark. You will need to know where to sleep and where to get water for the horses. It will be imperative to finding your way back to the Union lines."

"Can't I simply pretend to buy cotton?" I asked, aware of just how silly I sounded.

"Don't you think Blackburn might find that strange?" he asked. "Don't you think a woman—an outsider—driving a horse and wagon with nothing on it day after day along the same route will raise suspicion? They must be used to seeing your face, your wagon full of cotton, so that when the day comes in which you will bring Emmett back to Mobile Bay with that cotton, you will not be a stranger—to the people or to the land."

"Is there even that much cotton to be purchased?" I asked.

Phillips snorted.

"The amount of cotton grown on this land will render you speechless. Besides, as strange as it may sound, the South put an embargo on cotton at the start of the war, hoping it would make England desperate enough to come to their aid and end the war as soon as possible. Now, many of these planters have stockpiles of bales that they patriotically kept in storage until their government was forced to recognize that England would not be sailing to their rescue."

I gave Phillips a strange look.

"I thought the south wanted to sell their cotton to England. Not restrict it."

Phillips waved away my question.

"The political blunders of Jefferson Davis are nothing to think too hardly on. Just know that there is plenty of cotton to purchase."

"And if I need anything?" I asked.

"You'll write me," he said. "If it's urgent, you'll seek help at the St. Charles Hotel. If it's even more pressing than that, you'll have to sharpen your shooting skills."

I bit my lip and walked beside him in silence. When we arrived at the boardinghouse, Phillips turned to face me. He put his hands on my shoulders.

"You can do this," he said. "Trust yourself."

Chapter Thirty-Nine

The day after Phillips left, I ate spicy sausages for breakfast again. I had some faint appreciation for the rest of the flavors and was determined to adjust to the heat. Afterward, I wandered aimlessly up and down streets, heading east until I felt sufficiently lost. I decided to walk along the river, heading west until I found something I recognized.

I watched the boats on the riverbank as goods were unloaded and loaded again. Not just cotton but also corn and wheat and sugar. The men working were of all shades of white and brown and black. Heaving and sweating and grunting and spitting side by side. Their conversations were full of southern drawls and accents I had never heard before.

Finally, I came upon the sprawling garden in front of that church we'd passed upon our arrival, though it took me a moment to recognize it in daylight. A large crowd had gathered there, and as I approached, I spied a young, muscular Black man standing above the others. A speaker.

"And now they call us radical," he was saying. "As if the entire idea of this country isn't radical! As if the Declaration of Independence isn't the most radical document in the history of the world!"

Most of the listeners were Black, though many had very light skin. They clapped loudly.

"'We hold these truths to be self-evident! That *all* men are created equal!'"

"Yes!" a man in the front shouted.

"'That they are endowed by their creator with certain unalienable rights! That among these are life, liberty, and the pursuit of happiness!' Now isn't *that* radical?"

More cheers.

"Yes, they may call me radical because I *am* radical! Just like my father, who fought alongside Andrew Jackson in 1815 in the battle for *this* city!"

A man next to me nodded.

"Is it radical to believe that men who were born in this country—who have been loyal to this country, who own real estate, who pursue commerce, who provide skilled services to their neighbors, who are peaceful taxpayers—is it radical to say they should be allowed a vote?"

"No!" a young woman hollered.

"Men so loyal to this country that they begged to fight for it, that they picked up a musket and bled for it, that they watched their fellow soldiers die for it! Should they be barred from voting simply because of their skin color?"

This time the speaker shouted along with the crowd, "No!"

"Now." The speaker stopped and shook his head. "Now they pretend to be merciful—gracious, even—by turning us against each other. By offering suffrage to *some* Black men but not all."

The crowd was rapt with attention. Was this news to them? I leaned closer.

"They put their hands up in mock surrender." He raised his the same way. "And say, 'We will do it. We will grant suffrage to Negroes. But only the ones born free. Only the ones with skin nearly as light as ours.' Will we accept this?"

He looked at the us intently, slowly scanning the crowd, from one end to the other. Some shuffled their feet. Others shook their heads. A few looked to the men and women around them.

"I say never," the speaker hissed. "Never will I be tricked into trampling on my brothers of African descent for a right that has already been guaranteed to *all* men!"

A few men grunted in relief. "Never!" someone yelled.

"But what about intelligence?" the speaker went on, rubbing his chin. "They also want to allow only literate Black men to vote. What do we say to that?"

The crowd knew the game now.

"No!" they yelled.

"Do they allow only literate white men to vote?" the speaker asked louder, unable to mask his growing passion.

"No!" the crowd shouted again.

"I—a radical Black man—declare that we will settle for nothing less than what is rightfully ours under the radical document that gave birth to this country! Full suffrage for *all* men!"

The crowd clapped and cheered and whooped. The speaker grinned and raised one arm in thanks, looking suddenly humble and shy.

I turned to leave but caught a woman staring at me and smiling in a way that made me feel exposed. She sauntered over to me. She was short and curvy, and a long blond braid snaked around her neck and across her chest.

"Well, aren't you a mystery?" she said, extending her hand for me to shake.

"Pardon?" I asked, taking her hand.

"Name's Minnie," she said. "I saw you with the cotton man. I stay on the fourth floor of the boardinghouse. What's a cotton buyer doing listening to a Negro talk about suffrage?"

She raised an eyebrow. *Damn it*, I thought. *I'm already terrible at this.*

"I'm new to the city," I said. "I got lost and found myself here."

"And stayed and listened with eager ears," she said.

I opened my mouth, trying to come up with an excuse, but Minnie held her hands up.

"I'd rather not know your reasons," she said. "The mystery makes you interesting."

I studied her. I shouldn't trust her. Still, she was allowing me to keep quiet, and I intended to.

"And what do you do in the city, Minnie?" I asked. "Anything interesting?"

She laughed a warm, hearty laugh that reminded me of popping bubbles.

"You're saucy, too," she said. "I think we ought to be friends." She swiveled to my side and took my arm in hers.

"And to answer your question," she went on, as we began to walk, "I do many interesting things."

Chapter Forty

M innie would only tell me that she worked for a jewelry buyer. She seemed to study men wherever we went. What she was looking for, I couldn't say, but she watched them intently. Her room was right above mine, and despite my instinct to keep her at a distance, I was grateful to have her. We spent our afternoons together that week, and she showed me where in the city a woman could find herself and where she never should. She asked me if I had a way of protecting myself, and I told her I did.

"Good," she said.

"I'm not a very good shot, though," I said. "I haven't had to use it yet, and I hope I never will."

She shook her head. "That won't do. You need to practice. You need to be confident walkin' around this city by yourself."

So, she took me to an old warehouse next to a sugar mill on the outskirts of the city where we could practice.

"No one can hear nothin' out here," she said. The mill groaned and creaked as our shots pinged off the warehouse beams where she had tacked up newspaper advertisements. Minnie helped me adjust my shoulders and my feet, and my aim improved.

When I awoke on Friday morning, I was ready. I had not been invited to the daily meeting with Mr. Blackburn, but I knew the schedule now and raced to the riverfront after watching Reuben, Nicholas, and Jasper pass underneath my balcony. I double-checked that I had the permit and money Phillips had given me inside my satchel, along with provisions for the week.

I watched the ships pull into the city. Brigs and steamships. The Union soldiers inspected them, studying the crews' permits. I looked up and down the bank, waiting for the Irish lad, Nicholas. I intended to follow him. He seemed the safest of the three. The easiest to talk to, to get to open up. To get to share the secrets of the trade.

I finally spotted him, tottering slightly from side to side as he neared. He looked up and recognized me.

"Ah, the Irish Yankee," he said. He kept walking, and I fell in alongside him.

"Can I accompany you onto the ship?" I asked. He shrugged.

"I ain't gonna hold your hand," he said. For being so small, he could certainly move quickly. I sped up.

"You don't have to," I said. "I'd just like to chat a bit. Only on the ship. Then we can go our separate ways."

He stopped abruptly beside a brig and waited for the soldiers to complete their inspection. He shrugged again. Something at the edge of the water caught my eye. It looked like debris or a floating log. But then I saw an eyeball, and I gasped. Nicholas turned with interest. I stared at the log. It had certainly been an illusion. But then I saw another eye. And a snout with two holes.

"Is that . . ." I breathed heavily. "Is that an alligator?"

Nicholas snickered.

I stood as still as I could and stared at it. It did not move. It did not even blink.

"Is it dead?" I asked.

Nicholas crossed his arms and furrowed his eyebrows.

"Well, now, I don't know," he said. "You ought to go and pat it. Find out."

I looked at him, and for a moment, he was stoic. But then he burst into giggles like a little school girl. I narrowed my eyes at him, and he shrugged a third time.

"What?" he asked, smirking.

The Union soldiers stepped off the boat, and we clambered aboard. I tried not to look at their faces. They reminded me too much of Emmett. I tried to see faceless bodies moving along with no names. No wives or mothers. No identities.

"Where do you go for the cotton?" I asked, adjusting my hat so I wouldn't have to squint in the sun. "Mississippi? Alabama?"

Another shrug. Must have been a habit.

"Anywhere I want," he said. "Today, I'm going to Alabama. That's where this boat's going." He eyed me with a hint of irritation. "Does that suit you?"

I smiled. "Sure."

He stood with his elbows on the railing, hands dangling over the edge.

He spoke into the water. "If you bring some meat and hold it just like this from the bottom deck of a steamer, the alligators will jump out of the water and take it right from your hands."

There was no giggling this time, and I remembered what Phillips had said about Nicholas and chaos. I cleared my throat.

"Where in Ireland are you from?" I asked.

"My ma and da are from Waterford," he said. "Had me the day they stepped off the boat in Savannah."

"How did you make it to Louisiana?" I asked. Shrug.

"Da was in shipping," he said. "This was a better port. Been here since I was seven. I barely remember Savannah at all."

He spat into the river.

"And what about you, Miss . . ." He looked at me, waiting for me to finish.

"Miss Reilly," I said. "I'm from Cork."

"You remember it well?" he asked.

I didn't answer him right away. The ship rocked in the wake of another.

"Yes," I finally said. "I dream of it often. I suppose I might not remember it accurately. But my heart is still in Ireland."

He nodded, and we were quiet until we reached the fort at Mobile Bay. He grimaced when the soldiers came aboard. We showed them our permits, and they returned mine first.

"Damned Yankees," he muttered, as soon as they were out of earshot.

"Excuse me?" I asked. Shrug.

"Don't like the rebels much, either," he said.

"And how did you manage to evade conscription?" I asked. He reddened.

"Stayed in New Orleans," he said.

"With protection from the damned Yankees?" I asked.

He rolled his eyes and turned away from me. We slowly passed through the mouth of the bay and drew closer to the city. My heart began to beat faster as the gray uniforms of the Confederates came into view.

"Will they stop us?" I asked Nicholas. He shook his head.

"They know who we are," he said. "And they need us. They don't like it, but they'll let us through. Don't let them catch you with greenbacks, though. They'll arrest you for it."

My throat felt dry. I had sewn a pocket into my satchel for the greenbacks, but now that seemed insufficient. I hoped the Confederates wouldn't decide to search me. I turned from Nicholas to pull the wad out of its pocket and stuff it down the front of my dress.

When we stepped off the boat, we had to walk through a group of soldiers. They looked skinnier and much more ragged than the Union soldiers. They glared at us but said nothing. I followed close on Nicholas's heels through the docks and into the city.

"Phillips finally got himself a woman," Nicholas said, as he led me through the streets. The people here looked more desperate, too. They stared at us as if we were cows or pigs. As if they could taste us. I hurried to keep up.

"It's nothing like that," I said. "We are strictly business acquaintances."

Nicholas snorted.

"Well, of course you are," he said. "You aren't exactly Phillips's type." He grabbed his crotch and winked.

My face flushed. I was dumbfounded.

"How would you know?" I quipped. He glared at me.

We passed a corner store, a woman and a child sitting outside. They were gaunt. The woman's eyes were closed, and her head leaned back against the building. I looked away.

"I meant he's finally got himself a woman buyer," Nicholas said. "Y'all are like diamonds in this world. Ladies can get away with anything. You saw how quickly that Union soldier returned your papers. And the Confederates, if they ever do decide to search us—which almost never happens—they won't search a woman."

"Well," I said, wiping the sweat from my neck with a handkerchief. "I can use it to my advantage, then."

"If you can't, you're a dolt," he said. Then he shrugged.

Chapter Forty-One

Nicholas took off through the city, but I waited for Phillips's man at the agreed-upon spot. The city was hot with air you could almost touch. The dust was suspended around me, waiting to settle. I squinted into the sun, leaning against an abandoned shed. Finally, a man approached me.

"Come on, Miss Reilly," he said. He turned away, and I followed him. "I'm Allenby," he called over his shoulder. "I've got a wagon and some horses for you."

"It's nice to meet you," I said. He kept walking. Mobile was small compared to New Orleans, and it only took a few minutes for us to leave it. He led me to an enormous barn just north of the city.

The horses were hitched, and the wagon was ready to go. I paid him in greenbacks and got in. Mr. Allenby handed me the reins. His graying mustache drooped, and his skin was weathered from the sun. He was chewing on something, and his hat slumped back when he pushed it with his hand.

"If it rains at night," he said, "there's a latch at the back of the wagon. You can lift the boards up and crawl in. Just enough space for a person to lie down and be covered. You understand?"

I looked into his hazel eyes, but he betrayed nothing. Still, I understood. I nodded.

"Just bring it back here when you're done," he said. "It's all yours."

"Thank you, sir," I said. He pulled his hat back on straight and stepped off the road.

I headed north on the only road there was. The one Phillips had told me about. The river flowed past us to my right, rarely far enough away that I lost sight of it. I passed a few small farms. I thought I would ride first, see what I could, and try buying cotton on the way back. I didn't know how much the horses could carry. I didn't know anything about buying cotton.

I passed a sprawling plantation. The house was white with large Greek columns, as well as a red door and blue shutters. A handful of Black men and women worked in the fields—though not nearly enough, I imagined, to do all the work so much land would require. I heard some slaves had fled once the fort was captured.

I kept going. My hat covered my face, but my arms were uncovered and reddening. It would be a long week in this sun.

The ride was monotonous, and my thoughts drifted to Emmett. Was he suffering right now? Was he even alive? I imagined him tossed into a burial pit outside of a prison. I had been able to keep these dark thoughts away before, but here, on the dirt roads of Alabama, the only thing to do was to listen to clopping of the horses' hooves, the squeal of the wagon's wheels, the buzz of the flies, the chirp of the songbirds. I couldn't stop myself from thinking the worst.

When the river came close enough to the road that I could see the water hopping over the rocks along the bank, I led the horses to drink. I squatted next to them and cupped my hands in the cool water. I splashed my face and then did it again. I closed my eyes and breathed deeply.

"Please be out there," I whispered to the still air. "Please be alive."

I reached into my satchel and pulled out a perfectly wrapped piece of cornbread. It crumbled but tasted delicious, and I licked my fingers clean. The afternoon proved just as hot and boring as the morning had been. Some small farms, some large plantations. Some full of slaves, some abandoned entirely. I started talking—first to myself, then to Steven, and then to Emmett.

By the time the sun dipped low in the sky, I had yet to see anything resembling a town. Finally, a cluster of buildings appeared. I let the horses rest, stretched, and took in the town. It wasn't much. There was a post office and grocer with a loose shutter swinging in the hot breeze. A couple of small clapboard houses, one claiming to be a school. It was quiet. Eerily so. Any dreams I had of staying in a small roadside inn were dashed. A narrow, rocky road snaked off the main one to the west, and I peered down it and saw a large, looming building with a castle-like tower. Vines reached up its side like suffocating tentacles. I saw Confederate soldiers standing around it—though not very alert. What was it? It was the only building with any life at all.

A woman emerged from the grocer, and I raised my hand to her in a sort of wave. She squinted at me hard, as if she didn't trust her own eyes. She cautiously approached. I inhaled sharply through my teeth at sight of her frail arms, her hair so thin and straw-like. She eyed me suspiciously.

"Excuse me, ma'am, what town is this?" I asked. Her expression morphed to one of hatred before she spat at my feet.

"I ain't tellin' no Yankee spy a thing," she said, stepping so close I could see the pockmarks on her face, the yellowed whites of her eyes. Before I knew what she was doing, she pushed me with surprising force.

"Now git!" she said, as I stumbled back a few steps.

I returned to my wagon, watching her over my shoulder. Despite the warm breeze, gooseflesh dotted my arms. The town felt haunted. I would need to put some distance between myself and this place before nightfall. I didn't want to sleep anywhere near it. I needed to fall back into a heavy Irish brogue, too. When had I lost it? When had it morphed into something else? Something distinctly Yankee.

I rode until it was dark enough that going any further would be dangerous. I still didn't feel far enough from that place, but I pulled the horses off the road and rested anyway. I slept that night under a wide, reaching oak tree, my revolver by my hand.

I awoke ravenous. The sun was waking up, too but it was not cool like mornings in Massachusetts. I waved away the gnats flying about my head.

I tucked my revolver back into the dress pocket that Phillips had suggested I sew, and I ate a breakfast of hard, chewy bacon.

As I rode, I stared at an abandoned plantation, the cotton fields in full bloom. It was a blanket of snow in oppressive heat. No one to pick it. I imagined what Phillips would do if he could see it. Would he try to pick it all himself? I almost laughed at the thought. Where had these people gone? The white men who owned this place surely owned more than twenty slaves and were therefore exempt from fighting.

I had lost sight of the river entirely, but at the next town, I found a creek. Though there were a collection of buildings here, too, they were all abandoned. Not a single woman to frighten me away. A tree seemed to have taken over what used to be a store or tavern or office. Its branches leaned against the roof and grew into the windows. A squirrel ran along it, stopping to maneuver skillfully through the window's opening. I gave the horses some apples and set off again.

Finally, at yet another abandoned town, the road forked. I took the route east, which hugged the river I had thought lost. But the sun was already setting, and I would need to stop soon. And then, without any warning, the sky opened up on me, rain pelting me and soaking through my dress, wilting my hat, and pooling in my boots. I slept in a barn that night. The hay had not yet gone moldy, so it hadn't been abandoned for very long. I hung up my dress and socks and slept in my undergarments, worried the whole night that someone would enter and find me not only on their property but also nearly naked.

The next day was hot and dry, and it felt as though the rain had never happened. When I reached a town at sunset, I was surprised to see it functioning just as any town would. Women and children and a few men quietly entered and exited the post office and corner store. I slowed the horses and peered into each building—including a hotel. I gazed at it longingly but knew I ought to save my money. I purchased food instead. I considered paying in specie, but I hadn't seen any Confederate soldiers around. Perhaps I could pay with a greenback. The store owner's eyes grew wide, but she stashed it away quickly and whispered, "Thank you."

I slept outside again, and come morning, traced my way back to Mobile, trying to work up the courage to approach a plantation. Finally, I steered the horses off the road and up to the front steps of one of the larger plantations. I stood at the door and wiped my sweaty palms on my dress. My hands shook as I knocked, and I hid them behind my back. An older Black man answered the door.

"I'm here for . . ." I started. I cleared my throat and tried again. "I'd like to see if . . . there is any cotton I could buy?"

All my blood rushed to my face, and I wished I could shrink until I disappeared. But the man smiled at me.

"You wait right here, miss," he said.

"Thank you," I said.

I looked down at the porch, the white paint peeling, the wood splintering. A large white man with suspenders and a white beard appeared.

"Haven't seen you before, missy." He peered down at me

through his glasses.

"My name is Miss Reilly," I said, curtsying. "I'm a new cotton buyer in this area. I'm here to see if you have any cotton you'd like to sell."

He chuckled.

"Just sold my last bale to that other Irish fella. He's a day ahead a'ya. Probably got all the cotton up and down this road. You get here before him next time, I'll sell it t'yah." He winked. I forced a smile.

"Thank you, sir," I said.

"Name's Russel," he said. "Russel Thornberg. Better luck next time, Miss Reilly." He kept chuckling as he closed the door.

Of course Nicholas had already gotten it, I thought as I climbed back onto the wagon. I supposed I should have tried right away. But that would have meant tiring the horses out quicker. Covering less ground. I had no idea what relationships Nicholas and the other buyers had made. Which plantations were already promised to whom. I tried three more that day, all with similar results. On the second day, I got turned away five times. I was tired.

But then, I saw the shadow of a dirt road, forming a faint, winding path westward, toward Mississippi. I slowed the horses and squinted. I could see nothing at the end. Though I had only a few hours of daylight left, I decided to let the horses drink from the creek, and then, cautiously, we made our way along the road. Sometimes, it grew so faint, I accidentally directed them off the path, and I had to find our way back. Finally, something appeared ahead of us. A plantation, though the house clearly needed attention.

A handful of Black people worked the fields, no more than ten. Someone was home, at least. I knocked, but no one came. I knocked again and waited. I knocked a third time. Finally, a Black woman close to my own age opened the door slowly, only wide enough for me to see half of her face.

"I'm inquiring about cotton," I said. "I'd like to buy some."

She wet her lips and glanced over her shoulder before slipping out onto the porch.

"You want cotton?" she asked. She rubbed her right arm from shoulder to elbow.

"Yes," I said. "Have you got any to sell?"

She nodded.

"You a Yankee?" she asked. "You sound like you ain't from 'round here."

"Yes," I said. "I am."

We stared at each other for a moment. Then she looked up into a window of the house.

"Is the . . . the man of the house home?" I asked.

She shook her head.

"He ain't here no more, but my missus, she let me take care of this sort of thing," she said.

She wasn't telling the truth, that much I could see, but I smiled and tried to put her at ease.

"Well, why don't you take me to the cotton, then?"

She rushed off the porch, and I followed her around the side of the house.

"Do you know," I asked, as we walked, "that the Union Army took Fort Morgan? In Mobile Bay?"

"Yes," she said. Just yes. Nothing else. I wanted her to

know that I was on her side, as unlikely as that seemed. But I also wondered why she hadn't left. She led me to an enormous barn, six doors wide. She unlatched a set and opened them to stacks upon stacks of cotton. I gasped. What were they doing with this much cotton? Even if another buyer hadn't found this place, the owners ought to have sent someone somewhere to sell it.

"How much do you want?" she asked.

All of it, I thought.

"How much can my horses pull?" I asked. I didn't care if she knew how green I was.

"Four, five," she said, without hesitation. "You get two more horses, we could do ten."

I gazed at it all and nodded.

"How much does each bale weigh?" I asked.

"About 450 pounds," she said. "That scale over there say so."

She pointed at a scale on the side of the barn.

"Well, I can pay you fifty cents a pound." I paused to do the math in my head. "That's nine hundred dollars for four bales. In greenbacks."

The blood must have drained from her head. She looked a bit ashen, her lips pale.

"Are you all right?" I asked. She exhaled.

"Oh, yes," she said, composing herself. "That sounds 'bout right."

She glanced back toward the big house, and I wondered who was in there. What she was hiding.

"I'll bring my wagon around," I said. She finally smiled. I could see her teeth—but just barely.

"Yes, ma'am."

Chapter Forty-Two

The woman asked if I would come back, and I said I would. When I finally arrived back in New Orleans with four bales of cotton, Mr. Blackburn looked pleased and Nicholas annoyed. I was surprised to see him back so soon. He had at least a dozen bales to turn in, and I had no idea how he had done it.

"How far did ya get?" Nicholas asked.

"Monroeville," I said. He giggled that girlie giggle again.

"You'll have to make better time than that," he said.

"I brought back bales, didn't I?" I asked.

"Sure," he said, shrugging. "Probably stolen. Or rotten."

I rolled my eyes. "Cotton doesn't rot."

Mr. Blackburn handed me $1,350, and I pocketed it quickly. I knew I would need it again. That was how it worked. I bought the cotton, turned around, and sold it for a profit. I believed the papers called it "speculating." I didn't intend to keep any of the money, but I knew I would need it for the next trip. And the one after.

I went back to the boardinghouse and requested a tub

for a bath. But when I reached my room, I found Minnie fiddling with the doorknob. Or perhaps she had just been knocking.

"Are you . . . looking for me?" I asked. She whirled around and gave me a sweet smile.

"Why, yes, I was," she said. "I picked up your mail today." She handed me an envelope.

I looked at the envelope. It was blank.

"I came to knock on your door, see if you were back yet, and there was a man here," she said. "Creepin' right outside your room."

She raised her eyebrows.

"A man?" I asked. She nodded.

"I said, 'Looking for Miss Reilly?' But he ran off real quick."

My heart thumped harder.

"What did he look like?" I asked.

"Didn't see much of his face. But he was clearly up to somethin', and I didn't like the looks of it." She leaned in to whisper in my ear. She smelled like peppermint, and her hair grazed my cheek.

"Should I . . . take care of him?" she asked. When she pulled away, I studied her face. I would think her quite pretty if her large, wily smile didn't make me so uneasy. She had a small mole on her otherwise smooth cheek. Who was this woman, really? I couldn't ask her to kill a man—though I was tempted. I wondered if she had before.

"That won't be necessary," I said. "But thank you."

Her smile faded, and she stared into my eyes. She lifted her chin just a bit before sauntering away, hips swaying with each step.

"If you say so!" she called over her shoulder. But it didn't sound friendly. It sounded angry. I waited until I heard her footsteps going up the stairs before opening the door to my room. My hands shook a bit, and I slowed my breathing while waiting for my bath. Had Minnie been telling the truth? It had looked as though she herself was up to no good. There was certainly something very strange about her. Perhaps I needed to tell Phillips.

When the tub arrived, I lay in the cool water and quickly dunked my head underneath. It felt heavenly. I dried my body first and then my hair and lay across the bed, staring at the ceiling, admiring its beautiful detailing. The bed was so soft, I nearly fell asleep. But then I remembered the envelope Minnie had given me. I sat up and retrieved it.

Dear R.,

I trust that your first excursion went well. It will get easier. I have only a bit of information for you. Your husband is not at Salisbury Prison in North Carolina. I will need to find someone who can check South Carolina next, and then Georgia. I will keep you abreast of any further news.

I have included the map I promised you. I hope it is helpful.

Deepest regards,

P.

I unfolded the map. The major rivers were marked, as were three cities: Mobile, Selma, and Montgomery. This was not too helpful, but I would fill in the smaller towns myself as I learned them. I traced the river with my finger and marked a spot where I guessed Monroeville to be. It was about halfway between Mobile and Selma and nowhere even close to Georgia, let alone South Carolina.

My head swam with frustration. I slammed the map down on my desk and flopped face-first onto the bed. What was I doing? I would never get to Emmett this way. Phillips had not tried to explain to me just how large the South was, and I supposed he shouldn't have had to. But I had never been here. I had looked at maps before. I had seen how small Massachusetts was compared to these giants of the South. But it was different to feel it, after six days of travel. I felt how vast it was. There was no train I could take, no way to make this easier. It would take weeks—maybe months— to reach him, and then what? How would I get him out? I felt hopeless and foolish, with no plan but to sleep.

I dreamt I was on a ship. At first, I didn't know which one, but then I saw Ronan. Little, six-year-old Ronan. And I knew exactly which ship I was on. He was sitting cross-legged on the deck, petting a black cat that was asleep in his lap. I walked toward him.

"Rat Girl," I said. Ronan looked up at me and smiled.

"I caught her a fish, Rosaleen. I finally caught her one."

I sat beside him and stroked the cat between her eyes. "She looks happy," I said.

He gazed at her lovingly. "She is happy," he said.

I awoke before sunrise, my face wet with tears. It took me a moment to remember where I was and what I was doing. I was expected to leave again that day to buy more cotton. I dragged myself out of bed and gathered my writing supplies. I arrived on the streets as the stores first opened. I would need provisions again. I reached the river-front before Nicholas, though I did spot Reuben boarding a brig next to mine. I sat and waited for the boat to take me to Mobile. Two alligator eyes popped up from beneath the water, and I wondered if it was the same one from last week.

Nicholas threw himself down next to me. "Givin' it another go, are you?" he asked.

I smiled. "Until I'm as good as you," I said.

He shrugged. "That's not gonna happen."

This time, after I retrieved the wagon, I went straight to Mr. Thornberg's plantation. I didn't have to. I didn't have to go a mile past the secret plantation with the nervous woman. But I knew Phillips was right; I needed to get to know the land and the people. It could save Emmett's life. Besides, Mr. Thornberg had promised to sell to me if I got there first.

I pushed the horses to go faster this time, past the ghost towns and the Confederate castle. Still, we had to stop for the night before we arrived. I tossed and turned at the edge of a field, imagining Nicholas ahead of me.

I got an early start the next day, but the horses were slow and I didn't want to push them too hard. When we arrived, I practically ran up the large white steps.

Mr. Thornberg looked genuinely pleased to see me. He laughed a deep belly laugh.

"It's the new girl," he said. "You've made it in time, Miss Reilly. I do love a winner." He clapped his hands. "Let me see that wagon of yours." He put his large paw of a hand on my shoulder and stepped onto the porch. "I'd say those beasts can pull at least five bales."

I supposed they could. The woman had told me four or five. But that would mean I couldn't buy more bales from her. And I'd told her I would. Unless . . . unless I could bring these back to Mr. Allenby. I could pay him to store them for me until the end of the week. I pictured Nicholas's stupid smirk and agreed to buy five bales. Mr. Thornberg led me around to the fields. His slaves bent over the rows, picking the cotton and stuffing it into sacks and buckets. They looked unnaturally thin. Shoulder bones and collarbones jutting out. I swallowed the guilt creeping into my throat and looked away.

Two Black men led my horses and wagon behind us. They loaded five bales onto the pulleys and lifted them onto my wagon. I noticed how many more bales he had and remembered what Phillips had said about the stockpiles of cotton. Mr. Thornberg had lied to me that first day. He seemed like a man who enjoyed playing games. I handed him $1,125 in greenbacks. He hesitated for a moment, and I thought I had made a mistake. Perhaps the other buyers paid him in specie. But then he grinned and took it. I forced myself to smile. I did not like this man. I did not like giving him money.

"Pleasure doing business with you, Miss Reilly," he said.

I took the horses back the way we had come, and when we stopped for the night, I lay next to the cotton bales, trying to sleep. I could not find it, despite my exhaustion. So, I sat up, lit a lamp, took out my writing tools, and began to write a letter.

· · ·

Dear Steven,

I saw an alligator the other day. I can't draw as well as your da, but I'm going to sketch one for you. They are so motionless, it is strange. They stare at you with large, slitted eyes, watching everything. I imagine that when they do decide to move, they can be quite quick. They would need to be to catch their prey. They are beautiful when they swim, too. They glide so effortlessly, so smoothly. I miss you. Please tell me about school. About what you are working on in the shop.

Your loving ma,
Rosaleen

I drew the alligator next, taking the time to include its claws and tail. I realized that I had only ever seen Nicholas's friend in bits and pieces—never his whole body at once. A head and front legs. A tail and back. The rest was always hidden under the water.

I tucked the letter away and stared out into the dark expanse, the sky and earth meeting each other at some point I couldn't see. Enormous oak trees became dark masses, their branches melding into the ones beside them. They were the keepers of that spot, it seemed. Where the earth and the sky met.

Chapter Forty-Three

OCTOBER 1864

When I arrived at the end of the spotty dirt road, the plantation looked even sparser than it had before. The big house grew in front of me, and this time, I inspected its features. There were two levels, each with many windows, and all the curtains drawn. The second level featured a balcony with smaller replicas of the main doors below. I thought I saw a curtain twitch upstairs, but perhaps it only fluttered in the breeze. The day was slightly cooler than yesterday, and with a start, I realized it was October now.

My heart pounded. Whatever that woman and I had done the first time, it had been risky. I knocked anyway and stood back to wait for her. A moment later, her face filled the narrow window next to the door. She opened the door and crept out again.

"There ya are," she said. I reached out a hand for her to shake.

"Miss Reilly," I said. It almost came as easily as Mrs.

Doherty now. She stared at my hand for a moment before taking it and giving it a quick shake.

"Norma," she said. I smiled.

"You always comin' on Wednesday?" she asked, as we brought the wagon around back.

"I . . . I suppose I could," I said. "Do Wednesdays suit you?"

I saw the corner of her mouth twitch.

"Sure do," she said. One of the men in the field eyed us with a long, hard stare. Norma ignored him. I followed her to the big barn, guiding the horses. We hooked up the bales and hoisted them onto the wagon.

The earthy smell of the cotton reminded me of whiskey. I patted one of the bales and then forced a finger under the burlap and rubbed a bit between my fingers. It was dense like this, before getting carded in the mills. I thought of all the hands this cotton would pass through. First, the slaves, then mine, the treasury agent, the men on the ships, on the trains, in the cellar of the mills, and then each floor above it. Someday, someone would sew it and wear it. It might keep them warm for a long time.

Norma cleared her throat, and I looked up into her waiting eyes. I gave her a bit more money this time, which she immediately slipped into her apron.

"I'll be back next Wednesday, too," I said.

Just then, "Norma!" a woman's shrill voice cried from inside the house. "Where is Norma?"

Norma's eyes grew wide, and she turned from me without a word, hurrying back into the house.

I should leave, I thought. The men and women stared at

me now. A woman emerged through a side door carrying a large pot, a little girl behind her. Their eyes warned me to go. I climbed into the wagon and turned the horses around as quickly as I could. Though they were burdened by the new load, I sped them up to a trot until we could no longer see the house.

I thought of those people the whole way back to Mobile and wondered if I would ever know what was happening there. Was I putting Norma at too much risk? If she could sell cotton from under her mistress's nose, surely she could leave. They all could. Why had they not sought freedom?

It seemed the lowest parts of the state had been turned upside down with the arrival of the Union troops. Perhaps they simply didn't know what to do. But if I made one more purchase, one more payment, they could easily leave and have enough to reach someplace they could be free. If money was the worry, I could alleviate that.

But instead of feeling better about myself, I felt worse. I had also handed a stack of greenbacks to Mr. Thornberg, and I had, most likely, put Norma in serious danger.

By the time I reached New Orleans, I was irritated and angry. I didn't want to buy cotton. I wanted my husband back. I took my $3,375 in greenbacks from Mr. Blackburn and ignored Nicholas's indignant huffing. I needed to mail my letter, eat a filling meal, and sleep in a feather bed.

I was walking north on Canal Street when I ran right into Phillips. He raised his eyebrows.

"Well, aren't you a sight?"

"Yes." I blew out a deep breath, fluttering a strand of hair. "It turns out that buying cotton is dirty and tiring. I assume you need me for something?"

"Why would you assume that?" he asked.

"Because you don't coincidentally run into people," I said. "So, what is it? I'd like a bath."

He smiled.

"Was my map helpful?" he asked.

"Hardly. Alabama . . . the South . . . it's enormous, if you haven't noticed. I need more than three cities. I need Georgia. I need South Carolina." I looked around before saying quietly, "It feels hopeless."

"Chin up," he said, cautiously grabbing my filthy arm. "You won't need South Carolina."

I raised my eyebrows.

"No?" I asked.

"No," he said. "And I've got something else that might boost your spirits."

He led me back to the boardinghouse with a promise that he would mail my letter himself. Whatever he had to show me was urgent. We went to his room, and when the door opened, I spied two other people sitting by the fireplace. The woman turned to me.

"Rosa . . . sorry! Miss Reilly!" she cried.

"Lydia?" She stood, and I raced to give her a hug. "I'm sorry I'm such a mess! What are you doing here? Is everything all right?"

"Yes," she said, as she pulled away. "Everything is all right. How are you?" She took my hands in hers. "You must be terrified."

Tears stung the backs of my eyes. I nodded.

"Marie told you?" I asked.

"She wrote to me," she said. The man in the chair behind her stood, the leather squeaking. Lydia glanced at him and then back at me.

"I hope you don't mind me doing this," she said. "But I asked my friend here, Cunningham, to help you."

I furrowed my eyebrows, confused, as I considered him. He was a tall Black man with a strong chin and curly hair cut close to his head. He extended his hand, and I shook it.

"Nice to meet you, ma'am," he said.

"You as well," I said. "How do you know Lydia?"

"We're friends from the island. I find myself in Port Royal from time to time, and I met Lydia last year."

He looked at her and smiled wide.

"She sure does everything on that island," he said. "But I'm sure you know how she is. There isn't a problem she can't solve."

Lydia smiled back at him and then at me.

"He acts like I'm the mayor there or somethin'," she said.

Cunningham chuckled. "No, no. People come to *you* before they go to the mayor."

He was clearly taken with Lydia, and I wondered if she knew.

"Is that so?" I asked, still studying my friend.

"She's certainly more reliable," Phillips muttered behind me.

"So, how is it that you came here, to help me?" I asked Cunningham.

"Please sit first," he insisted. He gestured to his empty seat, and I sat. Lydia sat across from me, and he and Phillips remained standing.

"Lydia told me about your plan to get your husband out," Cunningham said, stuffing his hands in his pockets. "And I think it's a fine one. But it'll be tough getting him back here safely. They send dogs after the prisoners." He straightened a bit and hardened his jaw. "Just like they do the slaves. Those dogs will find him if you don't know where you're going and what you're doing."

"Are you from around here?" I asked.

"Not here, exactly," he said. "But from a plantation down South, yes. I work for the Union Army now. I've been in and out of Confederate territory for the past few years. I know what goes on down here."

"In and out of Confederate territory?" I wondered. "That sounds perilous. What do you do there?"

He glanced at Lydia and then down at his feet.

"I can't tell you that," he said, before looking back up. "The point is, there are helpers down here. At first, it was slaves helping other slaves escape. But in these war years, they've helped other people trying to escape, too. Your husband won't be the first."

"The slaves have helped prisoners?" I asked. He nodded. Lydia did not appear at all surprised by this information. Cunningham's thick eyebrows furrowed.

"The Union soldiers are fighting for their freedom, no?"

Some of them don't think so, I wanted to say, but I just nodded.

"Do you know where he is?" he asked.

I shook my head. "I'm hoping I will soon."

"He isn't in North Carolina," Phillips cut in. "Or South Carolina. My source assured me of this just this morning. Their records are shoddy, but from what he understands, there is no Sergeant Emmett Doherty at Salisbury or the Florence Stockade, and there never has been."

"That's good," Cunningham said. "Still. It'll take days—possibly weeks—to get him back to Union lines. I can get you to the people who can help."

"I would greatly appreciate that," I said. He smiled and adjusted his jacket. Just then, the keeper brought in four supper plates, as well as tea and whiskey.

"Thank you. We'll take it outside," Phillips said.

The four of us sat there eating and drinking, watching the city transform from day life to night life. Cunningham pointed to things below us and told Lydia stories. She laughed and listened and asked questions. She seemed perfectly at ease. I hoped Cunningham knew she was married. He seemed like a good man.

Phillips cleared his throat and raised his whiskey glass as if in a toast.

"To Miss Johnson, a most precious employee," he said to me. "And her . . . friend." He winked.

"So generous of you to allow this most precious employee to come here to New Orleans," I said after we drank.

"I gave her leave for the holidays, of course. Just a bit early."

I raised my eyebrows and lowered my voice, though Cunningham and Lydia were so engrossed in their conversation, they weren't paying us a bit of attention anyway.

"And she chose to come here instead of going home?" I asked. Phillips grinned.

"Indeed. Her presence has done much to assuage

Cunningham's suspicion. I believe he was quite wary of me. As is to be expected. His line of work requires it."

I took a sip of whiskey. "I imagine it does."

Chapter Forty-Four

M r. Thornberg was always excited to see me. I was some sort of novelty to him, so I played my part well. He wasn't the sort of man you would want to anger, so I made sure to always laugh at his jokes and blush at his compliments. I looked only at him and at the cotton and horses. I couldn't watch the slaves work. Besides, Miss Reilly wouldn't look twice.

After I left my first load of cotton with Mr. Allenby, I stopped the horses at the dirt road where Norma lived and thought I ought to leave it be. I didn't want to put Norma in danger. The horses were confused by my cues and impatient, but I made them wait a moment longer. What if Norma was counting on me, though? On the money? Something wasn't right inside that house.

I led the horses slowly down the road. I wouldn't knock today, I decided. I would wait. Norma would be expecting me. I didn't need to announce myself.

I steered the horses a bit further into the trees lining

the road, away from the house. I waited in the shade. The same man that had stared me down last time stood from his work and locked eyes with me. He slowly began to walk toward me.

"What you doin' here, miss?" he asked. My mouth felt as dry as the cotton in the field.

"Buying cotton," I said. He shook his head.

"That woman in there." He pointed at the house. "The missus. She done lost her mind. She don't even know who she is most days. That's why Norma thinks she can do what she's doin'. But the days the missus knows? Those days she could kill us all. You understand?"

I looked over my shoulder and then back at him. "Why don't you all leave?" I asked him. "The Union Army's at Fort Morgan. It's not more than two or three days from here."

"We know," he said. "It's where Walter went, we think."

"Who's Walter?" I asked.

"Overseer," he said.

"A Black man?" I asked. The field hand narrowed his eyes.

"You shouldn't come back here," he said.

"One more purchase," I said. "That'll be enough green-backs to last you all for some time. Then you can go to Fort Morgan."

I saw Norma hurrying toward us. She brushed past the man's arm, looking intently at him.

"Come on," she said to me. I led the horses to the barn, hugging the tree line as best I could, hoping to blend in. The field hand stayed where he was.

"What was Curtis sayin' to you?" she asked.

"He told me your mistress is insane," I said.

Her jaw clenched.

"Am I making things dangerous for you?" I asked. "I don't want to do that."

She spun on her heels and looked into my eyes. She sighed.

"Things are always dangerous for us, Miss Reilly. We stay, they dangerous. We leave, they dangerous. We make it to those Yankee boys with nothing in our pockets? Dangerous."

She opened the barn doors.

"Few of ours left when the news 'bout Mobile Bay came," she said. The doors squeaked as she pulled them open.

"But we heard it's still the same," she said. "We heard they say they'll pay us, but they don't."

She started to hook up the cotton bales.

"Even if they did," she said. "What sounds better to you, Miss Reilly? Ten greenbacks a month or what you're payin' us?"

"You couldn't have known I would come," I said.

Norma shrugged.

"I only know that we finally in charge around here. In a way. We the boss. We grow this. We pick it. We put it through the gin. Roll it up into bales. I wasn't 'bout to leave it. I didn't have a plan. But I was thinkin' when you came along."

We hoisted the last bale onto the wagon.

"You know 'bout Jesus, Miss Reilly?" Norma asked. I nodded.

"I think he sent you," she said. "You keep comin' on Wednesdays. I'll make sure the missus is sleepy."

I handed her the money.

"Please take care of yourself," I said. She smiled at me with all of her teeth this time.

"That's what I'm doin', isn't it?"

When I got back to the boardinghouse that evening, there was an envelope on my floor, addressed to Miss Reilly. It was from Mr. Joyce. I picked it up and collapsed onto my bed before ripping it open. Two letters fell out. I read the first.

Dear Rosaleen,

We miss you very much. We hope you are doing well. Steven is working on something for you. We received this letter yesterday, though you will see it was dated in July. It gave Steven much hope, though I didn't share it in its entirety.

All our love,

Mr. Joyce and Steven

I sat up quickly. My hands began to shake as I opened the second letter.

July 12, 1864

To my dear wife,

I am writing to tell you that I am alive but in enemy hands. We have finally arrived in Georgia. The prison is called Andersonville. There are a lot of prisoners here and ▓▓▓▓▓ ▓▓▓▓▓ ▓▓▓▓. *My mate Will is with me. He was injured at the battle near the Spotsylvania Courthouse. I stayed with him, and we were both captured. The Confederate surgeon took one look at his injury and* ▓▓▓▓ ▓ ▓▓▓▓▓. *I am trying to keep it clean, but it is hard. The water here is* ▓▓▓▓▓▓▓. *If any of our friends could send us food—Miss Martha, perhaps, through the Sanitary Commission—we would be grateful. The rations are* ▓▓▓▓▓. *It is hot here, so we are faring fine, but when it gets cold, we might need socks and blankets.*

I love you and Steven very much. Pray for me.

Love,

Emmett

I held the letter to my chest and sobbed. Whether I felt terror or relief, I couldn't say. Emmett was alive. Though this letter was three months old, I could only hope that was still the truth. I read it again, trying to decipher the words that the Confederates had blotted out, but could not.

Andersonville, I thought. I needed to tell Cunningham. His room was across from mine, and though I felt strange barging in without Lydia, this was urgent. I banged on his door. When he opened it, he looked around me down the hallway, perhaps for Lydia.

"I'm sorry to disturb you, but I just received a letter from my husband," I said.

"Of course," he said. "Please come in."

His room was tidy but brimming with things. There

were trunks lined against the wall, books stacked beside his bed and on his desk, and a pair of pants had been laid out on the bed.

"Is this the first letter you've received from him?" he asked.

"Yes," I said, sitting at the desk. "Though it was written in July."

Cunningham nodded. "And where did he say he was?" he asked.

"Andersonville," I said. He took a sharp breath.

"What?" I asked. "What is it? Should I be worried?"

"I'd say you're worried enough as it is, Miss Reilly. No, no. We'll get him out." He gave me a strained smile. "We'll get him out. Won't take more than a week to get there."

"What do you need me to do?" I asked. "Can we leave tomorrow?"

"No, ma'am," he said. "I'll need some time to prepare. To make us some maps. Get enough provisions."

"How can I help?" I asked. He gave me a crooked smile.

"Convince Lydia to stay here," he said. "She's got this crazy idea that she's comin'. But she can't. It's far too risky. She's used to helpin', but she won't be of any use to us out there."

"I understand," I said. I wanted to ask him more about her. About him. About the two of them. But I could see how he felt. It was written all over his face. "How many days, do you suppose, until we can leave?"

"Three, perhaps four."

I stood. My body felt like the inner workings of a clock, my insides moving around and around with nowhere to go. How could I simply wait for three or four days now that I knew where Emmett was? But I had no choice.

"Thank you," I said.

"I'm happy to help. Any friend of Lydia's is a friend of mine."

Chapter Forty-Five

I went to Phillips's room next.

"I won't be able to buy cotton this week," I said, as soon as he ushered me inside. "Emmett is at Andersonville in Georgia. I received a letter from him saying so. We're leaving in three days. Perhaps four. That's how long Cunningham says he'll need."

"Three or four days? Well then, you certainly *should* buy cotton this week," Phillips said.

I looked at him, befuddled.

"Why?"

"What else will you do? Sit around here and bother the poor man? You still have a cover to protect. The hardest part of this is still to come. Go purchase cotton. Cunningham will be better able to prepare without you breathing down his neck, trying to rush him."

I was furious at the man. My hands shook.

"What is this really about?" I demanded. "Are you simply dragging your feet? Are you using me? I know it's advantageous to have a woman buyer. Nicholas told me so."

Phillips looked as though he might laugh, but instead, his expression turned sad.

"I know you are desperate right now," he said. "You're not thinking clearly. But please remember that you are here now, about to save your husband's life, because of me."

A chill ran through my body. Though he'd said it softly and kindly, it felt like a threat. He was right, though. I *was* desperate. I did need him.

"How am I to know exactly where he is and not go to him immediately?" I asked, a tremor in my voice.

Phillips stepped toward me.

"The more time you spend out there, the more prepared you will feel. You need to do something right now. I see that. Think of your weak spots. Correct them if you can."

"Why? I have Cunningham now. He knows people who know every single inch of that land. In the dark, no less."

"And you still have an advantage over them simply because of who you are. You must keep your cover intact. You must visit those sellers who are expecting you. It is no longer only your own life and Emmett's that are in danger. Cunningham is risking his freedom. Everything he has. Do not be foolish and get careless now."

I took a deep breath and crossed my arms over my chest, grabbing each elbow. I looked out the window at the setting sun. He was right. We must be properly prepared. For Emmett's sake and Cunningham's. But I had always been lousy at waiting.

"You must believe that I am grateful for all you have done," I said.

The corner of his mouth lifted into a smile.

"Don't start groveling," he said. "It isn't like you."

I chuckled, releasing the tension in my chest.

"Go rest," he said.

"Not quite yet," I said. "I have to make it clear to Lydia that she is not to come. Cunningham asked me to speak with her. And he's right, of course. It's far too dangerous."

"Don't worry too much about Lydia," he said. "Talk to her, yes, but I will lock her in her room if need be."

"She really has become important to you, hasn't she?" I asked.

"The relationships she's made are invaluable. She is better at it than I had dreamed. They love Lydia. I cannot get that Port Royal cotton without her."

I thought then about what Marie had said. About Phillips not needing me. He *did* need me. And he needed Lydia now, too. He admitted it freely. I wondered what Marie would think of that.

I didn't trust myself to stay awake if I remained in my room, so Lydia and I strolled the city streets. The city was wonderful at this time of night. Though it was dark, the lamps illuminated the sidewalks, and children ran around their mas' skirts, laughing and squealing. Horse-drawn trolleys clomped and clattered down Canal Street. Union soldiers meandered along, presumably on patrol, though it looked much more like play than work. Music came from the open windows of pubs and inns, welcoming us.

"How long did Cunningham say it would take to reach Emmett?" Lydia asked.

"No more than a week," I said.

"We can do that," she said. "That's not so bad."

"Lydia . . ." I started. "I know you want to help us. But it's too dangerous for you to come."

She looked like she had bit into something sour.

"I know you know the dangers," I said. I stopped walking and touched her arm. "Better than I. Think of the girls." I paused. "Think of Zeke."

Her face fell. She looked tired now, but she nodded.

"You're right. The war isn't won yet. Confederate territory is no place for me." She looked like she had more to say, so I kept quiet. "I suppose I've gotten used to doing whatever I want. I like this feeling that I'm making a difference. The changes I've seen on that island. *I* helped with that, you know? I love my girls. I love the young women they're becoming. But I don't know if I've ever been prouder of anything than of what I've done on that island. Whole families learning to read. To write. Taking care of their own land and supporting their own families. It's hard not to feel as though the possibilities are endless for me. For all of us."

"That doesn't have to stop," I said. "Those families still need you."

"Yes, but it's a bit like a dream, isn't it? Eventually, I'll have to go home to Boston. I'll have to mend dresses for fine white ladies and spend my days cooking and cleaning up after the girls. After . . ." She swallowed, as if saying his name would summon him here, in the flesh. ". . . After Zeke."

Her eyes searched mine desperately for answers. Answers I didn't have. She *would* have to go home eventually. After a moment, she chuckled.

"Isn't that strange, that Boston feels stifling now? This big war, all these changes, and I'll go home to a place that hasn't changed one bit. A life that has stood still while I have been moving. Am I wrong to feel sad that *my* possibilities are not endless?"

"No," I said. "You aren't wrong. It's all right to be afraid. Even a bit despondent. You've changed, Lydia. But the people who love you will love this version of you, too. You've grown, but they'll grow with you."

"What if they don't?" she asked, so softly it was almost a whisper. I reached for her hand and squeezed it. Just then, I spotted a man out of the corner of my eye. A familiar-looking man. A large man. I let go of Lydia's hand and started after him.

"Where are you going, Rosaleen?" I heard Lydia ask, but I was already hurrying away and didn't have time to correct her error. I reached for my pocket, and my revolver bumped against my crinoline as I walked faster and faster, trying to keep pace with the man. He wasn't exactly running, but his strides were so long.

I tried not to push anyone over, but as he darted down an alleyway, I turned the corner quickly and ran smack into someone. Hard. We both stumbled, and when my eyes focused again, I saw Minnie rubbing her forehead.

"My! Miss Reilly!" she exclaimed. "You in a hurry?"

"I'm sorry, Minnie," I said. "I thought I saw someone I

knew." I craned my neck to look around her, but he was long gone now. No trace of him at all.

"Try calling their name next time. Goodness," she said. Her smile looked more like a grimace.

"I do apologize," I said. My own head was pounding, too.

"There you are," I heard Lydia cry, as she caught up. "What in the world did you run off for?"

"And consorting with Negroes again," Minnie said, looking Lydia up and down. "You are one strange cotton buyer."

Lydia gave me a concerned glance. Minnie's forehead was swelling.

"You should get that looked at," I said. "You'll have a bump tomorrow."

Minnie smiled now, but there was still some annoyance behind it.

"I'll look like I got my tail beat," she said. "Not great for business." But then she raised her eyebrows. "Or perhaps perfect for business." I didn't know what she meant by that, but I knew she wouldn't offer any more information. Especially not in front of Lydia, who looked uncomfortable.

"You want me to help you to a doctor? I'm sure the hospital right around the corner would take a look," I said.

She waved her hand dismissively.

"I've heard stories about those war surgeons," she said. "I think I'd prefer to take my chances." She stared at Lydia a little longer before saying, "You and your *friend* have a nice night." Then she strode off, in the same direction the suspicious man had gone.

I looked at Lydia, who was displaying a range of emotions. She had always worn her feelings openly.

"I'm sorry," I said, linking my arm through hers and turning back to the main road. "About taking off that way —and about . . . her." I looked behind us one last time. "I'll explain at the boardinghouse."

Chapter Forty-Six

I told Lydia about the suspicious man and about how I had met Minnie. She thought I needed to tell Phillips.

"Just because she helped you improve your shooting, doesn't mean she's your friend," Lydia said. "And now she's seen us together?" She shook her head. "You don't know who she might know."

I did need to tell Phillips. But by then it was nearly midnight, and though I expected to find him in his room the next morning, he was not there. So, I boarded the boat to Fort Morgan, a bundle of nerves. I bobbed my leg up and down, anxious about nearly everything.

I needed to think of the week ahead of me, of this last true cotton buying excursion, of what was left to do. *I must tell Norma that I won't be returning*, I thought. She would need to make arrangements.

Nicholas never boarded, and I guessed he was off to Mississippi this time. I was so lost in thought, I barely noticed the soldiers checking our permits. They didn't even ask for mine anymore.

As we pulled into Mobile, I thought of our upcoming trip to Georgia. I didn't know where precisely Andersonville Prison was, but it seemed Cunningham did. I wondered if Georgia was just like Alabama. I wondered if anything changed across this vast and sprawling sea of plantations.

The other passengers got off before me, and I startled when a man stepped right in front of me. It was Jasper. I smiled politely but tried to maneuver around him.

"I don't believe I've had the chance to introduce myself," he said. "Formally."

Now that he was so close, I could see that he was stunningly handsome. The "lose your breath for a moment" kind of handsome. He was grinning coyly. *Perhaps I'm not too old for him*, I thought. It gave me no comfort. I reached out a hand.

"Miss Reilly," I said. "Pleased to see you again."

He took my hand and kissed it.

"Don't you have a first name, Miss Reilly?" he asked.

No one had asked for a first name. My mind grasped for anything. A name written on the side of a merchant vessel beside us said Annie.

"Annie," I said.

"Well, Annie." He came around to my side and draped his arm across my shoulder.

"It can be dangerous for a lady like yourself to be out here on your own. Want me to show you around? I'll even let you have some of my sales."

I resisted the urge to roll my eyes and throw his arm off. I forced a laugh instead and tried to channel Minnie.

"How kind of you, Jasper. Perhaps next time. I've got to

get to a certain plantation. The seller has become a real admirer of mine. Loves *my* greenbacks the most." I winked, and he threw his head back and laughed. The top of his shirt was unbuttoned, and his muscular, hairy chest peeked out the top. We stepped off the boat now, no longer alone, and I breathed a little easier.

"Next time," he said, peeling himself away from me, "you're mine. Don't forget."

As I headed to Mr. Allenby's, I wondered if Phillips would be angry if I shot Jasper in the leg—or perhaps some other extremity.

I went to Mr. Thornberg's confident that it would be the last time I would have to do business with him. The last time I would have to perform that particular dance of ours. I thought of Emmett the whole time.

When I reached Norma's on the third day, I slowed the horses, thinking of what I would say. How I would break the news to her that she could no longer rely on me. The path was dustier than normal. It hadn't rained in days, and I had learned that was unusual here. So, it wasn't until I got up close that I realized the place was truly abandoned this time. No one worked the fields. No one came out of the side or back door.

I walked slowly around the house. I lightly touched the cotton bolls in the fields, careful not to prick my fingers. It was so quiet and still. Bees and butterflies flew from one plant to the next. Where was Norma? Was her mistress still inside? I stared up at the house. The thought of her wasting away in there caused dread to rise up inside of me. I didn't want anything to do with the woman, but no matter how wretched she was, she was still the owner of hundreds of thousands of dollars' worth of cotton. I could tell Nicholas about it. He could buy or steal the rest for all I cared. It was better than leaving it for the Confederates.

First, I would load one more wagonful. I brought the horses to the barn and opened it. There was still so much. Fifty bales at least. I kept looking over my shoulder and up at that window as I hooked up the bales.

Once the wagon was loaded and the horses turned around for a quick getaway, I knocked on the front door. Softly at first and then a bit louder. I turned the handle, and the door opened. There was a thin layer of dust on everything: the chairs, the table, the mantel, the piano. No one had cleaned this house for quite some time. Longer than a week.

"Hello?" I said. Silence. I did not want to find the woman dead in her bed. But I also couldn't simply leave. I crept up the stairs, touching the rail for a moment, forgetting the dust. I jerked my hand away, wiping it on my dress.

At the top of the stairs, the big room welcomed me, its doors opened wide like outstretched arms. *Come see*, they seemed to say.

"Hello?" I said again. Still nothing. I stepped into the room, holding my breath. The bed was large, with four posts and a dark-blue canopy. I saw a tuft of gray hair on the pillow before anything else and brought my arm to my nose to breathe into the sleeve of my dress.

The woman was puffy and gray. There was no expression on her face anymore. Her skin drooped and sagged. A fly landed on her cheek. On her bedside were bottles and bottles of laudanum. All empty. I hurried down the stairs before I became too lightheaded and took a deep breath of fresh air.

I glanced back at the house before climbing onto the wagon. I pushed the image of the woman out of my head, thinking only of Norma and Curtis and the rest. I hoped they had made it to safety. But Norma had been right.

Jasper wasn't on board for the trip back to New Orleans, and I was grateful. I wondered how many Confederate wives' beds he had warmed while their husbands were away fighting. How many widows he had comforted. I doubted he ever slept under a tree.

I was ready to rush off the boat to prepare for the trip to Georgia when I spotted Phillips and Mr. Blackburn waiting on the riverbank.

I went to Mr. Blackburn first, taking the money he owed me.

"Ten bales!" Phillips declared, looking genuinely happy. "Well done."

I smirked, and he jerked his head to the side, asking for a private word.

"Is everything ready?" I asked him.

"It was," he said. "But I just received this letter. It may change things."

He handed it to me. It featured General Butler's official seal, broken on the outside.

Dear Mrs. Doherty,

Sarah informed me of your letter. I am grieved to hear about your husband. I wish I could do more, but I cannot compromise the rigid stance we have taken regarding the Negro soldiers. I appreciate your understanding.

I was able to locate a Sergeant Emmett Doherty at Castle Morgan prison, located in Cahawba, Alabama. You can send any mail for him directly to me, and I will make sure it gets through the lines to the Confederates.

If there is anything further, please do contact me immediately. If the Confederates ever change their policy regarding Negro prisoners, I will arrange to have your husband on the first exchange.

All my best,

General Benjamin F. Butler

Alabama? I thought. Could it possibly be true? I looked at the date.

"Dated last week," Phillips said, as if reading my thoughts.

"What do you make of this?" I asked.

Phillips started walking, his hands clasped behind his back. His forehead was creased, deep in thought. I followed.

"They may have moved him when Sherman's troops occupied Atlanta," he said. "The Confederates get restless when they suspect a military operation could free thousands of prisoners."

"So, you think it is him?" I asked. "You think he's in Alabama?"

"It's possible," he said. "Though I suppose there could be

another Sergeant Emmett Doherty currently imprisoned."

"Yes, that would be unfortunate," I said.

Phillips looked at me. "What will you do?"

"I suppose I'll go to this Alabama prison," I said. "I cannot wait for confirmation through a letter or any other means. I must try now."

Phillips sighed.

"I hope he's right," he said. "But if he's not, when you return, we will try again."

When I went to knock on Cunningham's door, it was already ajar. I could hear whispering.

"Please be careful," I heard Lydia say. "I'm worried."

"You don't need to be," he said. "I've gone behind enemy lines countless times before. Remember? It's my job."

I didn't want to be caught eavesdropping, so I cleared my throat loudly and tapped on the half-opened door.

Cunningham appeared a moment later, looking sheepish.

"Miss Reilly," he said. "Is there something wrong? I thought we weren't meeting until later tonight."

"We weren't. But our plans will need to change. I have reason to believe my husband isn't in Georgia anymore. Do you know where Castle Morgan is?"

"Alabama," he said.

"That's right," I said. "I think he's there."

Cunningham nodded and opened the door a wee bit wider to reveal Lydia.

"I was just . . ." she started, shuffling around him.

"Won't you stay for the planning?" I asked her. She gave me a grateful smile. I wanted to put them both at ease. I needed Cunningham to concentrate.

"Of course," she said. Cunningham opened the door all the way, and we all sat around the table.

"So, that's closer, then. Correct?" I asked him.

"Yes, it is." He looked down at his bags. "I've packed too much now, but that's all right."

He gathered some drawing supplies and mapped out Alabama, showing me where we would stop and which roads we would take. He and I would board the same ship. Walk in the same direction once we got off that ship. Meet along the road when dusk fell each night. He showed me where I would turn off when we finally arrived in Cahawba.

Lydia and I left Cunningham's room just before suppertime.

"We were only talking," she said. "I hope you know that I wouldn't . . . I would never . . ."

"I know you wouldn't," I said, as we stopped at the door to her room. "But that man in there is quite possibly in love with you."

Lydia looked so sad in that moment.

"Does he know about Zeke?" I asked.

"Yes," she said. "Of course he knows."

She sighed.

"I won't see him anymore after this," she said. "I won't."

"I appreciate you bringing him here," I said. "I truly do. I couldn't do it without him."

She gave me a half smile. "Let's get Emmett home, huh?"

Chapter Forty-Seven

I knew I wouldn't be able to sleep after supper, and so, I wandered the streets until the only people still out were the ones up to no good. The man at the desk handed me a package as I came back inside.

I sat by my bedroom window and opened it. It was from Steven. He had carved a tree and written me a note.

Ma,

It's supposed to be the maple outside your window. I wanted you to think of home. Perhaps next time I will try an alligator. I would love to see one in real life. Caroline says that crocodiles are even bigger and eat humans! Now I must worry about crocodiles getting you, too. Please come home soon and bring Da with you. I love you, and I miss you.

Your son,
Steven

. . .

I turned the tree over in my palm, brushing its branches with my thumb. Tears formed at the edges of my eyes. I missed him so much I ached.

I fell asleep holding the tree and awoke what felt like a minute later to the first touch of sunlight creeping into my room. I was about to be late. I rushed to gather my things and practically ran to the riverfront, weaving in and out of people, occasionally bumping someone and yelling apologies over my shoulder.

Out of breath, I slid onto Nicholas's trunk beside him, just before the boat departed. He didn't even look up at me before he started jabbering on about something.

I hoped Cunningham was somewhere on the ship. I glanced around nervously. I had to trust that he was better at this than I was. I might have overslept, but he wouldn't have.

Nicholas talked the whole ride there, giggling and shrugging. I smiled along, but I was too nervous to truly pay attention. After the Union soldiers boarded the ship, inspected our permits, and waved us through to Mobile, I remembered to tell Nicholas about Norma's cotton.

"There's a plantation you should know about," I said.

He smirked.

"Why are you telling me about it?"

"It's abandoned," I went on. "A barnful of cotton. Bales and bales of it."

"This sounds like a trap," he said.

"It's not."

"Then why aren't you takin' it?" he asked.

"I am," I said. "But I have a previous commitment today.

Somewhere else. I thought we could take turns. We'll need to make multiple trips."

Hu studied me for a moment. Then he spat over the edge of the ship.

"I suppose I could go and see," he said, shrugging. "If I have time."

"Just don't go in the house," I said.

"Why not?"

"Trust me," I said. "You don't want to see what's inside."

He looked intrigued, but I didn't tell him anything more than where to find the plantation. He probably would go in the house. We disembarked, and I went to Mr. Allenby, who was waiting with horses and wagon ready as usual.

"I might be a bit longer this time," I said to him. He nodded but didn't look at my face.

I was to take my usual road and stop just past a town called New Wakefield. Cunningham's map had given names to the ghost towns. The day was just slightly cool, and I felt invigorated. Cunningham said our rendezvous each night would be quick. We would make sure the other hadn't run into any trouble. But traveling together was out of the question. I would have to reach Cahawba on my own. And so would he.

Cunningham didn't say a word to me that night—only tipped his hat as he rode by on horseback and slowly lowered to the ground a sack he had been carrying. My provisions for the trip were inside. He was wearing a raggedy outfit I had never seen before, and then, he

continued on out of sight. There was no one else on the
road anymore, with darkness settling in.

I decided it was as good a place as any to stop. I led the
horses to the river to drink before setting up under a tree
for the night.

The next day, I had to follow Cunningham's map even
closer. The road split at St. Stephens, then again at Jackson,
at Suggsville, and at Grove Hill. I was going mostly north
now, whereas before I had been going east. I didn't know
these roads.

"Try to follow the river," he had told me.

I knew more of the roads now than I had before, at
least, but I couldn't have found my way without his map. It
was the most important thing I carried.

That night, we stopped just past a town called Bethel. I
only glimpsed Cunningham's face for a second, and he
looked tense and alert. The plantations this far north were
not at all abandoned but were actively thriving. The fields
stretched as far as I could see—the Black shoulders, the
hats, the stooped backs too numerous to count. I hadn't
been this far north yet, but I should have come. There was
more than enough cotton for all the buyers here. No
wonder Nicholas had giggled at me.

When I arrived on the outskirts of Cahawba that
evening, I led the horses down a narrow path and into the
woods, just as Cunningham had instructed. The shadows
made my heart beat faster. Every snap of a twig sent me
looking over my shoulder. Finally, I saw a small light, and I
moved the wagon toward it. There stood Cunningham,
along with a woman. He took the horses, and I climbed
down as the woman squinted at me.

"This is Clara," Cunningham said, quietly.

"Hello, Clara," I said. "Thank you for helping me."

She nodded.

"Go inside and get you a plate."

The cabin was small and tidy. A loft with bedding over-looked the main floor. Three young faces sat at a table eating chicken and potatoes. They each had only a few bites left on their plates. When I came in, the oldest stood and took her plate with her.

"You can sit," she said. "I'm just about done, anyhow."

She shoveled the last scoop of mashed potatoes into her mouth, then took it over to a wash bin in the corner.

I looked at the other two. The youngest was a boy, about five years old. He stared at me with big blue eyes. I went to the bowls of food and made myself a plate. Then, I sat next to the other girl, who glanced at her brother.

"You better not let Momma catch you starin' like that," she said. "She told you to stop."

"I don't mind," I said. The girl didn't look at me but back at her last piece of chicken. She ate it quickly and licked her fingers, staring at the door as she did so.

"What's your name?" I asked the little boy.

"Felix," he said, in a tiny voice.

"I like that name," I said. "It's a pleasure to meet you, Felix. You can call me Miss Reilly."

He just kept staring. The middle sister flicked the back of his head.

"You say, 'Hello, Miss Reilly,'" she said. "You gonna get in trouble again."

Felix finally looked at her. He frowned.

"I'll tell Momma you were lickin' your fingers again," he said.

"Stop it, you two," the oldest said. She swooped over their shoulders to pick up her sister's plate.

"Felix, finish your supper," she said.

The middle sister sighed and got up from the table. The chicken was cooked just right. The juices warmed me, and though I tried to eat slowly, I could not.

"Your ma makes good chicken," I said to the children.

"Mmmhmm," the oldest agreed, as she scrubbed her sister's plate. "That's why they keep her in the kitchen at the big house."

She dried the plate and stacked it.

"She must be tired of cooking after doing it all day," I said.

The girl gave me a polite smile.

"She's teachin' me," she said. "I cooked it tonight."

"Oh my," I said. "I didn't know. It's delightful."

"Thank you," she said. Her smile grew into something more genuine.

Clara and Cunningham entered. My plate was already empty, so I relinquished my seat and carried my plate to the wash bin, where the oldest took it from me.

"You eatin', Felix?" Clara asked, scooping potatoes onto her plate.

"Yes, Momma" Felix said, pushing his food around his plate with his fork.

I stood awkwardly in the middle of the room. Crossed my arms. Uncrossed them. The middle sister sat cross-legged in a rocking chair next to the door and unraveled her braids.

"When's your man comin'?" Clara asked as she sat down.

"I don't know," I said. "He doesn't even know I'm here. And I don't know for sure that he's there. Though, I'm pretty certain he is," I added, quickly. She shot Cunningham a look, but he stared at his food, and if he noticed, he didn't show it.

"How you gonna find out?" she asked.

"I'm not sure," I said. "Perhaps I could pretend to be a Good Samaritan and see if the guards let me in with food or medical supplies for the prisoners."

Clara shook her head and swallowed her food.

"They don't let no ladies in that prison except the nurse, Miss Marks. I see her come and go all the time."

"Maybe I ought to see her, then," I said.

"I don't know about that," Clara said. "I don't know anything about her reasons for helpin' those men. She could turn you in."

Clara set her fork down and gazed off into the distance, deep in thought.

"There's a Mrs. Gardner," Clara said. "She lives on the other side of the prison. I hear her and her daughter pass things to the men through the stockade. I wouldn't tell her what you plan on doin' or anything, but she might let a note slip in."

I chewed my lip. Either of those women could turn on me.

"What do you think?" I asked her. "Should I try to approach her?"

Clara sipped her water.

"I think that's the best idea," she said. "You can write a

note to your man with instructions that he get her next delivery. Then he can send you a note back, and you'll know he's there. There'll be no stoppin' him after that."

Cunningham stopped eating, too. The whole room was quiet, staring at me.

She was right. He would come. I prayed in my head then that he was there. That he could do it.

"Yes," I said. "That's what I'll do."

Emmett

Chapter Forty-Eight

NOVEMBER 1864

T he middle finger on Malone's left hand had been blown off at Spotsylvania, leaving the two beside it dangling and useless. The Confederate field surgeon cut them off hastily and bandaged them. But later, when he still could not use his hand and the wound looked angry and inflamed, I knew the Confederate surgeon had not used the same care he would have with his own men.

I had first thought about amputating his hand myself at Andersonville, when we were given axes and told to chop wood. I turned it over in my palms, wondering if I could tie Malone down somehow and chop his hand off at the wrist. The bone might shatter, though, which would only cause more problems. Still, it was the only idea I had. But we were moved from Andersonville while I was still considering my plan.

Now, at Castle Morgan, his hand was black and yellow and swollen and had begun to rot where it hung. The blackness grew each day.

We weren't given axes here. They were forbidden. But a

commissioned officer who did work outside of the prison snuck me in a handsaw. If the surgeons wouldn't save Malone's life, I would.

Two men from camp—Big Charlie, the prison's gentle giant, and Jack the Irishman, who had come from Ireland just to fight in this war—helped to hold Malone down. I breathed heavily as I gripped the saw, trying to keep myself from shaking.

"Don't think too hard, Doherty," Malone panted. "Just feckin' do it."

I nodded but couldn't look into his eyes. Big Charlie gave Malone the brim of my cap on which to bite down. Jack pressed his knee against Malone's chest, and Big Charlie held his other arm; the roles could not have been reversed without Big Charlie crushing Malone.

I glanced over the shoulders of the men blocking us from the guards' view and then lined the saw up with Malone's wrist. I had tied a tourniquet just below his elbow, and his hand lay motionless, devoid of life.

Don't think. Just do it. It's only a cut of meat.

I began sawing. The blood spurted, covering everything immediately. I kept sawing. Malone shouted. I knew the guards would be coming soon. I worked faster, through the tissue, the muscles, the bone, until I made it through to the dirt underneath. I tossed the bloody saw into the fire just before the guards arrived.

When they saw the blood, they scrambled to find a stretcher. Malone's face was pale, and we pushed a shirt up against the gaping wound where his dead hand had been.

"They're going to take you to the hospital," I said. The hospital was outside of the prison. There wasn't much space there, and so only the most serious cases were taken to it. The sick stayed here, among the rest of us.

"I know," Malone breathed. "You did it, Doherty." He laughed quietly. "You did it."

"What the hell happened to this man's hand?" a Confederate guard shouted at us. He kicked the hand on the ground, to make his point.

"I think I might have pulled it off on accident, sir," Big Charlie said.

"Which one of you useless scum snuck somethin' in here?" the guard shouted again, ignoring Big Charlie. We all stared at him, silent. I tried not to smirk. My hands shook at my sides, and I gripped my pants.

Two other guards carefully picked Malone up and slid him onto the stretcher.

"See you on the other side," Malone said to me.

I knew the only men who would survive this would be those who kept busy. The thieves, scheming to steal from their fellow prisoners. The hopeful escapees, planning their routes. The ones who bartered with the guards for melon or peaches or peanuts.

I needed to occupy my time with something, and so, I asked Jack about his escape. He had escaped months ago but had been caught and dragged back.

"It's the dogs," he said. "They've been training those dogs since birth to sniff out the Blacks that try and run. Gettin' over the stockades is only one thing. Gettin' to Union lines is somethin' else."

"What was your plan?" I asked.

"The wrong one." He chuckled.

"Do you think Ernie made it?" I asked.

Ernie had escaped a few weeks before Jack and hadn't been brought back.

"Hope so," he said.

That afternoon, as I was thinking about all the successful and unsuccessful escapes, a guard called out to Big Charlie to retrieve a gift from Mrs. Gardner. The woman would often bring us green beans and potatoes and peas. Sometimes even books to read. The guards tolerated it and allowed one person of their choosing to receive the gift. Today, it was Big Charlie.

He returned with three potatoes and a book. Big Charlie was in my mess, and so I was pleased. But he was distracted, his eyebrows furrowed as he stared at something else he held. He whispered to Lyman and passed him the thing. Lyman opened it. It looked like a note. They whispered to each other some more. Then they both looked directly at me.

Big Charlie nodded in invitation, and so I went over.

"What is it, fellas?" I asked.

"It's a note," Lyman said. "It's for you."

"I don't understand," I said. Lyman held it out to me.

"Read it," he said.

Tell Sergeant Doherty the garden holds a beautiful rose for him. Please send a note back so his presence can be confirmed.

. . .

I blinked. Did this mean Rose was here? In Alabama? On the other side of these walls? It seemed about as likely as money raining from the sky.

"Do you know what it means?" Lyman asked. "Is it a code?" He stepped closer. "You plannin' something, Doherty?"

"Aren't we all, Lyman?" I asked, trying to grin.

But he just frowned. "You should let me in on it," he said.

"I have no idea what Mrs. Gardner means," I said. "But I do plan to find out."

Lyman nodded. "How you gonna write a note back to her?" he asked. "The guards pick who gets to cross that deadline and get the gifts."

"Maybe I'll ask Berman to let me return some books," I said. "We've got to have some of Mrs. Gardner's books around here."

"What if Berman's not on guard when she next comes to the wall?"

"Mrs. Gardner always waits for Berman before she comes," I said. "She knows he'll allow it."

This amount of thinking was making my head hurt. I needed to eat, though I knew it wouldn't satisfy me in any way.

"Worth a try, I suppose," Lyman said.

Lyman was probably one of the last people I would have picked to read that note. I turned away to cook my single piece of bacon. Big Charlie cut up the potatoes, and we cooked those, too.

As I lay in the sleep yard that night, I wondered how

Rose had found me and how she had gotten here. I needed to get to her. And I needed to start planning now.

The next morning, I asked a prisoner named Aaron if I could borrow his pen and ink. He had been a secretary when he was captured. He stood next to me while I used it, lest I run off with it.

I knew I couldn't just beg Berman for a favor. I needed to offer him something. I only had a few greenbacks left, but they would do. I offered him some and asked that he choose me to receive Mrs. Gardner's next gift.

"Your mess got yesterday's potatoes," he said.

"I'll give the food to another mess," I said.

"Why are you so eager?" he asked

"I want to thank her," I said. "I'm grateful for her kindness. And I want to return her books."

"Fine," he said, snatching the money.

That afternoon, I crossed the deadline for the first time —the same line that men had been executed for stepping over—to give Mrs. Gardner a note and a book.

It was not Mrs. Gardner, but her daughter, little Belle, on the other side. "Thank you," I said, earnestly.

"You're welcome," she said. She handed me four sweet potatoes and a bundle of green beans. I struggled to hold it all and squatted down next to a different mess to unload them. Then I walked away to plan my escape.

Chapter Forty-Nine

I spent the next three days talking to the men who were known for plotting escapes. They had never tried it, but they pointed and whispered and measured in foot lengths and knocked on walls and floors, and their eyes darted around like rabbits, watching the guards' movements. I copied them, making my own observations and calculations.

Even at night, I watched the guards. We all knew that Miller was the deadliest. We had seen him kill prisoners for the smallest infractions—if one was too slow or too jumpy or stepped too far out of line. He didn't warn them, just shot. He was young and eager to be praised for his vigilance.

The rest were either old men or cowards—men the Confederacy could afford to squander here. Most treated us with disgust and some with indifference. Some were cruel for no reason. Perhaps they wanted to be at the front. Perhaps they saw no honor in guarding prisoners.

Lyman followed me around those days—at first pretending he wasn't, and then no longer trying to hide it.

"You plannin' an escape?" he finally asked on the third day.

"Why? You gonna help me?"

He said nothing.

"That's what I thought," I said.

"You'll get caught," he said. I silently cursed Big Charlie for not choosing a different literate man to read the note. I had to breathe deeply and clench and unclench my fists a few times to keep from hitting Lyman.

"What are you getting at?" I asked.

"Just saying. It's not gonna work."

"Then I'll be right back where I started."

"Unless they kill you," he said.

"Go find something better to do," I told him.

He lingered for only another moment before leaving. I had been avoiding the water closet while he trailed me, because I knew it was how I would get out. It was the weakest point in the prison. An old warehouse in disrepair, the prison was shabby and coming apart. The wall were sturdy enough, but the roof barely held up on one side, and on the other side it had been torn off completely. The water closet was located on the end of with no roof at all. It was a small, somewhat enclosed space with only one guard assigned to it at a time. A guard who counted the minutes until he could be relieved from the stench. The question was, would I try to climb out of the top, over the wall, or go under the bottom, through the ditch that carried the waste away from the prison? Either way, I would still have the outer stockade to climb over. The dead zone to cross.

I studied the structure as I pissed. The walls were high and the ditch was shallow. Barely enough room for a man lying flat. Lyman was right. The odds were not good. But there was nothing else to do but try.

I knew I could trust Jack, so I asked him to help me distract the guard posted in the water closet.

"Your boots or your hat," he said. "You're lucky to still have both. I'll barter with the guard for them while you sneak away."

"I'd rather keep my boots," I said.

"Wouldn't we all?" he asked. "What size are they?"

"Size eleven," I said.

"That's why they haven't been taken from yeh," he said. "They'll be too big for the guards. Ehhh, I could try the hat. But I'm not certain it'll be enough. They might dismiss me straight away. Sure, it's an officer's hat, but it isn't a *commissioned* officer's hat."

"Can't you find some way to make it appealing?" I asked.

He smirked. "Sure, I can," he said.

"Thanks," I said, patting him on the back.

"And you'll want to go under the water closet," he said. "It's quieter. Maybe you could wait for rain. It'll make that hole deeper."

I had hoped to avoid crawling through the shite and piss, but he was probably right.

In three days, I would go—rain or no rain. We told Big Charlie, too, in case we needed him to cause a ruckus. A ruckus was always helpful. Big Charlie was up for most things, and this was no different.

But then, the night before my planned escape, it started

to rain. Not a soft rain, either. It poured in sheets. I lay in the puddles and mud beneath the open sky, watching the distant lightning, and I realized I could barely see a thing without it. Not the moon or the stars. I couldn't even see across the sleep yard. I could barely make out the men only feet from me or the guards patrolling the walk along the top of the outer stockades. After the lightning flashed, everything went completely black. Thunder roared in my ears. Now was the time, I realized. The storm would cover my movements perfectly.

The guards expected night escapes. As a result, they stationed more sentries on the walkway at the top of the outer stockade walls at night. I would wait a bit. I would go through the water closet, under the inner stockade walls, and across the yard to the outer stockade walls. And then, when I did climb up the wall, I would have to time it perfectly. I would need to have light feet when I reached the walkway. Make sure the sentries didn't hear or see me up there with them. I would have to grip the outer edge of the walk, lower myself down, and let go, jumping to the ground on the other side. I would have to do it all as fast as the lightning in the sky. I could, though. I could do it.

First, I prayed. I asked God to bring me to Rose. To make me as quiet as a mouse and as swift as a bird. To protect me and guide my feet. Then, after some time, when I started to hear the men around me snoring, I sat up. We had truly learned to live like animals. We slept in mud, exposed to the rain and lightning, and we didn't even much care.

I walked casually to the water closet, and as I did, I glanced at the sentries out of the corner of my eye. Each stretch of the walkway had one guard. I would only need to wait until he turned his back and started walking the other way.

Lightning struck while I was in the water closet. As soon as it was black again, I scrambled under the gap between the log walls and the mud into the ditch where the waste flowed out of the inner stockades. I held my breath. I had no time to second-guess myself. No time to turn back or be disgusted by what flowed around me. As soon as my feet were out the other side of the inner stockade, I ran to the outer walls of the prison. I pressed myself against the tall logs, trying to become as flat and as still as possible. I had no reason to believe they had noticed me. I waited for the lightning to flash again. My heart beat so hard. I didn't have to worry about the guards directly above me yet. It would be difficult for them to see me here. It was the ones on the adjacent walkways I had to worry about.

I looked up at the guard above me. He was more than halfway across the stretch, back to me. He would reach the end and turn soon. I couldn't wait anymore. I couldn't risk being seen.

I scrambled up the logs, grasping at nubs and notches. The guard still hadn't turned as I reached the top. The thunder covered my footfalls, but I knew the lightning would come again soon. I squatted, held onto the edge of the walk, and dropped to the other side. The distance was farther than I'd anticipated, and I hit the ground with a thud, rolling my ankle and smacking my shoulder into the ground. Pain coursed through me, but I tried to remain still. I prayed and prayed and prayed as I breathed steadily and lightning lit up the sky.

Chapter Fifty

The Alabama River was right in front of me, and I didn't know what to do. Was Rose with Mrs. Gardner? If so, I needed to get around to the other side of the prison. But that seemed like certain death. The sentries would surely see me. For now, I needed to create distance, and crossing the river was the best way to do it.

I limped as fast as I could toward the river, pain rushing up my leg. I dove in. The water was rushing, and the current pulled me quickly. I kicked my legs to get my head above water and then let myself float for a bit. The rain hit my face in large, angry pellets. I wanted to stay there. To let the river pull me all the way to the sea. But I couldn't, so I turned over, ducked my head underwater, and kicked furiously toward the eastern bank. I grabbed at tree roots, my shoulder still throbbing from the fall.

I hung on for a moment like that, trying to gather the strength to pull myself up. I was so tired. And weaker than I had ever been. My muscles screamed. The swim had exhausted me. I closed my eyes and pictured Steven's face. His honest and unapologetic plea for me to come home. For me to live. I grunted in the darkness as I pulled with my arms and tried to find some footing in the water. The thunder covered my yell as I wrenched my chest up onto the land. I grasped at more roots above me and pulled the rest of my body onto the bank.

I half grunted, half laughed into the dirt. I let myself lie there, but I knew that if I didn't get up then, I might not get up at all. So, I stumbled, dizzy and blinded by the rain, up the bank's slow incline and through the trees. I couldn't go much farther. Ahead, the trees thinned, and I didn't want to be in the open. I found a felled tree and lay beside it.

I slipped in and out of consciousness that night, not sure if I was dreaming or seeing visions. Every so often, the thunder would roar, and I would open my eyes, and for only a second, I would remember where I was.

The light of the morning began to creep around me, giving shapes and outlines to the things that had only been black holes the night before. I needed to move. To get farther away from the prison. But my limbs felt like bricks. My body shook in my wet clothes. I sat up slowly and squinted at the clearing. There was a road there. I didn't want to get too close. I kept moving south through the trees, getting farther and farther from Castle Morgan. I had no guess as to where Rose was. My only plan was to find Mrs. Gardner. That meant I would have to cross the river again. My teeth chattered. I felt like I was still moving against the current, every step painful and slow.

Something crunched nearby. I stopped and tried to hide

behind a tree. My heartbeat thrummed in my ears. For a moment, I was taken back to the battle in the wilderness, waiting behind trees for the enemy to find and kill me. But this forest wasn't nearly as dense, and I cursed it for that.

It was a man, coming closer and closer. I tried to hold my breath. My gaze darted around for a better hiding spot, but my mind couldn't catch up. My head could have been filled with mud. The man passed the tree I stood behind and then looked right at me. His hands were empty. He was unarmed. He was a Black man—a fieldhand, it seemed —with pants torn at the knees.

What do I do? I thought. *What do I say?*

But he smiled as if I were the exact reason he was creeping through the woods at this early hour. Perhaps he wouldn't tell anyone. Although, perhaps he would get a reward for turning me in.

"Come with me, Mr. Doherty," he said, his voice low. *Did he say my name?* I marveled. Had they put a search out for me already? It was still so early.

"You *are* Mr. Doherty, aren't you?" he asked, when I didn't immediately follow him.

"Who told you?" I asked. "Did the guards send you?"

His face softened.

"I'm a friend of your wife's," he said. "We've been looking for you every morning and every night. Come quickly, because they *will* send someone for you soon."

I glanced over my shoulder. But nothing was there. The world was still waking up.

"Can you take me to her?" I asked.

"Yes," he said.

"How will we cross the river?" I asked. "I don't know if I can swim it again."

He shook his head. "We won't have to," he said. "Follow me."

This time, I did. The man moved like a shadow, never tripping or stumbling. I started to think he was an apparition. Something I had dreamed up.

Then he stopped and squinted at the road to our right. I did too. It looked empty.

"We need to cross here," he whispered. "You go first. Hold your head high. Act like you belong."

I stared down at my clothes, grateful for the first time that my uniform had been taken from me. I looked like a Confederate. He watched me, waiting for a response or an action. I nodded. We crossed the road casually, me first, chin up, the man behind me, face down. I didn't know where to go after I crossed, so I kept walking through a small clearing and into the trees. I felt less exposed in the trees. The man caught up with me and didn't tell me to turn around.

"I thought Rose was with Mrs. Gardner," I said.

"She's been around there," he said. "We've all been waiting for you, not sure which side you'd come from. I'll send word to her that I found you. The rest will be coming back soon, anyway."

"The rest of who?" I asked.

"The slaves of this plantation," he said, gesturing toward the south. "Clara and Jesse and Miles and Alice. They've got to get to work soon."

My head buzzed, and the pain of walking had become nearly unbearable. I didn't understand what he was saying.

When we reached a cottage in the woods, the man gave me dry clothes.

"Who are you?" I asked him.

"Cunningham," he said. "Now, put on these dry clothes and rest."

Chapter Fifty-One

I fell asleep as soon as I lay down on the straw pallet in the corner. I couldn't remember the last time I hadn't slept directly on the hard ground. I expected I would wake up at Castle Morgan and find out this had all been a dream.

But instead, I awoke to a gentle touch and the sight of Rose's face. Tears ran down her cheeks, and I couldn't tell if they were tears of pain or relief. I could see both in her gaze.

"I'm well, Rose," I said. "I'm all right."

She began to sob. She lay next to me and nestled up against my body. I began to cry, too. I couldn't believe it. She was truly here. We lay like that for a long time, clutching one another, refusing to let go.

"How did you find me?" I finally whispered into her hair.

"Phillips found out you were a prisoner," she said, speaking into my chest. "And General Butler found out where."

"I have never liked Phillips more," I said.

Rose chuckled.

"I'm here buying cotton for him," she said. "That's how we're getting you back to Mobile Bay."

"*You're* buying cotton . . . from *them?*" I asked.

"I would do anything for you," she said.

"Would you get me a bath?" I asked.

She giggled. "I promise."

We didn't get up until Cunningham returned. He looked embarrassed to interrupt, but he held a pair of scissors.

"Thought you might like a haircut," he said. He must have noticed the lice crawling all over my head. I would have been ashamed if I wasn't so relieved.

"Yes," I said. "I would be grateful."

He led me to a tub in the back and let me bathe before cutting my hair and beard.

"You'll rest again tomorrow," he said. "We leave the next day."

"Are you sure?" I asked. "We can leave tomorrow." He looked as if he wanted to agree, but he shook his head.

"The journey will take a few days. You'll need more strength than you've got now."

That night, I greedily ate the hearty dinner and then promptly vomited it all back up. Carla rubbed my back and told me the other escaped prisoner had done the same. I wondered if it had been Ernie.

"Try again, but not so much this time," she said.

I felt ashamed. Like a small child or a sick old man. But I did as I was told and kept the second portion down.

The next day, my ankle swelled, and Rose propped it up by pushing all of the bedding together. She fed me grits and soup and told me what she had been doing in New Orleans. I fell asleep a few times, but she didn't mind.

By supper, I felt properly hungry again, and I didn't vomit anymore. Rose and Cunningham spoke of the way to Mobile Bay.

"He'll go under the boards," Rose said.

"And what happens when the dogs come?" Cunningham asked.

"I'll . . . I'll tell them I'm a cotton buyer," she said.

"And they won't question that?"

She looked at me, worried.

"I have my permit."

"The dogs find everyone," Cunningham said, swallowing his food. "I think we need a better plan. Perhaps we'll travel at night instead. It's the way we're used to working."

"And how will that help with the dogs?" Rose asked.

"You're a cotton buyer," I said, interrupting them. "So, buy cotton. Then you won't have to rely on them believing you. They'll see it with their own eyes."

"Emmett, those bales weigh 450 pounds," Rose said. "Once they're on the wagon, we can't get them off until they're loaded onto the ship. Not without the help of at least four men."

But Cunningham looked at me, pleased.

"And neither can they," he said. We both smiled.

"What if they bring a whole group of men?" Rose asked, trailing at my limping heels as Cunningham and I packed the wagon. It was late, and we worked by lamplight.

"They won't," Cunningham said. "They're short of men down here and too confident in the dogs."

"What if we need to get to you and can't?" she asked, her voice laced with panic.

I stopped moving and grabbed her by the waist, gathering her in my arms.

"You won't," I said. "I'll be perfectly fine."

"You'll be unable to move," she said. "There's barely enough room for you to lift your arms to feed yourself. I doubt you can even roll over."

"Rose, I'm not getting caught and dragged back to that prison," I said. "I'm coming home with you. This is the only way."

"I hate it," she said.

"We're so close," I said. "We can do this."

Cunningham returned to the cabin, taking the lamp with him and leaving us in the light of the moon. Rose rested her face against my chest. I kissed the top of her head.

"Go sleep," I said. "You'll need your rest."

She nodded, then looked up and kissed me. Her warm, comforting lips stirred something inside of me that I had not realized was missing.

"I love you," she whispered, before going off to bed.

Cunningham woke us while it was still dark. Carla and the children were just stirring, too, and wished us luck on our journey. Rose had lined the inside of the wagon hatch with a blanket. It seemed warm for a blanket, but I didn't argue or remove it.

I kissed her before climbing in. My water and food were inside. When the boards came back over me, it was completely dark. We would set off first and Cunningham would trail us, just close enough to keep us in his sights.

The ride was turbulent until we reached the road, and then the movement almost lulled me to sleep. But just as the sun was beginning to rise and seep through the cracks between the boards, Rose started speaking to me.

"The roads are still empty," she said. "You ought to read the latest Paddy letter. I finally called out Donahoe by name. I blamed him for the riot deaths. I hope people can see just how vile that man is."

She wouldn't be able to hear my response, so I just listened.

"I think Cunningham may be in love with Lydia," she went on. She had told me how the two of them came to New Orleans. That Lydia was waiting there now. "That must be difficult. Unrequited love. . . ." She seemed to get choked up, because she stopped speaking for a moment. Then she cleared her throat and went on.

"I don't know if I'll be successful buying cotton today. I don't know anyone this far north. But certainly tomorrow. I hope the dogs don't find us before then."

Perhaps they won't even look for me, I thought. I was only one person. But they had looked for Jack. And they had found him. What if they found me? What would they do to Rose? The thought sent blood rushing to my face.

The horses slowed, and the rocking of the wagon quickened. We were stopping.

"Quiet in there," Rose said. She stood right above me, her hand pressed against the boards. I put mine there, too. And then she was gone. I slowed my breathing. Tried not to move at all, even though I had an itch. I felt as though I lay there alone for ages, though it was probably only a few minutes before the horses began to move again.

"I can only purchase two today if you must have specie," I heard Rose's voice saying.

"Yes, I must," another woman said. "I'm no criminal."

The wagon lurched this way and that. I held my hands out to the side, trying to brace myself so I wouldn't thump around. Then, the wagon stopped. I couldn't hear Rose anymore, or the woman. I only heard two men.

"That one hooked?" one asked.

"Uh huh," the other said.

Then, a dark object was lowered right over my face. It grew and grew as it got closer, until the boards above me groaned with the weight. I hadn't thought I would mind being trapped, but I found myself taking shorter, quicker breaths. If the boards gave out for some reason, I would be crushed, suffocated. I couldn't see the second one coming, but the boards protested this weight, too.

It was dark for me again. I closed my eyes and thought of Steven. My breathing slowed.

Chapter Fifty-Two

The dogs didn't find us until near the end of the second day. I didn't hear them, at first, because everything sounded so muffled. But I felt the horses speed up. They must have been close to reaching their limits before the wagon turned off the road and abruptly stopped.

Then, I heard the dogs. Even inside the floor of the wagon, their barking was loud and menacing. I heard Rose scrambling and prayed she wouldn't get bit.

"What is the meaning of this?" I clearly heard her say. She must have been yelling.

I heard a man's voice but couldn't make out what he said.

"Well, *I'm* clearly not a Union soldier!" Rose said.

Then, a third voice joined the chorus. A deep, booming voice.

"Well, I do declare! Who is making such a ruckus on my property?"

The first man spoke again. I only made out "hunt" and "apologize."

"Ridiculous!" the voice boomed. "Miss Reilly is a loyal buyer, here for my cotton—as she is every week!"

The dogs were underneath me now, sniffing furiously and emitting a high-pitched, pleading whine. I held my breath.

"Gentlemen, the only cotton we will be moving today are the bales in that warehouse back there that belong on this wagon of hers. I suggest you call your dogs off my property before I fetch my shotgun and take care of the useless beasts myself! This is a lady we're talking about, for goodness' sake!"

More muffled talk, and then a sharp whistle pulled the dogs away. I heard Rose speaking quietly.

"Miss Reilly, I do apologize," the booming voice said. He was no longer shouting, but I could still make out his words just fine. "What a disgrace!"

Rose said something else, and they both laughed.

"You aren't seeing another seller behind my back now, are you?" the voice asked.

Rose replied.

"There are always bales for you here, sweetheart," he said.

That man needs a hobby, I thought, curling my hands into fists. The wagon moved again, and then three more bales were loaded. The boards groaned again, as if in warning.

It was nearly impossible now to hear anything except an occasional bellowing laugh. I waited impatiently while, I assumed, they talked. I ran my hands along the cracks in the boards, feeling the coarse canvas, the soft cotton poking out here and there. My head ached, and I started to feel as though I were spinning. I reached for the food and nibbled on some chewy bacon.

Finally, we moved. I drank again. My bladder hurt. Carla had advised I wrap a cloth around myself like a baby, and I did. But I didn't enjoy soiling myself and tried not to. I tried not to think of how terrible I would smell when Rose got me out.

I slept that way for two more nights and days, only eating and drinking when I started to feel queasy. When we reached Mobile, the cotton was finally unloaded. I heard Rose speaking to another man. Her voice was higher than normal. I couldn't make out anything either of them said. But when Rose started to move the horses again, I felt like I could finally breathe. The boards had held up. I hadn't been crushed by the cotton. We walked a short time to what I could smell was a barn.

"I think I'll need it for one more day," Rose said. She had dropped her flirtatious act, and her voice now sounded shaky and concerned. This must have been someone she trusted.

"Aren't there any roads that go around the bay?" she asked.

"Only to Pensacola." The voice was gruff. "I've got a boat, though."

"How did you . . ." She didn't finish.

The boards lifted. Even the dim light of the barn felt too bright. The man's face was wrinkled and weathered, and he stared at me, neither smiling nor surprised. He offered a hand to help me up.

Next to him, Rose breathed a sigh of relief but still asked me, "Are you all right?"

I nodded. But my legs wobbled. My head swam. The man handed me a pair of pants, a shirt, and a hat.

"Thank you, sir," I said. He nodded and left the barn. Rose stayed but turned to give me privacy. I was grateful.

"Mr. Allenby is a man of few words," she said, her back to me.

"But he's a Union man," I said, stepping out of my pants and cloth and into the new pants.

"It sure seems so, doesn't it?" she said. I slipped the shirt on.

"I'll be right back," I said.

I balled up my old clothing and walked unsteadily out of the barn. Mr. Allenby was waiting for me and pointed to a fire a few yards away. I threw the clothes in. Some Confederate's old pants. I smiled as they burned.

A large rowboat waited for us by a shallow embankment just outside of the city. We climbed in with our heads down. I didn't look up to see if anyone noticed.

When I picked up the oars, my weak arms trembled. *I could get us away from the shore,* I told myself. That much I could do.

But the pull of the water was so strong and the oars so heavy. I was sweating and out of breath before I had rowed us at all. I glanced up at Rose and Mr. Allenby. They wore similar looks of concern. Rose put her hands atop mine.

"Let me," she said.

I slowly handed her the oars and scooted back. I felt broken. Foolish. I bit the inside of my cheek. I was ashamed to be this way.

The Union soldiers at the fort fired a warning shot as we neared. Mr. Allenby waved a white handkerchief as high above his head as he could. He stood, tilting the boat. They didn't fire again, but when the boat touched the beach, four soldiers were waiting, muskets raised.

"Please!" Rose shouted at them. "My husband is a Union soldier. A prisoner. He escaped. Please help him!"

She didn't wait for an answer but stood and helped me to shore. I thought her either brave or crazy. My body shook so hard, I couldn't stop it. I stumbled onto my hands and knees, Rose touching my back.

"Regiment, soldier?" one of them asked. I sat back on my heels.

"Twenty-eighth Massachusetts Infantry," I said, breathless. "Sergeant Emmett Doherty. Captured at Spotsylvania. Imprisoned at Andersonville and then at Castle Morgan."

They lowered their muskets slowly and one by one came to my side to help lift me to my feet.

"How did you escape, sir?" one of them asked.

"In a storm," I said. I wanted to tell them more, but I was just so tired. They led me to the port where ships were coming and going.

"Sir!" one man shouted at a ship. "One of ours! He escaped from Cahawba! He needs medical attention!"

I didn't look up for the answer. Black spots danced in front of my eyes. The ground rose. They led me onto the ship. Rose shouted behind us, and a moment later, the soldiers set me down on a tarp. Rose's soft hands promptly covered mine. I tried to see her but everything was blurry.

"I'm here," she said, softly. "I'm right here."

Rosaleen

Chapter Fifty-Three

DECEMBER 1864

For the next five days, I went from the Union hospital in New Orleans to my boardinghouse and back. I ate and slept and sat beside my husband. The army said that once he was strong enough, he could go home to Lowell to recover. After that, he was to report again for duty. He still had two years left in his contract. The thought made me want to scream. Hadn't he given enough? Hadn't we all given enough?

I thought of Mr. Thornberg, who had sacrificed nothing. He left the suffering for his slaves to endure. Men like him believed that countless lives were worth sacrificing, so that he could continue to own human beings. The man embodied everything I had been fighting against for years. And the man had saved my husband's life. Unknowingly enough, but still. The thought filled me with disgust and anger and, worst of all, appreciation. I didn't want to think about Mr. Thornberg ever again, and yet, I would think of him many times. In the coming months. The coming years. Mr. Thornberg haunted my conscience.

I tried to simply sit with Emmett and feel grateful for his presence. I ran my fingers along the calluses on his hands. I rested my head on his chest and felt the beating of his heart.

They had splinted and bound Emmett's ankle; the bone had probably fractured. I prepared for our trip home, buying things we might need, trying to think of how to best make Emmett comfortable. I took my clothes to be laundered for the last time and was nearly out the door when I spotted a Black woman hauling a load of clothes into the back room. I saw her face for only a moment, but I recognized it.

"Norma?" I asked. She froze, her back to me.

"It's me . . . Ro— Miss Reilly," I said.

She peeked over her shoulder, and her eyes opened wide. I walked to her slowly.

"How did you get here?" I asked, incredibly relieved to see her. She glanced around warily.

"Come with me," she said. "We'll talk outside."

She led me to a back door, and we slipped out.

"I can bet you were lookin' for me again," she said. "I'm sorry I wasn't there."

I shook my head.

"I'm glad you got out. Are they paying you well here?"

"Well enough," she said. "And I got plenty stashed away. Thanks to you."

I was glad I was carrying my money with me now. I gave her nearly all of it.

"It's yours," I said. "I took some bales when I went back and you weren't there."

She looked at the greenbacks in her hand and smiled.

"This'll help with Curtis's boy," she said. "He ain't workin' no more. He's in school now. I just about fainted when I saw them teachin' our children at school. But they are, and so we send 'em."

"He made it here, too?" I asked. "Did everyone?"

Her face fell.

"No," she said. "Not everyone."

"I'm sorry to hear that," I said. "This war will be won soon, I pray."

"And it'll be a long road," Norma said. "For all 'a us. But I'm hopeful." She smiled again, this time wide enough to show those beautiful teeth.

"I wish you the best, Norma," I said.

"You too, Miss Reilly."

It was nearing dinnertime when I left the laundry alley and went back to the boardinghouse to eat.

I ate on the balcony and watched the people passing below. It surprised me how much I would miss this city. The beautiful buildings, the vibrant people, the smells of tangy, spicy, delicious food. It felt like a city that could explode at any moment—with violence or with jubilation.

I was just finishing up when Cunningham knocked on the door.

"Please," I said. "Come in."

He accepted and stood awkwardly in the middle of the room.

"I'm leavin' tomorrow," he said. "And I wanted to say goodbye and good luck to you and your husband."

"Thank you," I said. "We truly could not have done it without you."

He smiled politely.

"Here," I said, gathering my satchel. I took some greenbacks out of it and held them out to him. He furrowed his eyebrows, staring at them. I thought he would refuse, but finally, he took them.

"You pay better than the Union Army," he said. I laughed.

"Where will you go now?" I asked. He grinned.

"You know I can't tell you that," he said. "But I suppose it will be wherever they need me."

"Please stay safe," I said. "You're very brave to keep going out there."

He sighed and looked past me, at nothing. Then, he looked down at his feet before meeting my gaze.

"There's nothing else for me to do," he said. "There was never any question I would do what I'm doin'. As soon as they asked me, I didn't hesitate. This war won't be about me and whether I make it through. It'll be about what this country becomes. Whether it lives up to the place it set out to be. Whether children who look like me will have a future in it or whether they'll be regarded as property forever. What was I gonna do? Stand idly aside?"

A chill went up my spine. I thought of the conversation I had had with Lydia back in Boston, when she told me Zeke wouldn't enlist. A whole lot made sense then, and my breath caught. *Oh, Lydia,* I thought.

"You're a true patriot, sir," I said. "And I hope that you do make it through this war. Our country needs men like you, and I'm proud that I got to know you, even if only for so short a time."

Cunningham ducked his head.

"Those are kind words," he said, smiling. "Thank you." When he looked up into my eyes again, I added, "Lydia is blessed to have met you, too."

His smile faded, and he nodded. "Goodbye, Miss Reilly."

When I visited Emmett the next day, I asked the nurse when he would be discharged. She had given him crutches, and Emmett practiced walking up and down the hallway with them. She watched him with arms crossed.

"Looks good to me, ma'am, but we'll have to have the doctor sign off, and he's awfully busy this morning."

I left the hospital for dinner, determined to find the doctor when I returned that evening. I missed Steven. It was time for us to go home.

I ate dinner with Lydia on my balcony. I knew she must have been feeling something after Cunningham left, and I didn't want her to be feeling it alone. She told me stories about the island. About the families there. We laughed at the miscommunications she had had when she first arrived. At her bumbling and confusion.

"But they were all so patient with me," she said, shaking her head. "All those families. More patient than the Yankees I worked with, who probably wondered how in the world I had been hired to teach. No experience. No credentials."

"What you did was more important," I said, swallowing

my food. "You made those people feel seen and heard. You made them feel like they weren't any different than you. I bet that was special to them."

"I'm going to be so sad to leave them," she said.

We both fell quiet, looking out onto the street.

"I don't think I loved him," Lydia finally said. "Not in that way. I think I loved *me* when I was with him. I think I loved the person he made me feel like I could be. And now I'm worried that the man I *do* love, despite . . . despite everything, I'm worried he won't even recognize *this* Lydia. Might not even get to see her. If I go back there, this Lydia might be gone forever."

"There are people in Boston who need new Lydia," I said. She shifted in her chair.

"Sure," she said. "There are. But once this war is won, there are going to be millions of people who have lived their whole life never knowing what it means to be free. And yes, there will be white folks who help them. But it's like you said: Will they truly see them? Will they truly hear them? Listen to their wants and needs? I will, Rosaleen. I will do that, and I want to do that."

"I'm certain that plenty of those people will come to Boston for a new life, and you will be there to welcome them," I said, trying to find some thread with which to stitch Lydia's life back together. I suddenly felt guilty for helping to plant this thing inside of her, though I was immensely proud of her, too.

"Perhaps," she said. It was a quiet and sad "perhaps," and I knew she didn't believe it.

Chapter Fifty-Four

The doctor finally signed off on Emmett's papers and officially recommended that he be sent home to Lowell to finish healing. I packed my things and the porter took them to the carriage, where Phillips and Lydia waited for me. We would collect Emmett together and be at the docks in time to depart that afternoon.

As I made my way down the narrow stairs, I felt grateful for so many things. But mostly that my husband was alive, that he was coming home, and that we would be a whole family again—if only for a little while. I couldn't wait to take care of him. To nurse him back to health. To lie by his side and feel his breath on me. We boarded the carriage and made our way to the outskirts of the city where the Union hospital and barracks sat on the banks of the Fishers Canal.

Two Union soldiers helped Emmett out of the hospital and toward the carriage. He strained with concentration until he paused and spotted me. Then, he broke into a grin and hobbled over.

"Shall we race to the docks?" he asked.

I chuckled. "No racing for you. Only resting."

He leaned into me and whispered, "How restful, exactly, do I need to be, Nurse Doherty? Are all bedbound activities approved?"

I giggled and nodded. I loved that fool. The soldiers helped him into the back of the carriage and we all took our places. Lydia and Phillips sat beside one another facing Emmett and me, his crutches laid across our laps. Emmett squeezed my hand. He was starting to regain some strength, though his cheekbones still protruded and he looked little like the Emmett that had left us only a year ago at Christmas.

A breeze came through the window of the carriage, and Lydia pulled her shawl tighter around herself. The sky was a dirty gray, but it could do nothing to dampen my spirits. I watched the city grow around us again as we neared the docks. Suddenly, a woman came running onto the road.

"Help!" she yelled. I recognized her.

"Minnie?" I asked out the window.

"Oh, Miss Reilly!" she exclaimed. "I'm so relieved to see you! Please, won't you come help this poor dockhand? His arm has been crushed. Can't you bring him to a hospital?"

"Yes," I said. "Yes, of course, Minnie." I shouted to the driver, "Sir! Please follow this woman to the docks."

"Yes, ma'am," he yelled over his shoulder.

"It's a good thing you no longer need to disguise yourself," Phillips grumbled. "You're terrible at acting callous."

The driver followed Minnie down a very narrow street and then another.

LISA BOYLE

"Where is this woman taking us?" Phillips asked, pulling out his pocket watch. "We've got a ship to catch."

At the end of the tight maze, rather than finding large ships and shipments and men in a hurry, we found nothing. An abandoned, creaking dock and, in the water, the outlines of alligator eyes. I looked around frantically for Minnie.

"Minnie?" I shouted. "Minnie?"

And then, the carriage door opened, and Emmett was yanked outside and wrenched to the ground.

He cried out in pain. I stumbled after him—over Lydia and Phillips, getting tangled in Emmett's crutches. By the time I was out of the carriage, he was already being dragged down the dock by a large man. A man whose profile told me all I needed to know. He was that same man I had seen twice before.

"Stop!" I shouted. "Let him go!" But the man kept going. I ran as fast as I could, my heartbeat thumping in my ears, my revolver bumping against my leg.

I couldn't shoot the man while he dragged my husband. What if I missed? I reached for my revolver anyway, raised it, and shot into the water. The large man ducked and then spun around. The alligators stirred from their sandbar slumber and quickly dashed into the cover of the bayou.

"Stupid bitch," he spat.

"McDermott," Emmett choked out.

The man was pulling Emmett by the back of his shirt, and Emmett tore desperately at his collar, trying to create enough space to breathe.

"Shut up, Doherty!" the large man shouted. "Shut the hell up! I'm not listenin' to any more of your bloody

370

nonsense. *You're* the reason this war went to shite." He punched Emmett in the face. I gasped and my aim wavered.

"Men like you are the reason that everything *I* was fighting for is gone." He hit him again, giddy with anger. "A traitor is what you are. And a big mouth. No more. I won't hear one more word out of you. Today, you're no more than supper." He swept his arm out to the side, pointing toward the water. "That's the only noise I want to hear. The snapping of your skinny bones." I could see Emmett's eyes rolling.

"Let go of him now," I said. "Or I will shoot you."

"No, no, my dear," Minnie whispered into my ear, as she pressed the barrel of her gun to my side. "None of that."

The man chuckled and bashed Emmett in the face again. Blood trickled from Emmett's mouth, and his head lolled to the side.

"Looks like all your hard work—all your fookin' sneakin' around—was for nothin'."

I willed myself to ignore the burning in my arms. To keep them from shaking. To ignore Minnie's gun at my side. I aimed. I wouldn't let him take Emmett. And then, before I could do anything else, a shot rang out beside me, a cloud of smoke billowing. Minnie turned as I heard the click of the next round being chambered.

The man Emmett had called McDermott stumbled back a few paces, staring straight into my eyes. He released Emmett. He looked surprised. The blood began to drip from his beard before his hands shot to his throat, and he tipped over into the river.

The alligators threw themselves atop him. The water splashed with twisting tails and flailing arms. The man's shouts muffled into gurgles, and the water turned dark.

I turned to see Phillips and Minnie aiming their revolvers at each other. I raised mine again, this time at Minnie.

"Lower your weapon, Minnie," I said. She glanced at me and started to maniacally laugh.

"Go ahead!" she cried. "I'd like to admire those skills we worked on!"

Phillips darted into action. He grabbed her hands and wrested the revolver out of them just as she shot another round into the air. Her hair slipped out of her braid, strands hanging in her face. She stumbled and then grounded herself again. She looked up at us through the blond mess of tangles and grinned.

"Well, this has been fun," she said. "Wouldn't you agree?"

"What in the bloody hell, Minnie?" I said, still pointing my revolver for some reason. "Why?"

She raised her eyebrows and smirked.

"I saw Hugh here followin' you one day, snoopin' around. Don't you remember? I told you he was at your door. I decided I wanted to be a part of whatever little game he was playin'. You didn't want me involved. But I wanted to be. This city has become so *boring* since the Union took it. What's a girl got to do to have a little fun? Not much, apparently, when it came to Hugh McDermott." She winked and licked her lips.

Phillips put both guns away and grabbed Minnie by the

back of the neck. She tried to yank herself away, and he squeezed harder. She winced.

"Wait. Don't y'all want to know about the money?" she asked, eyeing Phillips. "'Bout who was payin' him to follow you around?" She stuck her finger at me. "I'll tell ya—if ya let me go."

I opened my mouth to answer, but Phillips cut me off.

"No," he said. "I'm tired of hearing your voice, actually." I had wanted to know. But I trusted that Phillips could find out just as easily. He was right: We wouldn't be bargaining with this foul woman. I went to Emmett.

"Are you all right?" I asked, helping him to his feet. He was already bruising and swelling from the force of that man's blows. One of his eyes was closing. He only nodded. He looked dazed.

I helped him slowly stumble and hop to the carriage, while Phillips tied Minnie's hands behind her back.

"This is gettin' to be a bit much," she said, sounding much angrier now.

"Oh, I certainly don't think so," Phillips said. "The army will have a wonderful time punishing you for assisting in an attempted murder of a soldier. Not to mention all the other lovely criminal activities you've probably been engaged in." He leaned into her ear but didn't whisper. "I hear they send women to Ship Island prison."

A fearful look passed over her face so quickly I barely saw it at all.

"I'm sure it'll be a laugh," she hissed.

Chapter Fifty-Five

We took Minnie to the St. Charles Hotel and left her with General Banks's men. Our ship was growing impatient at the docks, but they would never think to leave without Phillips.

I was helping Emmett onto the ship when a voice called, "Miss Reilly!"

I turned to see Nicholas, looking puzzled. "Haven't seen you in some time. Whatcha doin' there?"

Emmett studied my face with a slight hint of annoyance. I was sure he was tired of strange men being so fond of me. I smiled apologetically.

"I'll be right back," I said. He looked like he wanted to argue. "Nicholas is harmless. I promise."

Lydia took over while I went to Nicholas. A confused grin was plastered across his face.

"I fed your friends this morning," I said, pointing to the river. "They'll be full for some time."

Nicholas's expression changed to one of amusement.

"Whaddya mean by that?"

"It was a large meal," I said.

"Bigger than me?" he asked. I nodded, and he giggled.

"You're somethin' else, Miss Reilly. Never have met a Yankee like you before. Leadin' me into a dead woman's house to steal cotton? And now this?"

I looked at the ship. Emmett and Lydia were inside now, out of sight. Phillips stood on the deck, watching us without actually looking.

"I won't be back," I said. "I'm going home now. So, the rest of that cotton is all yours." Nicholas's eyebrows went up, and he whistled. Then he stuck out his hand. I smiled and shook it.

"It was a pleasure," he said.

"Good luck out there," I said.

He shrugged. "Don't need no luck."

I spent the voyage home with Emmett. I was exhausted and happy to lie about in his arms. At first, he didn't want to talk about the war. But I assured him that I was there whenever he was ready. That I would always be there, no matter what his stories revealed. So, he told me things in bits and pieces. That he was worried about his mate, Will Malone, who was at the hospital at Castle Morgan, and that he hoped he would make it through the war. About the Confederates they'd captured in the woods, right before Emmett and Will were captured themselves. About Will's songs. I could tell he was only skimming the surface, but I listened intently.

When the ship docked in Boston, we boarded another

carriage to take us to the train station. My legs itched to walk, but it was too far for Emmett and his crutches. We parted with Lydia, who planned to spend the holidays with Zeke and the girls. Plus, Gil was home on furlough, she had told me. I could see her apprehension when we said good-bye. She hadn't been home for more than a year, and I prayed that their reunion would be full of joy and happiness.

The train to Lowell arrived late, and I could tell Phillips was annoyed.

"Who do you suppose was paying him?" I asked Phillips, as we boarded the train. I knew he had been thinking over the incident this whole time. Phillips grunted.

"When I find out, I'll tell you," he said.

When we arrived in Lowell, Phillips said goodbye, and Emmett and I got into one last carriage to take us home.

"I hate these bloody carriages already, and it's only been a day," he grumbled.

"You'll heal quickly," I told him. Mr. Joyce was expecting us, but Steven was not, and when we arrived, it took Emmett some time to get his crutches in order and to hobble to the door that Mr. Joyce held open. Mr. Joyce held out a hand for Emmett to shake.

"Welcome home, lad," he said. Steven came running from somewhere inside the house.

"Who's here, Grandda?" he asked. When he saw us, he stopped in his tracks. His face broke into a toothy grin, and he rushed at Emmett so quickly, I thought he would knock him over. But Emmett laughed, and I bet he would have welcomed it. They stood there for a long time, Steven's face buried in Emmett's chest, Emmett holding onto a crutch with one hand and gripping Steven tightly with the other. Cocoa walked slowly up to them, her tail wagging quick and low. She bumped their touching legs with her snout. When Steven turned to me, I could see his face was wet. I wiped my own before saying, "Let's have your da sit, huh?"

Mr. Joyce helped Emmett to the couch, and Steven hugged me next.

"Thank, Ma. For bringing Da home," he said. Then he looked up at me. I had forgotten how tall he was. I smiled and kissed the top of his head.

"I said I would, didn't I?"

Three days later, there was a knock at the door, and I asked Steven to please see who was there. I had just finished helping Emmett clean and replace his splint, and Mr. Joyce was out somewhere, I wasn't sure where. I heard a muffled, happy exchange as I walked down the hall and through the kitchen. I stopped briefly to wipe a coffee ring from the table.

"Da is doing very well," Steven was saying. "He's much better on his crutches now. He was clumsy at first."

I put the rag down as Mr. Joyce came into the room and put his hat down where I had just wiped. He grinned at me and gestured to the door. "Ran into someone at the train station," he said.

Curious, I hurried to the door and grabbed it, pulling it open a bit more. Marie and Gil stood there with Jane—who was no longer a baby but a happy, bouncy, small child

—and Levi, who smiled big enough for me to see his missing two front teeth.

I scooted Steven to the side as I clung to my friend in a hug. We said nothing at first. Just held one another. When we pulled away, she said, "Lydia told us Emmett arrived home safely. We came to celebrate."

I smiled as tears formed in the corners of my eyes.

"I am so happy to see you," I said. I looked at Gil. He was quite dashing in his uniform. "You look wonderful, Gil."

He nodded. "Thank you," he said.

"Please." I stepped aside. "Please come in."

I received a package from Phillips the day after Marie's visit. There was a note on the outside.

Come and see me when you've cooled off. —P

My hands shook as I opened the package. It was a copy of *The Boston Pilot*.

To the Irish of Boston,

It is with great sorrow that I report a harrowing deception among us.

You may have read letters during this war signed by a so-called Irishman named Paddy. You may have been swayed by his words. Convinced he was exactly who he said he was and believed exactly what he said he did.

But the writer is a fraud. She is a woman—her name is Rosaleen Doherty—and she is a cotton speculator. She has been deceiving her hometown of Lowell for years, and now, she has deceived you, too.

It brings me no pleasure to tell you that this despicable woman has neither morals nor integrity and has been making herself rich off of the Negro slave.

It is for the benefit of our community to disregard her and the things she has written and to do what we know is best and true: to put the needs and well-being of the Irish first.

Your editor,
Patrick Donahoe

I gripped the chair next to me and let out a sharp curse.

Chapter Fifty-Six

I read the newspaper two more times that day and then put it away forever. I felt hollow. Empty. I tried to gather the anger and hatred that I knew simmered somewhere, underneath my exhaustion, but it was too heavy. I had lost so much and gained so much, and now Paddy was gone. It felt like I had disappeared, as well. Donahoe had won. I should have told Phillips about Hugh McDermott. But I hadn't.

I knew I had not disappeared, though. I was still there. Still breathing. And so, I watched my family together, happy and alive, and I knew that despite everything, I had done what was right. I had saved my husband. Our family was whole again. Nothing was more important than that. Not even Paddy.

I busied myself writing letters to everyone I could. General Barlow, General Banks, General Butler, even President Lincoln, asking for my husband's contract to be cut short. And if not that, then perhaps a post near home guarding the Confederate prisoners on Georges Island or keeping camp in Cambridge. I outlined his service, explained his trials in painful detail. Emmett didn't know. Most days he laughed and joked with Steven, tried to walk as much as he could, and told us stories. But some days he was quiet. Subdued. Changed. It worried me. On those days, I often found him with Mr. Joyce, head bowed, speaking to God. Trying to find peace. Or perhaps, forgiveness.

He tried to comfort me a few times about Donahoe's letter, but I wouldn't let him. I told him it was worth it to have him home. To have him alive. And I meant it. I grieved Paddy and was glad I was not grieving Emmett. Still, a part of me felt dead, too, now, and I didn't know what to do next.

A week later, when I left to see Phillips, I thought for the first time about what that letter had meant for him. His bosses surely understood what he had done. Were they angry with him? Had they reprimanded him?

Maggie greeted me at the door and hugged me right away.

"It's so wonderful to see you," she said. "And Emmett is home now?" She squeezed my shoulders.

I smiled and nodded.

"He is. He is well," I said. I thought of her John, then. She had told me no news of him, and I had been so caught up in my own calamities I had not asked.

"How is your John?"

She shrugged and sighed, an apologetic smile creeping onto her lips.

"Still fighting," she said. "He came home for a bit last

year and then went off again. Reenlisted. I received a letter from him just yesterday."

"We will pray that he makes it through this war unscathed," I said.

"Oh, I'm sure none of us will make it through this war unscathed." We stared at each other, and I felt the truth in her words. We were already different. All of us.

When I walked into Phillips's study, he was writing something, and so I waited in the doorway, arms crossed, leaning against the frame.

"Come in," he said, without looking up. I did and sat. Finally, he looked at me.

"How are the editors at *The Commonwealth*?" I asked.

"Don't worry about the editors," he said. "I'm even more important than you can imagine. They won't do anything to me."

I smiled, despite my mood. Phillips was still Phillips. Reminding me—reminding himself—just how important he was.

"So, Donahoe was paying him," I said.

"Seems as though this Hugh McDermott found out who you were when he stole a heap of letters you wrote to Emmett," Phillips said. "McDermott tried to sell them outright to Donahoe, but Donahoe wanted to squeeze as much out of it as he could. So, he paid McDermott to follow you."

I sighed. "I suppose that's it for me," I said. "And I'm sure I'm of no use to you anymore, either."

Phillips looked amused.

"You truly aren't yourself right now," he said. "That's all right. When you're ready, I will help you to see what's next for you. This is not at all the end, but rather, the beginning."

"And how is this the beginning?" I asked.

"You don't need Paddy anymore," he said. "Think about everything you've done. You are a hero, truly. As is your husband. Hiding behind another's name is no way to gain the prominence you seek."

I shook my head. "I don't seek prominence."

"But you seek to be influential," he said. "It's time to step outside of Paddy. To tell your story. Your true story. Leaving me out, of course. If you write it, I will publish it myself. A book of your life. About who you are. Why you did what you did. About what happened during this war. It will be wildly successful. No one will care then about a foolish newspaper editorial. It will be about Rosaleen. Her courage. Her fight. Her *Irish* story."

I was speechless.

"You would publish my story?" I nearly whispered.

"I would be honored to," he said. The only sounds, then, in that large study were the ticking of the clock and those of Phillips filling his pipe.

"Many people might be angry at me," I said. "At my family."

"I know," he said. "But remember, I take care of my people. You will have protection."

I swallowed hard.

"Think about it," he said.

⁓

I lay beside Emmett that night as he tried to scratch his foot through the splint.

"Damn this cursed contraption," he muttered.

I rolled over and kissed his cheek.

"What did Phillips say today?" he asked.

"He wants me to tell my story. Says the Irish need to know the real Paddy. To know that *she* is with them. He said he'll publish it as a book."

Emmett stopped scratching and put his foot down. He lay still for a moment.

"Is that what you want?" he asked. "All that attention?"

"I want what I've always wanted," I said. "To make a difference. To help those who need help. Give a voice to those unable to speak. We both know that it's nearly impossible to do that without power. And what else, if not that, have I been spending all these years trying to do?"

He looked at me.

"I don't *want* power," I said. "But I want to be able to influence those who have it."

Emmett touched my cheek.

"You'll do that if you tell your story," he said. "Don't you believe me when I tell you you're the most amazing woman in the whole world? Others will be as awed by you as I am every day."

I leaned over and kissed him softly. He closed his eyes as I pulled away, and I gazed at him, amazed still that we had truly brought him home.

"Can I ask you something, then?"

"What?" he murmured.

"Will you help me?"

"Hmmm," he said. It sounded like a hum. I could tell he

was falling asleep. I kissed his cheek and held his hand. I knew in a few hours, he would wake up screaming, covered in sweat, his breath coming in short spurts. He dreamt of the battles and the prisons, and though I could never understand his pain, I would always be there with him when he felt it. That, I had promised him. And so, I waited until I heard his snores before moving to the desk.

I had a few hours until he would need me. So, I picked up my pen, dipped it in ink, and started from the beginning.

Author's Note

While most characters in this book are fictional, some did exist, including: Brigadier General Thomas Francis Meagher; Major General Benjamin F. Butler; Sarah Butler; Major General William Tecumseh Sherman; Major Andrew Lawler; Major General Ambrose Burnside; Colonel Richard Byrnes; President Abraham Lincoln; General-in-Chief Ulysses S. Grant; General Robert E. Lee; Jefferson Davis; Salmon P. Chase; Major General George Gordon Meade; Colonel Thomas A. Smyth; Brigadier General Francis C. Barlow; Major General Nathaniel P. Banks; Patrick Donahoe, editor of *The Boston Pilot*; the Boston Associates, the elite businessmen of Massachusetts, the funders of *The Commonwealth* newspaper, and Phillips's bosses; Reverend Theodore Edson; Miss Marks, a nurse who tended to prisoners at Castle Morgan; and Mrs. Gardner and her daughter, Belle, who passed food and books through the Castle Morgan prison stockades until Mrs. Gardner was arrested.

When the American Civil War began in April of 1861,

the economies of the North and South states were inextricably linked. Cotton was the backbone of the South's economy, and while 80 percent of that cotton was shipped to England, the rest was purchased by the Northern states for their cotton mills. The South believed their cotton would help them win the war, mainly by swaying England to join their side. England built ships and weapons and sent ammunition to the South. However, cotton was only one reason England sided with the South; they also identified more with the South's politics, though England had outlawed slavery in 1833. England was reluctant, however, to send their army or navy. They were already fighting a war with France, and when President Abraham Lincoln issued the Emancipation Proclamation, England realized the war was now about more than preserving the Union and they could not support the South in their efforts to preserve slavery.

The cotton trade during the war operated in much the same way as is described in this book. At the start of the war, citizens were allowed to apply for permits to purchase cotton in Union-occupied southern cities. At first, they were allowed to use specie (coins or gold or silver pieces) to purchase the cotton, but as the war progressed, the rules and guidelines changed many times, and eventually only greenbacks (the Union government's notes) were allowed to be used. They then sold the cotton at auction. The Purchasing Act that Phillips mentions in the summer of 1864 stipulated that only government treasury agents could purchase cotton, but President Lincoln quickly modified that act to allow anyone who owned or "controlled" cotton to bring it into Union-occupied territories.

The Port Royal Island Experiment, as it was called, is also a true-to-history event. When the residents of the South Carolina islands fled, they left behind some of the best cotton land in the country, along with the enslaved people of the islands. The North sent teachers, pastors, and businesspeople to help the former enslaved grow their own cotton. However, most of that land was bought up by white Northerners at unfair auctions that favored the wealthy. Approximately four to five thousand acres were bought by the island's former enslaved, who owned and cultivated the land successfully for generations after the war ended.

When New Orleans was captured by General Benjamin Butler's forces in April of 1862, Butler set up the Union headquarters at the St. Charles Hotel. He also redistributed wealth and land to the poorer inhabitants of the city, both white and Black, free and recently freed. He opened trade lines and allowed cotton to come into the city to be sold. Butler was also the man to declare escaped slaves "contraband of war" in the spring of 1861, as depicted in this book. He argued that the enslaved people were being used in the South's efforts to wage war by digging trenches, chopping trees, etc., and were therefore considered "contraband" and would not be given back to the Confederacy. After this declaration, enslaved people began to flock to Union lines in search of freedom. More than a year ahead of the Emancipation Proclamation, this decision drastically altered the direction of the war.

At the beginning of the war, prisoners were exchanged fairly regularly. Both sides operated on a similar policy as had been used during the War of 1812 and the Revolutionary War. However, it soon became clear that neither side was equipped to handle the sheer number of prisoners that large battles began to produce. When news about the state of prisons and prisoners began to spread, exchanges began to stall. Each side retaliated against the other by withholding rations, subjecting prisoners to harsh punishments, and more. Finally, in December of 1863, all prisoner exchanges ceased. The final straw for the Union was when Jefferson Davis threatened to sell all captured Black prisoners into slavery and execute the white officers of those Black regiments. Benjamin Butler had been involved in prisoner exchanges the previous year and penned an editorial in the summer of 1864 explaining that prisoner exchanges would not begin again until the Confederacy treated Black prisoners the same as their white counterparts, eligible to be exchanged.

Though never official Confederate policy, there were many instances of Confederate officers and troops giving no quarter to surrendering Black soldiers and instead shooting them on the spot. Marie describes Gil witnessing this at the Battle of Olustee in Florida. She also mentions Fort Pillow, which is the most widely known instance of Black soldiers trying to surrender, only to be killed instead. Many Black troops used Fort Pillow as a rallying cry, and one white soldier recalled, "When [the Black soldiers] charge, they will not take any prisoners if they can help it. Their cry is, 'Remember Fort Pillow!'"

While the Union Army began to recruit and train Black soldiers in southern-occupied territories in 1862, the first Black regiment to be formed in the Union and made up of Northern men was the 54th Massachusetts Infantry, which is Gil's regiment. The 55th Massachusetts Infantry was formed soon after, followed by the 5th Massachusetts Cavalry. Black Union soldiers in the South were often recruited from "contraband camps." Sometimes, spies—like Cunningham's character—were recruited this way, as well. Black spies would cross into and out of Confederate territory throughout the war, bringing news of troop movements to the Union Army.

Enslaved people in the South helped Union prisoners escape on multiple documented occasions. One escaped Union soldier said, "It would have been impossible for our men, held as prisoners in the South, to make an escape without the aid of Negroes." These prisoner accounts describe the willingness of enslaved people to house them, feed them, and walk with them throughout the night, leading them to the next guide, until they reached Union lines.

In the novel, Emmett is first imprisoned at Andersonville in Georgia, the most infamous of the Confederate prisons. Opened in early 1864, more prisoners died in Andersonville than any other prison during the Civil War. The death rate at Union prisons was 12 percent, and the death rate at Confederate prisons was 15 percent. At Andersonville, a third of the prisoners did not survive. The head of the prison, Captain Henry Wirz, was the only person to be executed for his crimes after the war. Andersonville was at its most crowded during Emmett's imprisonment, the month of August 1864. When the Union Army captured Atlanta, most of the prisoners were transferred to other prisons.

Cahaba (called Cahawba at the time) Prison, or Castle Morgan, was an old cotton storage warehouse converted into a Confederate prison. It closed down and reopened many times throughout the war. Its busiest month was October 1864, at the time of Emmett's escape. At that time, the prison held 2,151 men—more than quadruple its capacity. Emmett's escape was inspired by the real accounts of escaped prisoners from Cahaba.

The Irish Brigade was commanded by Brigadier General Thomas Francis Meagher. The 28th Massachusetts Infantry was the fourth and last regiment to join the brigade. The green boxwood sprigs worn at Fredericksburg, the speech Meagher made to "Mrs. Meagher's regiment" before the battle, the march through the field the day after the battle to identify Irish Brigade bodies, are all true-to-history events. The novel also features other battle stories taken from history as well, including the 51st Pennsylvania asking for their whiskey rations to be brought back before taking Burnside Bridge at Antietam; General Meagher defying General Burnside's "no fire" edict the night before the Fredericksburg campaign; and the soldiers celebrating General Grant's decision to go south rather than north after the Battle of the Wilderness.

All the songs that Will Malone sings in this book were written before or during the Civil War and would have been sung among the troops of the Irish Brigade. The lyrics come from David Kincaid's compilation album *The Irish Volunteer*, and include the songs: "Opinions of Paddy Magee," "My Father's Gun," and "Free and Green."

The opinions of the Irish before and during the war varied. At the start of the war, Irish enthusiasm was at its highest, with churches and newspapers urging men to enlist. However, as the war progressed and the Irish

Brigade saw an enormous number of deaths, support for the war began to decline. Most of the Irish were Democrats and did not support the Emancipation Proclamation, nor did they support allowing Black soldiers to fight. The draft riot that claims Ronan's life is also a true-to-history event. The draft riot in New York City lasted four days and is still the deadliest riot in American history. An angry Irish mob murdered many Black citizens and white soldiers during those four days following the announcement of the draft lottery. The riot in Boston was much smaller and only lasted one day, as described. Those who were killed were, in fact, the Irish who were trying to break into an armory.

And yet, many of the Irish troops proved incredibly courageous throughout the war. Not only did they incite fear in the Confederates but admiration for their bravery, as well. Lincoln once kissed the green flag of the Irish Brigade in thanks for their valor. The president was also known to be a fan of the writings of "Private Miles O'Reilly," an Irish soldier writing under a penname during the war, who often defended Lincoln.

Patrick Donahoe and *The Boston Pilot* both existed in history, and the first three quotes in chapter three of this book are direct quotes. All other excerpts were inspired by Donahoe's articles.

To research this book, I visited the following battlefields: Antietam National Battlefield, Fredericksburg Battlefield, Wilderness Battlefield, Spotsylvania Battlefield, and the Chancellorsville Battlefield Visitor Center. I am incredibly grateful to the park rangers who assisted me at each of these battlefields, talking for nearly an hour with me, printing out the 28th's regimental history, pulling out maps showing where and when each regiment was throughout the days of the battles, and answering my follow-up emails. Special thanks to Peter Maugle for sending me links to the national parks' maps months after I visited. I am incredibly grateful for your help.

I frequently referenced the 28th Massachusetts Infantry's website at http://www.28thmass.org, as well as the American Battlefield Trust website at http://www. battlefields.org. I also referenced maps of Alabama found at the David Rumsey Map Collection online, maps of New Orleans found at the University of Alabama's website, and images of New Orleans during this time period found at www.washingtonartillery.com.

I read the following books: *Battle Cry of Freedom* by James McPherson; *The Immortal Irishman: The Irish Revolutionary Who Became an American Hero* by Timothy Egan; *Irish Green and Union Blue: The Civil War Letters of Peter Welsh*; *Lincoln and The Irish: The Untold Story of How the Irish Helped Abraham Lincoln Save the Union* by Niall O'Dowd; *The Irish in the American Civil War* by Damian Shiels; *Civil War Boston: Home Front and Battlefield* by Thomas H. O'Connor; *Hardtack and Coffee: Or, the Unwritten Story of Army Life 1861–1865* by John D. Billings; *Cahaba: Captive Boys in Blue* by Dr. Jesse Hawes; *The Negro's Civil War: How American Blacks Felt and Acted During the War for the Union* by James McPherson; *A Stillness at Appomattox* by Bruce Catton; *While in the Hands of the Enemy: Military Prisons of the Civil War* by Charles W. Sanders, Jr.; *Hell Itself: The Battle of the Wilderness, May 5–7, 1864* by Chris Mackowski; *Trading with the Enemy: The Covert Economy During the*

American Civil War by Philip Leigh; *Lincoln's Scapegoat General: A Life of Benjamin F. Butler, 1818–1893* by Richard S. West, Jr.; *A Season of Slaughter: The Battle of Spotsylvania Court House, May 8–21, 1864* by Chris Mackowski and Kristopher D. White; and *Simply Murder: The Battle of Fredericksburg, December 13, 1862* by Chris Mackowski and Kristopher D. White.

As always, I would like to thank my beta readers for their dedication to the success of yet another Paddy book. Thank you so much to Latia Sanders for your valuable feedback and your unwavering support. To the wonderful Annabelle McCormack for your encouragement, honesty, and your willingness to always commiserate with me. A huge thank you as always to my husband, Tim, for being my rock, my manager, my alpha reader, my biggest fan, my toughest critic. All of it. You make me better every day. And thank you to all my supporters and followers on Bookstagram. My connection with you all has been so fulfilling and rewarding!

About the Author

Lisa Boyle was born and raised in Finksburg, Maryland. She received bachelor's degrees in journalism and international affairs from Northeastern University in Boston, Massachusetts. From cheesemonger, to educator at the U.S.S. Constitution Museum, Lisa has done a little bit of everything. She now lives in North  Carolina with her husband and daughter. *Signed, A Paddy* was the recipient of the 2022 Eric Hoffer First Horizon Book Award, the 2022 Eric Hoffer Historical Fiction Book Award, and the 2022 IPPY Best Regional Fiction, U.S. Northeast, Bronze Medal.

Want to read the FREE prequel? Sign up for Lisa Boyle's newsletter at www.lisaboylewrites.com, and get your link for *To My Dark Rosaleen*, a short story that takes place five years before *Signed, A Paddy*.

Did you love this book? Don't forget to leave a review!

Made in United States
Orlando, FL
14 March 2024

44780421R00243